<u>Proud Lion</u>
An Accidental Detective Adventure

by

Nathanael Miller

Copyright 2020 Nathanael Miller
All rights reserved

ISBN: 978-1-953475-01-5

For my parents.
They taught me to read, to write, and to dream.
Most importantly, they taught me to work.

Table of Contents

Chapter 11
Friday, Sept. 23; 10:00 hours; Naval Station Norfolk, Virginia

Denouement
Friday, Oct. 28; 19:30 hours; Chesapeake, Virginia

Fantail
Wednesday, May 9, 2018; 15:30 hours; Philadelphia

Appendices

USS *Ponce* (LPD 15) operating in the Arabian Sea, Dec. 4, 2010. (Official U.S. Navy photo by Mass Communication Specialist 1st Class Nathanael Miller / RELEASED)

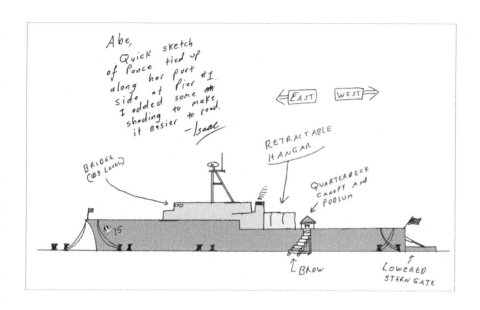

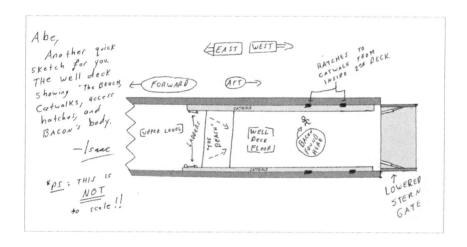

9

Acronym and Nickname Dictionary

The Navy has its own unique lexicon. The following terms are used in this book.

List 1: Navy terms

ARG
Amphibious Ready Group (task force of amphibious assault ships)

BM
Boatswain's Mate (enlisted seamanship specialists)

CMC
Command Master Chief (senior enlisted advisor to a CO)

CNO
Chief of Naval Operations

CNRMA
Commander, Navy Region Mid-Atlantic

CO
Commanding Officer

Crows
Informal nickname for petty officer insignia

Det
Detachment (small team sent from a command for a specific mission)

DoD
Department of Defense

DINFOS
Defense Information School

Dwell time
Time spent at home for sailors who deploy as part of specialized teams.

ECP
Entry control point

IKE
USS *Dwight D. Eisenhower* (CVN 69)

LCPO
Leading Chief Petty Officer (senior enlisted leader, pay grade E7)

LPO
Leading Petty Officer (front-line supervisor, usually in pay grades E5 or E6)

MA
Master-at-Arms (enlisted active duty security personnel)

MC
Mass Communication Specialist (enlisted mass media specialists)

MCC
Shorthand for Chief Mass Communication Specialist, an MC who has been promoted to chief petty officer (pay grade E7)

MMR
Main machinery room (a ship's engine room)

NWU
Navy Working Uniform (semi-formal enlisted uniform: khaki shirt worn over black trousers or a black skirt with black leather shoes)

Proud Lion
Official nickname of the former USS *Ponce* (LPD 15)
List 1: Navy terms (continued)

PT
Physical training

PTSD
Post-Traumatic Stress Disorder

p-way
Shorthand for "passageway," the corridor on a ship

OIC
Officer-in-Charge (runs part of a multi-center organization for the CO)

OS
Operations Specialist (enlisted shipboard warfare ops technicians)

QM
Quartermaster (enlisted navigation specialists)

SEA
Senior Enlisted Advisor (a chief, senior chief, or master chief who is senior enlisted advisor to an OIC or other lower-level senior leader)

SECDEF
Secretary of Defense

SECNAV
Secretary of the Navy

SINKEX
Sink Exercise (use of an obsolete ship as a target for live ordnance)

TAD
Temporary Additional Duty (a job for another chain of command)

UCMJ
Uniform Code of Military Justice (the military's internal laws)

Work-ups
The period of time a ship or team is in training for deployment

XO
Executive Officer

YN
Yeoman (enlisted administrative specialists)

List 2: Fictitious terms appearing in this book

AFSC
Atlantic Forces Surface Command

COMCAM
Combat Camera East Coast

NEPAC
Navy Expeditionary Public Affairs Command

Fo'c'sle
Wednesday, May 9, 2018; 14:21 hours
Philadelphia

A lone figure walked along the pier towards the old ship, ignoring the birds, breeze, and sun. The ex-USS *Ponce* floated quietly ahead of him at her berthing in the Philadelphia boneyard, her future as uncertain as his.

Navy Chief Petty Officer (Retired) Isaac T. Shepherd chuckled as he remembered reporting aboard *Ponce* in 2010. He had mispronounced her name as USS "Ponz" when checking in. The Officer of the Deck had quickly (and most emphatically) corrected him. The ship's name was actually pronounced "pon-SAY."

Every Navy ship has a few nicknames. Some are official; many are not. *Ponce* was known by many of the typically salty nicknames one would expect, everything from "Old Bucket" to terms of dubious endearment used only when her sailors were severely drunk. The ship's official nickname, "Proud Lion," was taken from her crest. The crest was anchored around a purple rampant lion, which was itself an homage to the coat of arms of Ponce, Puerto Rico, *Ponce's* namesake city.

A gull cried out above *Ponce's* mast, angry that another gull had snatched a fish from its beak. The cool breeze drifted across the ship's weather decks, a slight chill bequeathed to the air by the Delaware River. The sun, bright and hot, created an oddly cheerful ambiance amidst the silent steel sentinels in the water.

Shepherd was tired, but didn't he feel lost, only uncertain. Like his old ship, he too had retired the previous year. Ironically, his own retirement ceremony had only been a few weeks prior to *Ponce's*.

Ponce was now one of the many somnolent members of the inactive fleet of decommissioned ships in storage at the Philadelphia boneyard, each awaiting its final fate. Most of these old war horses would find their end at the end of a scrapper's torch. Not a happy fate to contemplate, but an unfortunately practical one.

Luckily, I've got a more promising future ahead of me, Shepherd thought as he casually walked the length of the pier. *I just don't quite know what I want to do with it yet, but it's waiting for me.*

Shepherd heard the distant sound of a forklift trundling along the far end of the pier as he approached the ship. His eyes scanned up over the hull, past the bridge to the 04 Level.

Shepherd had always found it amusing that Navy ships had two designations for the "deck" one stands on. The main deck, or "weather deck," is just that—the main deck. Below this are the *decks.* Above the main deck are *levels,* designated 01, 02, etc., and pronounced "Oh-1, Oh-2," etc.

The 04 Level on *Ponce* was the highest one could go without climbing the mast. Nearly a decade earlier Shepherd had often retreated up there to read in the evening light and cooling sea breezes of the Middle East during a rather memorable deployment.

Shepherd's sea-green eyes peered through his bifocals. Now sporting a neatly trimmed steel gray beard, his hair was still military short. Some habits are just hard to break, after all.

Shoving his hands into his pockets, Shepherd came to stop under the faded number "15" on the ship's port bow. He wore an old brown corduroy sport coat with the rank insignia of a chief petty officer as a lapel pin: a gold anchor with the letters "USN." A canvas haversack was slung over one shoulder and across his chest.

Memories crowded his hyperactive brain. Some were of being fired on by Iranian small boats, which nearly started World War III. Some were of the ship's captain committing suicide on the pier after being arrested for murdering a Marine.

Pleasant memories also jostled for attention. These included hanging over the ship's bow to photograph a pod of dolphins enthusiastically jumping through the bow wave as *Ponce* approached Jordan. He recalled camping with the Marines in Kenya. Finding lion tracks crisscrossing the camp in the mornings had been as noteworthy as winding up in the middle of a troop of baboons that decided to cross a dusty street he was walking along.

None of us ever did figure out how those bloody lions managed to sneak through camp unnoticed when we were surrounded by Marines standing guard, Shepherd thought with a wry smile.

He leaned back on a bollard, closing his eyes and recalling the memory of a pure sapphire sea split asunder by *Ponce* as she strove to catch the far-off horizon. He always loved being on deck in the wind as *Ponce* chugged through the water with all the pluck of a dump truck on an interstate highway.

He brought himself back to present-day Philadelphia. It was all over now. Everything.

"Hello, old girl. It's good to see you again," Shepherd said quietly to his ship. "It took longer than I expected, but I'm here, just like I promised."

It might have been a sailor's superstition, but he sure *felt* like the ship was happy to have a visitor. The visit was overdue, like a visit to a terminally ill friend, but he had finally made it.

"I guess both our marathons are finished now," Shepherd said. "Time for me to figure out where I'm going next."

No more uniforms, no more ranks. No more standing watches or scrambling across flight decks. No more hanging out of helicopters or climbing stringy boarding ladders up the sheer cliff of a ship's side in the middle of a pitching sea.

No more murders. No more playing detective. No more dead bodies or bad guys.

A dead body in the barracks more than 20 years ago in Spain had started it all. A dead body in a Virginia Beach hotel last year had ended it all. Between those two bodies had been a string of corpses, including the three deaths associated with *Ponce* that Shepherd had confronted within the space of six years. This was one of the reasons he added the boneyard detour to epic road trip he was now on. He needed to be alone with *Ponce* to process the memories of Carl Bacon's murder.

A shadow zipping along the pier caused him to glance up. He watched a lonely tern fly across the harbor and perch on the mast of the rusting ex-USS *Shreveport*. *Shreveport* was one of *Ponce's* sisters in the now-defunct *Austin*-class of amphibious transport docks, or "LPDs," as the Navy classified these mid-sized amphibious assault ships.

Every ship has ghost stories which resonate through out the ship's life, becoming part of the fabric of the ship's own spirit. *Ponce* was no exception. Shepherd had seen *Ponce's* resident ghost twice during his time on the ship. The first time he saw the spirit of the long-dead sailor was in 2011. Shepherd thought his imagination had played a trick on him and there had been no one stepping into the compartment ahead of him, a compartment with no exit save the hatch Shepherd used to enter it...

Of course, when Chief Ortiz and I saw the ghost together on watch back in 2012, well...

Shepherd absently wondered if the ghost was going to find *Ponce* a boring place to haunt now that the ship was largely forgotten in the boneyard. Or, had that unfortunate spirit found a companion in the ghost of Carl Bacon?

Shepherd would have loved to go aboard *Ponce* again, but it was not to be. The only people allowed on board now were the boneyard personnel when they did periodic maintenance checks.

Still, Shepherd's powerful mind could see every deck, every passageway, and every compartment. Mentally he put himself up on that distant 04 Level and looked down over the ship's fo'c'sle as he went back in time, back to Carl Bacon's murder in 2016.

What a case that was, Shepherd thought sadly. *What a mess...*

Prologue
Tuesday, August 9, 2016; 19:57 hours
Naval Station Norfolk

Carl Bacon was dead.

Dead as a doornail.

Deceased.

Pushing up daisies.

Playing a harp on a cloud.

Pick any cliché, but Carl Bacon was dead.

Agents from the Norfolk Field Office of the Naval Criminal Investigative Service were certain Bacon died of a terminal case of murder. They concluded he succumbed to an attack that apparently resulted in death when his body made a ginormous *splat* on the hard, wooden well deck floor of *Ponce*.

The investigation was swift and brutal. Everyone on board the old ship was questioned over the next several days. A narrative was seized upon by the NCIS agent leading the case, and he moved with alarming speed to identify and have the local Judge Advocate General bring the suspect to trial.

Operations Specialist 2nd Class Jarvis Cline was arrested quite publicly a week after Bacon's death. NCIS agents, along with multiple Navy Masters-at-Arms, surrounded the sailor on *Ponce's* mess decks during lunch on August 16th. Cline was roughly cast to the deck and restrained, all the while screaming for help.

A crowd of speechless spectators watched as he was frog-marched off the ship, cell phones out and recording. The lead NCIS agents, a short, muscular man, stopped by the Quarterdeck to take a call when his own phone rang. He didn't bother to lower his voice or step out of the line of view of the crowd.

"Yeah, little pervert came squealing like a pig," The agent said to whomever he was speaking to. "No, this is a slam dunk. Little creep didn't like the boy macking on his sweetheart. Yeah...yeah...yes, we got him dead to rights. He fragged his boy alright. We wouldn't have arrested him if we couldn't prove it. Yeah...the pervert's going down hard. Just what his kind deserves."

The dozens of cell phones recording the event were jostled about as their owners breathlessly began to upload the video and their own interpretation of events to dozens of social media accounts. Not half an hour later, a local Norfolk newspaper reporter, trolling through Navy-related social media accounts, saw the raw video of Cline being dragged off *Ponce*. The reporter immediately dialed an anonymous contact on base. The anonymous contact excitedly relayed a story that nearly fit the facts. The reporter then called NCIS and confirmed the arrest of Cline before drafting and uploading his story to the paper's online edition.

The spark was lit, and the media firestorm went off like a bomb. Even before NCIS could issue its own official statement, local radio and TV stations were broadcasting remarkably similar (and similarly botched) reports. These reports would be picked up by the national networks and blasted across North American. Excited talking heads on TV reacted with indecently joyful glee as they reported a story they just *knew* would make their careers.

The glut of media attention blazed like a spotlight on the Navy brass in Washington, D.C., that same day. The chief of naval operation's aide, scrambling to appease the wrath of Admiral Thomas Donovan, hastily called his own contacts in Norfolk, and then drafted a statement for the admiral. Bypassing the normal review process by the CNO's public affairs and legal teams, the aide brought the statement to the admiral. The admiral barely glanced at it and gruffly told his aid to issue it.

"...in military news Petty Officer Jarvis Cline was arrested today on the charge of murdering Petty Officer Carl Bacon aboard the amphibious transport dock USS *Ponce*. Sources close to the case have said Cline was jealous because Bacon apparently had an affair with Cline's girlfriend, Petty Officer Brandy Sniffer..."

"...this is just another case of the toxic masculinity that pervades the patriarchal structure of the military. Jarvis Cline would not be dead right now if military culture didn't perpetuate a stereotype that makes young men like this Petty Officer Sniffer feel they have to live up to hyper-aggressive standards of behavior..."

"Petty Officer Jarvis Cline was hauled into Navy custody today. He's been charged with murdering his roommate at their house in Norfolk. Cline has a long history of violence and had been restrained several times over the past year when he attempted to harm his roommate..."

"...the aircraft carrier *Ponce* saw one of its own arrested for murdering one of its own earlier today. Apparently Jarvis Cline, one of the ship's senior officers, was arrested for murdering another crewman in the ship's wheelhouse over an argument about a boyfriend..."

"...the weather over the Hampton Roads area will be hot and humid, but showers are expected as we move deeper into August. In local Navy news, Petty Officer Jarvis Cline was taken into custody today on suspicion he murdered his girlfriend after learning from his roommate she had had an affair in Cline's house while he was deployed to the Middle East on the battleship USS *Ponce*..."

"...in a statement issued within hours of the arrest of Petty Officer Jarvis Cline for murder, Admiral Thomas Donovan, chief of naval operations, said every sailor in the Navy is accountable for their actions, and he has ordered Cline to be punished to the fullest extent of the law..."

The wonder of it all was that everyone managed to spell Jarvis Cline's name correctly.

The Navy propelled the case to court-martial in record time. Cline went on trial for his life September 5th. The courtroom on board Naval Station Norfolk was packed as the proceedings began.

Prosecutors working for the Judge Advocate General's office laid out a clear narrative during their opening arguments at the court martial. Their intent was to demonstrate the unmitigated guilt of the defendant aboard a rickety old warship and put the accused murderer away faster than old socks.

The jury was told that, like all amphibious assault ships, *Ponce* had a flight deck, multiple berthing and storage compartments below decks, and was capable of operating landing craft out of a deep "well deck" that could be flooded with sea water.

These factors made her the perfect platform for use as a test bed during the final years of her service life. *Ponce* had been fitted out with numerous experimental new technologies in 2012 and sent back to sea for four years. These technologies included everything from a prototype laser weapon to new antisubmarine warfare defenses. *Ponce* tested the new tech for four years until finally returning to Norfolk in 2016 to begin the long decommissioning process. The ship would be stripped of every usable fitting and part over the next year until she was retired in late 2017.

Prosecutors went on to tell the jury the turmoil resulting in Bacon's death began long before *Ponce* came home from its final mission.

Operations Specialist 2nd Classes Jarvis Cline and Carl Bacon had rented a small house in Norfolk not long after the ship came home. The fact of these two living together as roommates was seen as nothing short of amazing since the two sailors had initially seemed to hate each other. Following their arrival on board *Ponce* in 2014, they had both been demoted a pay grade following numerous fights with each other.

Their final fight seemed to have done them both some good. Following several anger management courses they stopped drinking and developed what could only be described as a tight-knit relationship.

A *very* tight-knit relationship, the prosecution emphasized.

Unfortunately for both (but more so for Bacon), bad things can happen to good people, the prosecution said.

Annoying and inconvenient, but, there it is.

Prosecutors informed the jury the evening of the murder was a duty day for the two sailors. Bacon was supposed to relive Cline at 19:45 to stand the 20:00 – 00:00 Messenger of the Watch. Prosecutors reminded the jury an on-coming watch typically shows up 15 minutes early to ensure any items or special information that needs to be "turned over" is turned over in a controlled and precise manner.

At 19:45, the other watch-standers were doing their turnovers as sunset approached. The day was sunny and the temperature was still been hovering at 80°, with 86% humidity giving everyone outdoors and instant sweat bath.

Five minutes later, Bacon still had not shown up for his watch. The officer of the deck, Chief Quartermaster Thomas Shifter, told Cline to quickly find Bacon. As Cline was Messenger of the Watch, he could leave the Quarterdeck to take messages around the ship with no breach of protocol.

The defense rose and began their opening arguments. Cline's lawyer, a famous, high-powered civilian attorney engaged by Cline's mother, said Cline made his way through the ship's mess deck looking for Bacon. Having failed to find either the human Bacon or the edible variety in the chow line, Cline dropped to the second deck and headed aft along the starboard side.

At this point on *Ponce* a single passageway runs the length of the aft part of the hull. Traversing this passageway, Cline passed through berthings and other spaces. Inboard of these spaces was a catwalk running the length of the cavernous well deck about 25 feet above the wooden deck floor. A similar catwalk ran opposite along the port side. Each catwalk could be accessed by a ladder from the well deck floor at the catwalks forward ends, and from inside the ship by only two hatches from the compartments in the second deck. These hatches were located towards the aft end of the ship.

Cline's lawyer told the jury the sound of boots scuffling on the deck further aft, and a thud that could have been a sack of gourds being tossed off a truck, hastened Cline's speed.

Feeling the hairs on the back of his neck stiffen, Cline came to the end of the line—the starboard aft line handling room where the ship's starboard mooring lines were stored (the jury was reminded the ship was tied up along her port side). Seeing nothing and no one, Cline started back forward. On a whim, he popped out onto the catwalk from the forward of the two access hatches. *Ponce's* stern gate was lowered, allowing the dying sun to bathe *Ponce's* well deck with hot sunlight. Cline looked aft and saw a few sailors painting fittings on the fo'c'sle of the USS *Mesa Verde*, which was tied up aft of *Ponce*. Something glinting below him drew his eyes downward.

Running to the Quarterdeck in a panic, the defense said. Cline was breathless, sweating, and covered in bruises he said were from banging into pipes and fittings in his haste. Gasping through shallow breaths, he relayed to Shifter he had seen Bacon lying dead in the well deck, a large pool of blood surrounding his head like some ghastly halo.

Years of training and experience enabled Shifter to react quickly. Going into autopilot mode, he got *Ponce's* on-board medical team moving, ordered the ship locked down so that no one could board or leave, and contacted the commanding officer. Captain Benjamin Smith, ashore at his home, also reacted fast, directing Shifter to call shore-based EMTs and NCIS. Smith told Shifter he would be back on the ship in half an hour, and to give NCIS full cooperation until he arrived.

Cline's lawyer then described how the lead agent, NCIS Special Agent Shey Cremer, came aboard *Ponce* shortly after the first responders, questioning everyone as Bacon's body was being photographed before being taken off the ship. Built like short, muscular tank, Cremer had long since perfected the slightly abrasive persona of a hardened cop, using it to good effect.

He prodded and verbally bullied everyone for several days, but he found all their stories remained consistent. The stories were too consistent for Cremer's taste, most especially Cline's story.

Cline's lawyer said that, despite the prosecution continually highlighting the sailors' history of violence, the idea that Cline had killed Bacon was not seen as credible enough to secure an arrest warrant. In fact, everyone Cremer spoke to indicated Cline and Bacon had developed a singularly tight and *exclusive* relationship. Witnesses described Cremer himself as "seeing stars" every time that came up.

At this point, the defense alleged Cremer's biases indicated he saw such relationships as signifying deviancy, violence, and even sociopathic behavior. The defense maintained that Cremer had focused on Cline due to Cremer's own prejudices. Cline's lawyer said this motivated Cremer to create a narrative allowing him to finally receive an arrest warrant for Cline in contravention of the facts.

The prosecution then called forth Operations Specialist 2nd Class Brandy Sniffer. Sniffer testified she had been on the ship's port side catwalk and had seen Cline kill Bacon. She recounted to the prosecution lawyer how Cline attacked Bacon and the two men fought, yelling so loudly their voices echoed around the well deck until Cline pushed Bacon to his death. Sniffer tearfully said she had been reluctant to come forward because she was afraid of Cline. According to her, Cline had been jealous of Sniffer and Bacon's romantic relationship and sought her for himself.

The prosecution went further, firmly telling the jury that no forensic evidence had been found that could have definitively cleared Cline. Logically, the prosecution said, this meant Sniffer's testimony should carry greater weight since she was the one person to have actually seen the fight.

Bacon's parents and sister refused to leave San Francisco and fly to Norfolk for the court-martial. The journey would be emotionally too difficult, they told local media. They could only hope the Navy would give them justice by destroying Cline for the corruption and murder of their boy. The prosecution read a deposition from Mr. and Mrs. Bacon to the jury on September 8, detailing their conviction Carl had been coerced into an unnatural relationship by Cline. The Bacons' deposition said Carl had never shown or discussed any interest in same-sex relationships, instead dating girls during his formative years before joining the Navy to see the world.

The defense fiercely objected to the Bacon family deposition, but the judge overruled their motion. The judge agreed with the prosecution's argument that such information was necessary for the jury to understand the personal behavioral histories leading up to the murder.

Cline's mother had traveled from Arkansas to be in the court room (his father had long since passed away). Mrs. Cline flat out refused to talk to the press, but was consistently seen shaking her head during the prosecution's arguments, especially whenever Cremer was on the stand. She actually leapt to her feet, yelling at the judge after he overruled the defense's objection to the Bacon family deposition and had to be led out of the courtroom. Sobbing hysterically, she continued to scream at the judge that her son was being railroaded simply for being gay.

Sitting in the gallery was another increasingly distressed observer. The man had already begun to wonder if there was something he should do. Admiral David E. Jones, Commander, U.S. Atlantic Command, reached the end of his rope when he saw Mrs. Cline dragged out of the courtroom by two aggressive bailiffs who showed no mercy to the distraught and terrified woman. Bystander he might be, but Jones decided to act.

Stepping in the late afternoon sunlight following the court's recess for the day, Jones walked straight into the gaggle of press that had been allowed on base for the circus. Long considered a top candidate for eventually becoming Chief of Naval Operations himself, Jones strove to remind his fellow citizens of a basic legal principle.

"I strongly condemn any rush to judgment against Petty Officer Cline," Jones said to the gathered media. "Obviously, the prosecution believes they have enough evidence to convict Petty Officer Cline, but their belief is *not* a verdict of 'guilty.' That will be up to a jury of our citizen-sailors to decide. It must be remembered that Petty Officer Cline is *innocent* unless he is *proven* guilty during the trial. This is one of the foundational principles of our entire justice system, and is the underpinning of many of our civil rights. The fact that we are protected from punishment based purely accusation must be cherished and protected, or else none of us will ever be truly safe."

That didn't go over well in the Five-Sided Puzzle Palace... er, the Pentagon.

Jones received an irate call that night from the CNO, ordering him to retract his statement and issue a new one saying the Navy would indeed convict Cline for murdering his shipmate.

Jones refused, and refused to be worried by threats to end his career (he'd been through them before, as a matter of fact). Jones felt deep in his bones that *something* was just not right in the whole affair. He couldn't quite put his finger on it...beyond an innate distrust of Shey Cremer bred decades earlier.

Long ago, then-Cmdr. David E. Jones' career had been in tatters after a series of murders swept through the squadron he commanded in Spain. He had been saved by a young sailor who, despite being falsely accused of the murders, solved the case. The oddly resilient young man had seen a tiny detail in a phone call that turned the whole thing around. Jones never forgot the suffering that sailor went through, nor just how quickly investigations can shift on a dime when a most unlikely fact is revealed as a key piece of evidence.

Jones intended to continue his intervention, but he needed to remain low-key to avoid the appearance of prejudicing the proceedings himself. The admiral made a late-night phone call that activated a small network of contacts. The court-martial would go on as it should, but the admiral decided the Bacon murder needed a second look. *Something* just didn't add up, so Jones mobilized the one person he knew who would not rest until the truth was exposed.

Admiral Jones unleashed the Accidental Detective.

Chapter 1

Friday, September 9; 13:11 hours
Norfolk, Virginia

"...Rear Admiral Joyce Durham, Commander, Navy Region Mid-Atlantic, issued a statement this morning that says, 'The Navy has a zero-tolerance policy for this kind of violence. Our men and women in uniform are, as a whole, dedicated to preserving life and protecting our fellow citizens. It is an unconscionable betrayal for Jarvis Cline to have murdered a fellow sailor, and we will ensure he suffers the full penalty under the law for his action. The Navy will not tolerate the presence of murderers or sexual predators within our ranks, and I want to assure all the women out there, especially those in uniform right now, that your safety from deviants like Petty Officer Cline is a top priority for Navy leadership.'"

"...Navy sources close to the situation confirmed today that Admiral David Jones, Commander, Atlantic Command, refused a direct order from the CNO to retract his statement of last night and issue one aligned with the CNO's own statement on the Navy's intent to punish Jarvis Cline for murdering Brandy Bacon on the destroyer *Ponce...*"

"...the senator said he's outraged by the Navy's lax standards in selecting its sailors, and he fully intends to punish the service for letting a sexual predator like Jarvis Cline into its ranks by withholding funding for key quality-of-life upgrades unless his demands for service-wide sensitivity training are met..."

"Isaac, you're a damned idiot!" Master Chief Petty Officer John Stiles said, looking across the table at the younger man. A short pause ensued before he repeated his statement for emphasis. "Isaac, you are an *idiot.* You're almost guaranteed to be selected for senior chief petty officer next year, but you're just going to freakin' quit and waste your goddamned anchors?!"

Stiles, in his mid-50s, had a slender frame supporting leathery skin weathered by years spent in the sun. His khaki uniform bore a colorful rack of service ribbons on his left side above the shirt pocket—a rack so big it was a wonder he didn't fall over.

Stiles was a 26-year Navy veteran and on the fast track to fleet master chief—a fleet commander's senior enlisted adviser. He was currently serving as the senior enlisted adviser to Commander, Atlantic Forces Surface Command.

Across the table sat the slightly younger man with oddly bright sea-green eyes peering through military-issue wire-rimmed glasses. Chief Petty Officer Isaac Shepherd's hair was, even at 44 years old, far more salt than pepper. Shepherd was decidedly much burlier than the slender Stiles, possessing a barrel chest and slightly rounded face with a strong jawline, capped by a somewhat weak chin that appeared to be trying to retreat from his face.

Shepherd plopped down his cheeseburger on the plate. Unlike Stiles, Shepherd was dressed in the blue "Aquaflage" working uniform affectionately (derisively?) known as the "Blueberries." Modeled off the Marine Corps' digital camouflage pattern uniform, but done in the blue and grays of the Navy.

"John, if your endgame is to get me to reconsider retiring next year, then you really should consider trying *not* to come off like an arrogant ass," Shepherd said, his voice as firm as a brick. "After 20 years of serving my country, I've earned the right to make a career decision without you, or anyone else, declaring I'm 'wasting my anchors.' You know as well as I do it's not how long you wear the anchors, it's what you *do* with them while you're an active duty chief."

Stiles was taken aback. Shepherd had always possessed a certain inner strength, but the past couple of years had seen the younger man develop a downright confrontational streak. Lately, Shepherd had also become rather cranky, and Stiles began to wonder if his approach was the wrong way to go. To buy himself time, Stiles took a bite of his steak and chewed, looking at Shepherd and waiting, putting the pressure on Shepherd to say something.

Shepherd wiped his mouth on his napkin and stared back, content to let the silence grow.

The two men were eating at The Pancake House, a popular a local staple located on Granby Street near the naval station. The diner was packed with people in uniform, all on their lunch breaks. The scent of fresh coffee waltzed with the smell of freshly cooked hamburgers while french fries sizzled and cold salads delivered bursts of botanical flavor.

Shepherd decided to use the awkward silence to his advantage by taking the off the top bun of his burger and dousing it with a fresh tide of black pepper.

Stiles finished chewing his steak and swallowed a spot of water to wash it down. He deliberately did not watch Shepherd reinforce the already thick layer of black pepper on top of the ketchup, mayo, and salt he had already put there. What was it with the man and his black-pepper-on-burgers fetish, anyway?

The silence grew increasingly uncomfortable for Stiles. He was used to being in control, but he felt that control quickly slipping away. Metaphorically blinking first, he broke the impasse and spoke again.

"You don't care about making a difference for the Navy anymore?" Stiles pressed the issue with a hard edge still in his voice.

Shepherd swigged his own iced tea (unsweetened as he didn't need the sugar) and shrugged. Up until now he had been enjoying the lunch. Shepherd and Stiles had never been close friends, but Stiles had been a treasured mentor ever since Shepherd was advanced to chief in 2012. Now, however, Shepherd was getting pissed off.

"John, among everything else I've done, I spent nearly seven years *teaching,* both at DINFOS and here at NEPAC East," Shepherd said, folding his hands and staring Stiles dead in the eye. Shepherd's baritone voice had gone cold. "I've graduated nearly 5,000 students from all pay grades, branches of service...hell, some civilians and even some international students. That alone gave me more influence in the military than most chiefs ever get to have, including *you.* Knock off this 'you're quitting' crap or else I'm pulling chocks and going back to work!"

Now Stiles was *really* taken aback. No one—*no one*—had spoken to him like *that* since he put on master chief years ago. Anger flared...and then Stiles' better judgment got the better of him.

He looked at Shepherd from a different perspective, realizing he really *hadn't* considered how much Shepherd had accomplished as an instructor...or anywhere else, for that matter. Besides, cranky or not, Shepherd had grown up a lot in the last four years. He wasn't the insecure, frightened young man Stiles had met in 2012. Stiles quickly shifted his rudder and decided a tactical retreat was in order until he better understood the man across the table from him.

Stiles held up his hands in a let's-make-peace gesture. "Ok, ok. I never was an instructor myself, so I never really thought of it like that."

"Damn straight!" Shepherd snapped, his voice and back still tight and eyes narrowed. Shepherd's eyes were an unusual feature that only he and his two identical brothers shared. "I'm not 'quitting' as you so crassly put it."

"Then what do you call it?" Stiles asked, but his tone and posture made it a genuine question, not an accusation.

"I call it time to find out who Isaac Shepherd is without the uniform. I've been laser-focused on the Navy since I was six years old. I've run a good race, but it's time for me to move on to new challenges," Shepherd's temper calmed as he sensed Stiles backing down.

"Y'all need anything?" Their waitress stopped by.

"Hmmm?" Stiles looked away from Shepherd. "Oh, no, thank you."

"I'm good," Shepherd said, smiling at her.

The young lady departed, her eyes lingering on Shepherd momentarily before turning away to continue her rounds.

"That girl is going to be really disappointed if she tries to give you her phone number," Stiles snorted.

"Say what?" Shepherd asked, oblivious.

"Isaac, she's been eyeballing you ever since we sat down. She's interested."

Shepherd actually looked a bit put off, "Well, sorry, but *my* interests lie elsewhere."

Stiles clunked his elbows on the table and folded his hands.

"About that, how are you suddenly gay if you were married and have a daughter?" Stiles blurted out the question. Evidently he'd been wanting to ask that for a long time.

This is ridiculous! Do I really have to go through this again?! Shepherd thought angrily.

"For one, I'm not 'suddenly' anything," Shepherd said, his voice tightening again. "You know what the world we grew up in was like. Jennifer knew I was gay when we started dating, but we thought we could make a mixed-orientation relationship work. Obviously, we couldn't. As to Martha, she's my step-daughter. Her father, Jenn's first husband, died when Martha was only two."

"If you really knew you were gay, what made think you could sustain a marriage?"

"Stupidity and society," Shepherd snapped as his temper now fully erupted. The words flowed in an angry torrent. "The world we grew up in made people like me the punchline of girly-man jokes, or else the perverted villains of movies...and then there was my own obsession with appearing 'normal' to avoid being labeled a pervert. Hell, John, you yourself made quite a few gay jokes and insulted quite a few selectees on the IKE as 'fairies' and 'wanna-be faggots' during my initiation season!"

Stiles recoiled in shock. He was *definitely* not used to be on the defensive.

"As to me," Shepherd shook his head, clearly restraining himself from a greater tirade, "Well, just accept that I thought I could live by someone else's script instead of reality, and now have to spend the rest of my life living with the consequences of the dumpster fire I caused. The divorce is just about a year behind us, so Jennifer can at least try to find a normal guy, and not a fraud like me."

Stiles didn't know what to say, and it was an experience he certainly didn't enjoy.

"Now, why don't we get to the *real* reason you asked me here today, John?" Shepherd said, an iron curtain descending behind his eyes. "In four years, you've never asked me to meet you anywhere to discuss professional matters except your office.

What's so important you deviated from the norm and want to discuss a professional issue with me out in public?"

Stiles glanced out the window, and then back to Shepherd. It was obvious to a blind man Shepherd would shut down any further discussion of his career and personal life. Stiles shifted gears to the matter at hand.

"Isaac, I need the 'Accidental Detective' to take on one more case."

"You need *what?*" Shepherd clearly had not expected to hear *that* moniker again.

Stiles was pleased to see he had surprised Shepherd. When dealing hyperactive, hyper-intelligent, and hyper-intuitive man like Shepherd, the rare moments when one caught him off guard were moments to be savored.

"You're the 'Accidental Detective' for a reason, aren't you?" Stiles asked. "For the past 20 years you've stuck your nose into murder mysteries and assorted terrorist incidents. As far as I know, you've solved them all."

Shepherd snorted.

"You can thank Abraham Gray for that nickname," Shepherd said. "I'm done with all that and ready to move on."

"I know, but you've been following the Cline court-martial, haven't you?" Stiles asked.

Shepherd nodded unhappily. "Yeah. Nothing new there. Typical political cowardice we unfortunately see in all too many senior leaders. So what?"

Stiles looked directly into Shepherd's eyes with an intensity that could have frozen an iceberg.

"Isaac, someone we both know and *highly* respect believes Cline might be innocent."

"Really?" Shepherd's eyebrows lifted and settled about midway up his forehead. "So a mysterious 'someone' wants me to stick my nose in where it doesn't belong? Granted, I've done that a lot over the last 20 years, but that's one of the reasons I'm retiring. I'm done playing detective."

"Ok, then," Stiles said. "But I'd hate to see Admiral Jones' face when I tell him you're not a player."

Stiles' delivery was so deadpan that it took a moment for the import of Stiles' sentence to hit Shepherd.

"Admiral Jones?" Shepherd asked blankly.

"Yeah," Stiles said, smirking as he caught Shepherd off-guard twice in as many minutes. *I think I just set a record!*

"Admiral Jones?" Shepherd repeated, his voice now slightly higher.

"Yes. Admiral Jones. Commander, U.S. Atlantic Command." Stiles went on. *"That's* why we're meeting here at The Pancake House; we're just two chiefs out for lunch. The noise level in this place is a nice way to camouflage a conversation."

"I see," Shepherd said, struggling to hold onto his poker face.

"He asked for you specifically," Stiles nodded. "Apparently, he has a great deal of faith in your ability to find out the truth, whatever that truth actually is. But, hey, if you don't want the job, I'll tell him—"

Shepherd started laughing uncontrollably. A few heads turned at the booming staccato.

"John, you bastard! You know I'd never, *ever* turn down a request from him! He was the greatest CO I ever had!"

Stiles smiled, savoring his victory.

"Ok, ok. Well played, you bastard! I'm in," Shepherd conceded, his eyes sparkling with mirth. "Tell the admiral to expect a hefty bill; I charge by the hour! So, where do I start?"

Stiles raised his eyebrows, "You tell me; you're the 'Accidental Detective.' The most I know are crime shows on TV. Where do you usually start?"

Shepherd laughed at himself. "To phrase my question more accurately, does the admiral have any specific information for *me?"*

"No," Stiles said. "When we spoke last night Jones told me he just had a feeling that something wasn't right, but it was only a feeling. He doesn't trust one of the agents involved in the case. Some numb-nut named Shey Cremer."

Shepherd's face went white.

Stiles read Shepherd's body language. "I take it you know him?"

"I do," Shepherd said. "I was appalled to find out on the news he was the leading NCIS investigator. The bastard falsely accused *me* of murder 20 years ago. He's been a thorn in my side ever since and definitely has it in for me."

"Why?"

"Why did he accuse me of murder, or why does he have it in for me?"

"Both," Stiles responded.

"I found a dead body in my barracks 20 years ago. Quite often, the person 'finding' the body is the culprit," Shepherd explained. "More basic than that—he found out I was gay. His favorite name for me ever since is 'faggot.' That should tell you a lot about him."

Stiles nodded, feeling acutely uncomfortable again. "I see. Anyway, the admiral just has a feeling he can't pin down, so he asked me to contact you. This has to be done as quietly as possible; there's already enough publicity surrounding the trial that's made the Navy look like a bag of crap."

"Well, gut feelings can be a very good starting point for looking at a case from a fresh perspective." Shepherd said, wiping his mouth and then dropping his wadded-up napkin on top of his plate. "Ok, I'll see what I can turn up."

"You going to call that NCIS friend of yours?" Stiles asked.

"I have too," Shepherd said, pushing back his chair and stretching his long legs. "This isn't the 19th century. One doesn't just stumble into the machinery of law enforcement like you see in the movies. If it wasn't for Abe Gray and a few others who've put up with me, I'd have had *no* career as an 'Accidental Detective,' but would probably have toured some of the finest brigs in the Navy."

"You need to be discreet, Issac," Stiles reminded Shepherd. "Jones is on the hot seat right now. I've heard the CNO is *pissed* and sped right past 'pressuring him' to 'ordering him' to retract his original press statement. The CNO wants Cline's ass buried as soon as possible. Jones refused."

Shepherd nodded, signaling the waitress for their checks. "He's never been one to back down when he believes he's right. That's one reason I want to be like him when I grow up."

"I got this," Stiles said, taking both checks from the waitress, who did not take her eyes off Shepherd. "Call it a retainer on your...your 'services.'"

The two men got up and headed to the register. Stiles paid before they stepped out into the humid Virginia afternoon. Putting on their covers, the two began walking to their cars.

"Just so you know, the admiral will be calling your command today," Stiles said quietly, a trickle of sweat already appearing on his temple. "He's going to smooth the way with your leadership so you can do what you need to do."

"That'll be helpful," Shepherd said. "It's hard enough having to deal with the OIC at my own NEPAC center, but having the CO of whole worldwide shebang across the street makes things rather...rather interesting, politically speaking."

Stiles stuck out a tough, and callused hand. Shepherd gripped it with an equally tough, callused hand.

"Thanks, Isaac," Stiles said. "Odds are Cline is guilty as hell, but the service needs his trial to be run fairly and the evidence gathered properly. Just keep a low profile; any appearance of impropriety will harm all of us. And, please, don't place yourself in any unnecessary danger."

"Not that I've ever done *that*," Shepherd said, rolling his eyes.

Shepherd parked *Sarah Jane,* his whimsically-named small, blue SUV, and headed to the NEPAC East building. The parking lot was strangely empty, even for an early Friday afternoon. Besides *Sara Jane,* the parking lot was occupied by only a few other cars and the somnolent NEPAC East duty van. He would not have been surprised to see a tumbleweed blow lazily across the lot in the dusky, damp breeze of the afternoon. Shepherd noticed an SUV with a sticker reading "coexist," but the letters of the word were made up of various characters and symbols associated with video games. He smiled, knowing who that vehicle belonged to.

The Navy Expeditionary Public Affairs Command East building was located in what used to be an old photo lab on what had been Naval Air Station Norfolk, an air base established in 1917 along side the old Naval Operating Base Norfolk, which had also been established in 1917. In 1998 the two bases had been merged into the modern Naval Station Norfolk, the largest naval station in the world. Naval Station Norfolk was so big it dictated traffic patterns across Hampton Roads even on the weekends.

A 1932 art deco building sat on the other side of 3rd Avenue directly across from the building housing NEPAC Ease. The building had once been a barracks, but now housed the HQ of the worldwide NEPAC organization. The command was made up of three centers: NEPAC East in Norfolk, Virginia; NEPAC West in Bremerton, Washington; and NEPAC Japan in, well, Japan.

NEPAC existed to put public affairs officers and enlisted Mass Communication Specialists onto the Navy's ships when they deployed, as well as send them to shore-based exercises and special assignments. In the modern Navy, only aircraft carriers and large-deck amphibious assault ships (the ones that looked like mini-carriers) have media centers, and those are only manned at half-strength when the ship isn't on a deployment. A select few other ships have a single MC assigned to them, but still often needed extra manning when deployed. The NEPAC detachments brought these capacities up to full strength.

Shepherd was currently the "dual-hatted" leading chief petty officer of both Production and Operations Departments. In his capacity as Ops LCPO, he oversaw training, equipping, and deploying nearly 50 public affairs officers and MCs to (currently) three carrier strike groups, three amphibious readiness groups, an odd assortment of land-based European exercises, and one hospital ship providing medical care to the east coast of South America.

His other responsibility was ensuring the Production Department got things done. Production was manned by sailors home between deployments. Fortunately, he had found a terrific Mass Communication Specialist 1st Class to act as the leading petty officer of both departments.

Shepherd quietly entered the Production Room. Two computer banks were set up on two rows of tables. One bank was made up of PCs connected to the Navy's internal network. The other set of computers was where the magic happened—Apple computers the MCs used for production work.

Sitting at the LPO's desk was a muscular young black woman who looked powerful enough to beat a U.S. Marine at arm wrestling. Her desk had very few personal items on it, but amongst them was a trophy and a couple of video game figurines.

"MC1 Robertson!" Shepherd said just a bit loudly, causing her to jump.

"Jeez! Dammit, Chief, you gave me a heart attack!" Dionne Robertson said, putting a hand to her chest to steady herself.

"Where is everyone?" Shepherd asked, smiling mischievously.

Robertson was wearing the Navy Service Uniform of a khaki shirt over black trousers and black leather shoes. Her crows glinted on her collars and a small ribbon rack adorned her left breast area.

"OIC cut everyone loose," She answered.

"Then why are you still here?" Shepherd asked. "Why don't you use the extra time to get ready for that romantic getaway to Cape Charles with your new boyfriend?"

"We're both already packed. Unfortunately, Jacob's ship has an audit going on," Robertson replied. "He won't be getting off work until 17:00, so we'll head to the B&B later tonight. I figured I might as well use the time to tie up the supply report. Somewhere our numbers got fouled up after that last shipment of memory cards. I want to do this one myself while it was quiet."

Indeed, next to her right arm, was a pile of memory cards. She was clearly checking each card's serial number verifying it against a spreadsheet on her monitor.

"So someone *forgot* to keep track of the *memory* cards?" Shepherd quipped. It was a feeble joke, even by his abysmally corny standards, but, hey, why not?

"Cute," Robertson said. "We've got that bi-annual audit coming up next month, you know. I don't feel like telling the inspector general we lost a few thousand dollars' worth of memory cards, but the only way to straighten out this mess is to verify each one by hand."

"Sounds like fun," Shepherd said dryly. "But I do appreciate you jumping on that. I was going to talk to you about it next week. Still, keep track of the time you're taking to do this. I'll comp you for the time spent."

Shepherd had long kept his eye on Robertson, ever since he had been been her instructor at DINFOS when she was training to be an MC. She was an unlikely sailor, what with her early career as a professional middle-weight mixed-martial arts competitor. She boasted several gold medals, and even sported a silver from the Olympics. Ultimately, she got bored with competition and joined the Navy to do something fun.

Shepherd was certain Robertson would be selected for chief somewhere in the next two years.

"Roger that!" Robertson said happily. "How was your lunch with Master Chief Stiles?"

"Not what I expected," Shepherd said. "It wasn't bad, but did he asked me to look into a problem for him."

"Did he read you the riot act for dropping your retirement papers?"

"If he didn't, I damn well will!" Boomed a voice that made both sailors jump.

"Dammit, Ben!" Shepherd groused, restarting his heart. "Didn't you transfer upstairs to COMCAM last year?! *I'm* the only one authorized to scare the tobacco juice out of people around here now!"

Chief Benjamin Foltz tromped into the production area, his own khaki uniform looking a bit droopy from the August humidity.

"Sparky, I made chief a year before you," Foltz said, an evil grin on his face as he used Shepherd's old Navy nickname from his aviation maintenance days. "I get to scare you whenever I damn well want!"

Shepherd laughed, clasping Foltz's hand. "You haven't come downstairs for a few weeks now. How's COMCAM treating you?"

Combat Camera East Coast was located on the second floor of the building housing NEPAC East. COMCAM's mission was to support special forces missions.

Shepherd and Foltz had been partners running the NEPAC East training program for
two years until Foltz transferred to COMCAM the previous May.

"Well, we got the final word," Foltz said, settling into a chair. He was a spare, angular man who could have played a grown-up version of Shaggy from the *Scooby Doo* cartoons. His voice carried a light twang left over from his central Pennsylvania roots. "COMCAM is shutting down next year."

Shepherd nodded, unbuttoning and removing his blouse. Hanging it over the back of a chair, he plopped down and leaned back, hands behind his head.

"Wow," Shepherd said. "That's been a two-year fight. What finally put them over the edge?"

"Let me guess," Robertson spoke up, "They've been refusing to help fill public affairs missions, and, since special forces are using drones and helmet-mounted cameras now, they just ran out of missions to justify their existence."

"I'm impressed, Dionne," Foltz said, and he looked it. "You nailed it exactly. The CO refused to 'lower his command's status' to 'mere public affairs fluff'—his words, by the way, not mine—so Big Navy decided to shut down COMCAM."

"Never underestimate Dionne," Shepherd advised Foltz. "Her sagacious perspicacity seldom fails to notice the nuance of a situation."

Shepherd was betting the overblown vocabulary would annoy Foltz, and Foltz didn't disappoint him.

"Spark, if you don't start using normal English, I swear I'm going to throw my shoe at you!"

Shepherd and Robertson burst out laughing. Foltz tried to look angry, but failed miserably and finally let a chuckle loose.

"So, John busted your ass over dropping your retirement papers, Spark?" Foltz leaned back, putting his feet up on a table.

"Isn't it kind of uncool to try and hard-sell someone on staying in?" Robertson asked.

"Different people have different styles, Dionne," Shepherd said. "Stiles is pretty much your traditional, old-fashioned master chief. Besides, he'd be failing if he didn't at least *try* to make a case to keep me in. That's part of leadership, you know: doing your part to try and keep the service manned. Of course, the other part is knowing when a person is finally done and helping them transition out in a responsible way."

"And Spark here has never made a bad decision in his life," Foltz drawled.

Shepherd shot him a bemused look, but Foltz was busy polishing his halo.

"So, the master chief *didn't* accept your decision?" Robertson asked.

"Oh, no, not that," Shepherd shook his head. "Sorry; that wasn't the impression I meant to convey. No, John pushed me to stay in, but when he was satisfied I really mean to retire next year, he let it go. He thinks I'm an idiot for getting out now, but, at least, I'm an idiot he respects."

"Well, he and I at least agree on the 'idiot' part," Foltz said to the ceiling.

Robertson quickly turned her laugh into a cough.

"Don't you have a drill you need to go put through you ear or something?" Shepherd laughed.

Foltz smiled, "I'm just yanking your chain, Spark."

"Oh, I know!" Shepherd said, gearing up to zing Foltz again. "After all, your inability to match pace with my indefatigable wit only attests to your mundanity of thought."

"Indefa—*what?!*" Foltz said. He reached down, pulled off his black leather shoe and tossed it at Shepherd.

Shepherd laughed as he caught the flying footwear, tossing it back to Foltz.

Robertson smiled, "I've known a few seamen and third class petty officers I thought were idiots for getting out after only one hitch. But, then, like you said, it's their choice."

Shepherd rose to his considerable height and pulled his blouse back on before heading out. At 6'4", he towered over most people and had a devil of a time finding pants long enough for his legs anywhere but in a specialty shop. More than once a Navy uniform supplier had been flummoxed when requesting a uniform item for him.

"Dionne, I'm going to be out of the office for a few days next week. If you need anything, call me on my cell," Shepherd said. "I'll let the OIC and the rest of our leadership know."

"No problem!"

"You busy this afternoon, Spark? I've got a load of wood to split, and an extra sledge hammer you can use on the wedge." Foltz said as he also got up. Foltz's own 6'2" frame was visibly shorter than Shepherd's, but his wiry build created the illusion he was taller.

The two started heading down the hall as Shepherd buttoned his blouse.

"I can't," Shepherd said, not realizing their voices were traveling back to Robertson. "I've got to head over to NCIS and talk to Abe Gray."

"*Another* case?!" Foltz said. "You said you were getting out of the murder business."

"I did, and I meant it," Shepherd said as they reached the back door. "This one got handed to me by someone I can't say 'no' to."

Chapter 2
Friday, September 9; 15:07 hours
Naval Station Norfolk, Virginia

"Isaac, you're an idiot!"

Shepherd's face contorted with irritation, "Just *how* am I an idiot, Abe?"

NCIS Special Agent Abraham Gray's gray-blue eyes peered out from under a head of neatly groomed shock-white hair. The 50-year-old special agent was a tall man himself at 6'1." Regular exercise and a healthy diet enabled him to retain a slender frame and exude youthful energy. Gray boasted a reputation as being one of NCIS' most brilliant investigators, although his mind didn't quite pulse with the same power as Shepherd's.

Sitting on an ancient, faux-leather, government-issued couch, Gray ignored the ancient faux-leather squeaking in protest. Not surprising, that squeaking—the couch was probably issued during the administration of the President Theodore Roosevelt.

"Isaac, the trial's *already started,*" Gray said. He wore an impeccable blue suit, red tie, and American-flag lapel pin. The combination of white hair, upright carriage, and sartorial preferences sometimes resulted in Gray being mistaken for a political candidate.

"The evidence being presented is almost purely circumstantial, as I know you know," Shepherd said, his own large frame resting on another government-issued sofa that looked like something straight out of a World War II movie. "Come on, old friend. I know circumstantial evidence and one eye-witness can reasonably convict a person. Still, you have to admit the whole circus in that courtroom looks like, well, a circus. Is it *not* theoretically possible Cline is innocent?"

The two men were sitting in the small, airy lobby of the NCIS building on board Naval Station Norfolk. Located near the piers, the building had a grand view of a parking lot, fire station, McDonald's restaurant, and the masts of ships sprouting like weeds into the sky. The receptionist, sitting behind bulletproof glass at the front desk, did not hide her disdain as she stared at Shepherd.

Gray crossed his arms and looked out the windows. "What I want to know is why you suddenly decided to dive into this one, Isaac? When we had you over for dinner last week, you told me and Sarah one reason you're retiring is that you want to stop playing detective."

"I meant what I said," Shepherd answered. "However, a certain factor got my attention."

"What factor?" Gray demanded.

"Admiral Jones."

Gray dropped his arms and sat up straighter. "Admiral Jones asked you to look into this?"

Shepherd nodded, "Not directly, but through John Stiles over at AFSC. According to John, the admiral isn't satisfied with what he's seen at the trial."

"This puts me in a bit of an awkward position," Gray said, looking as if he had just sat down on an angry hedgehog. "I'm not about to ignore a request from Admiral Jones any more than you are, but I'm also a special agent in one of the bureaus *helping prosecute the case.* I can't just go reopen the investigation."

Shepherd shrugged, "I'm aware of that, and I'm sorry to put you in such a delicate position."

Gray cocked his head, disbelief dripping from his expression.

"Well, ok, I'm not actually sorry," Shepherd admitted. "Still, you know there's no way I can get access to anything without your help. I guess we'll just have do this thing very quietly."

Gray dropped his head into his hands, exasperated. Finally shaking his head in apparent surrender, he looked back up.

"Ok, ok," Gray said, "I'll talk to Charlotte about this and get back to you."

"Thanks," Shepherd said, getting up. "Look, odds are the evidence *will* prove beyond a reasonable doubt Cline killed Bacon. But, we both know it never hurts to take a second look at the evidence. Innocent men and women have been wrongly convicted before, so I guess this will just be a check to ensure *that* outcome doesn't happen."

Gray also stood and shook Shepherd's hand. "I'll let you know what Charlotte says later this evening."

"Thanks," Shepherd said. He stretched and rubbed the back of his neck. "Hopefully this won't take long. NEPAC East has a double change in our leadership to get ready for in December. My OIC transfers out the same week as the CO of NEPAC turns over command to our next skipper—a Capt. Messenger, I think. I'll need to be focused on those events. Also, Chief Season is underway right now and I'm helping with that a little."

"Chief Season" was a six-week long intensive training period for the 1st class petty officers selected for advancement to chief petty officer.

"You're not keeping Chief Season at arm's length this year?" Gray asked, surprised. "I thought you'd be too busy planning for retirement to get into the reindeer games?"

"I'm mostly staying out of it," Shepherd said, picking up his cover. "This year the pinning ceremony got pushed back a week to Sept. 23, so next weekend I volunteered to set up a heritage event on the *Wisconsin* with Cody Rupp and Ben Foltz."

Gray nodded, "That should be fun. Alright, just stay out of trouble until I can—!"

"What in the HELL are you doing here?!"

Gray and Shepherd both nearly coughed up their spleens in shock as Special Agent Shey Cremer blasted through the receptionist's door into the lobby, his voice bellowing like a wounded elephant's.

"What the *hell* are you doing here?!" Cremer demanded again, stopping and staring up at the much taller Shepherd.

Shepherd noticed the receptionist smirking. Evidently, she'd been the one to alert Cremer to the his presence.

"That's really none of your business, Cremer," Shepherd said, an edge to his voice.

"Abe, I've already let Charlotte know this accidental wannabe is here," Cremer growled. "It doesn't take a genius to figure out he wants to meddle in the Cline prosecution."

"Wow, Cremer," Shepherd said with sarcastic enthusiasm. "Your deductive skills are firing on all cylinders today! And here I thought you didn't have enough brain power to toast an English muffin."

"Isaac!" Gray snapped, rolling his eyes. "You *know* that doesn't help."

"It helps *me* feel better," Shepherd was all innocence.

"You get your faggot ass out of this office!" Cremer ordered.

"Shey!" Gray snapped, "Don't *ever* use derogatory slurs like that! Especially around me!"

Cremer snorted, "You are directed to leave, *Chief* Shepherd. Abe, Charlotte wants to see you. Now."

Gray sighed wearily, "Isaac, we'll talk soon, ok?"

Shepherd reached out and shook Gray's hand again. "Ok."

"Off to the gay bar?" Cremer sneered.

"Why? Are you looking for a date, big boy?" Shepherd said in a silky voice. Blowing Cremer a sarcastic kiss, Shepherd popped his cover onto his head, and left.

"What the *hell* is wrong with you, man?!" Gray's anger broke over the much shorter Cremer. "I don't give a *damn* what your personal feelings about Isaac are; you go around using derogatory slurs like that and you'll open us up to a lawsuit!"

"Whatever," Cremer huffed.

Charlotte Webb, Special Agent in Charge of the NCIS Norfolk Field Office, was a thick, solid black woman. She did not suffer fools and hid a rebellious streak under her formidable facade. She was known to be wise, scrupulously fair, and had a reputation for trying the most unconventional means available if it meant legally gaining the evidence she needed to convict a suspect...or prove their innocence.

This was the second time Gray had worked for her. He first met her when she had taken over the NCIS resident agency office on board Naval Station Rota in Spain nearly 20 years ago. He had been as delighted to be professionally reunited with her as he had been unhappy when Shey Cremer also joined the Norfolk field office the same time as Webb. Gray never made the mistake of taking Webb's support for granted. Webb was cautious and just as likely to direct Gray to keep out of the Bacon case as she was to have him reevaluate it with Shepherd's help.

"Abraham, Shey," Webb gestured to the chairs opposite her desk. Her office looked out over the waterfront. Bright sunlight filtered a zig-zag pattern through the blinds across a bookshelf laden with law books. "Please, sit down. Shey tells me Isaac Shepherd was here. It doesn't take Sherlock Holmes to guess it's about the Bacon case. Is that true?"

"Correct," Gray said.

Webb smoothed her red blazer and leaned back, folding her hands atop her gray skirt. "That's it? Just 'correct?'"

Gray shrugged, "You asked me a question, and I answered it."

She raised a single eyebrow, to all appearances irritated. Gray knew her too well, however; she was actually amused at his insouciance.

"I would like a bit more detail, Abraham." Webb was often just as formal in her use of names as Shepherd was. Gray sometimes wondered if they'd picked up the habit during their graduate course work.

"Admiral Jones requested Isaac reevaluate the case against Cline," Gray said. "Jones is *not* making a case that Cline *is* innocent, but feels the case is based on shoddy case work and thinks the circus atmosphere surrounding the trial is soiling the Navy's reputation. He fears the Navy is creating the appearance that senior leaders are keelhauling a junior sailor just to protect themselves. To be honest, Charlotte, I agree."

"Bullshit!" Cremer spat, enraged at Gray's direct swipe at him. "'Shoddy case work' my ass! Just because I moved fast to nail a freaking *murderer* doesn't mean my work is shoddy! This situation does *not* need your pet puppy interfering!"

"'Pet puppy?'" Gray snapped. "Shey, do you *ever* listen to yourself?!"

"Enough." Webb said quietly. Such was the force of her personality that she did not need to raise her voice. Both men fell silent.

She fixed Gray with her eyes, "Abraham, you know very well I'll move Heaven and Hell if I believe there's a chance an innocent person is in jeopardy of being wrongfully convicted. You need to *convince* me there *is* a reasonable doubt in this situation. While Shey's...enthusiasm...is sometimes, in my opinion, excessive, the case he helped build is tight enough the JAG went to court with it. His work does include finding doe eye-witness, I must add. What argument can you make that would convince me we need to reevaluate the situation?"

Cremer crossed his arms and looked rather smug.

Webb ignored him and went on.

"To use an expression Chief Shepherd often uses, we have a 'metric butt-ton' of other casework to do already. You must give me a logical reason that convinces me to reallocate our resources."

Gray sighed. "Charlotte, the only 'logical' reason I can give is that it *is* logical to take a round turn on our own work if we don't have forensic evidence."

"'Round turn?'" Cremer asked.

"A mariner's term," Gray said. "A 'round turn' means adding extra loops of a line around a bollard or a cleat or a piling to ensure the line is secure. Sailors also use it to mean double-checking a job to ensure it's done right. You've spent *25 years* around the Navy and never picked up that term?"

Webb redirected the conversation before Cremer could reply to Gray's latest verbal jab. "That's not good enough, Abraham. You have three cases that I can think of right now that need your attention. Carla has four. Shey has four, *not* counting his assistance on the Cline prosecution. Claudia has four—"

"You said it yourself, Charlotte," Gray said, interrupting her. "I have only three cases, everyone else has four. I have the time to review the evidence against Cline and make sure we're tracking on it."

"You want to work *against* me while I'm helping prosecute a case?!" Cremer barked.

"Shey," Webb silenced Cremer. She was always amazed by the depth of her skills as an actress. No one would ever guess she despised Shey Cremer as much as she did the members of the Ku Klux Klan who terrorized her family in Tennessee when she was a very small child. Her facade led most people to conclude she simply believed Cremer's exuberance needed to be reigned in now and then...

...until the day Cremer handed her something she could use to kick him out of NCIS, that is.

"Abraham," Webb said again, "You aren't convincing me."

Webb studied Gray's face closely as she talked. She knew him well enough to know he had an ace up his sleeve; she was just waiting for him to play it. "So far I see no evidence that is *not* happening, despite the media frenzy and the CNO behaving...the CNO making ill-advised public statements."

"Shey *has* helped amass a very tight case against OS2 Cline," Gray said, barely able to keep a straight face as he said it. Still, better to keep peace as he zeroed in on the *real* problem now that the preliminary sparring match with Cremer was over. "The issue is the fact that all the evidence on the prosecution's side is circumstantial. Yes, there is a witness who believes she saw the murder. Yes, Cline and Bacon had a history of fighting. Yes, Cline had anger management issues. I grant all that, but there's *no* direct forensic tie here placing Cline at the scene of the Bacon murder, and we all know honest witnesses testifying in good faith can still be mistaken."

"Abe, you know very well a large number of cases are won on circumstantial evidence," Cremer growled. "These punks we take down are too smart to leave anything so direct as a webcam recording of them perpetrating their crimes."

"Shey makes a very good point, Abraham," Webb said.

Gray nodded. "I concede all that, but I must again point out that we have *no* forensic evidence in this case. If Cline *did* push Bacon over the catwalk railing after fighting, why didn't Cline leave any uniform fibers on Bacon? Why is there no evidence of DNA transfer if the two men were in a *physical* altercation? Why were no fibers or biological material from Bacon found on any of

Cline's uniforms? Cline still had the uniform from the night of the murder in his laundry bag when he was arrested. Why were there no fibers or biological material from Bacon on *that* uniform? Frankly, the prosecution's narrative is statistically impossible."

"We have an eyewitness!" Cremer spat out in disbelief. "You think that's not important?!"

"Shey," Gray smoothly circled back to his earlier point, "We've all seen 'eye-witnesses' who were simply mistaken, and 'eye-witnesses' who were outright liars. I'm *not* accusing Petty Officer Sniffer of anything, but I *am* curious why a violent fight left no forensic evidence behind? Is it possible Sniffer saw someone who, from the other side of the ship, resembled Cline? There's also the problem that her story of a love triangle is vastly at odds with a lot of the perceptions held of the Cline/Bacon relationship expressed by the people you interviewed."

Cremer did not see the piercing look Webb shot Gray after his remark about the lack of forensic evidence supporting Sniffer's testimony.

"So, then *you* do the review," Cremer sneered. "We don't need that amateur ass sticking his nose into our business. He's a *public affairs* dork, for god's sake! What does *he* know about law enforcement?!"

"Other than his dual degrees in history and criminology?" Gray seized the opening Cremer accidentally gave him. "Other than the fact that he solved the Symko case in Spain 20 years ago when *you* were incorrectly accusing *him* of the murder? Or the fact that he solved the Blake murder on the *Carl Vinson* back in 2001? Or that he was the one who broke the terrorist plot on Guam with the *Pacific Blaze* in—"

"Enough, Abraham, your point is well taken," Webb silenced the litany. "You still have yet to convince me, but you are making progress."

Cremer's jaw dropped.

"Doing a review can only help protect us, especially with the lack of forensic evidence." Gray said. "You know very well the defense is going hammer that point home to the jury. This is the TV-addicted 21st century. *Everyone* on that jury has probably watched enough crime shows to know that forensic evidence is generally key to getting a conviction or acquittal in the modern world."

Cremer looked like a steam boiler nearing explosion. Webb looked cool as a glacier in winter. Gray looked like a presidential candidate sitting for an interview.

Gray crossed his legs, folded his hands on his lap, and concluded his pitch. "If we don't cover all bases and this case goes south on us—by which I mean Cline is acquitted—it'll look like we tried to railroad an innocent sailor. Hell, Admiral Donovan's *already* generated a huge backlash with his remarks. TV commentators are comparing his statement to the way the Navy tried to blame two innocent sailors for the *Iowa* explosion back in 1989."

"What if the press gets wind that Chief Shepherd is nosing about the case?" Webb asked. "That will look just as bad for the Navy."

Gray held up his hands in defeat, "I can't argue against that point, Charlotte. What I can offer is that you *know* Isaac. He knows how to be discreet...especially if I'm there to back him up. I still think it's a win/win for us. Isaac and I either prove Shey's on the right track, or else we prove we really *are* going after the wrong person, in which case NCIS becomes the hero of the hour by rescuing Cline from a false conviction and bringing the real murderer to justice."

Webb sat quietly, obviously weighing Gray's argument. The lack of forensic evidence had been bothering her for some time, and 21st century juries did expect forensic evidence. Gray's forthright argument forced her to consider her own doubts.

"Charlotte," Gray said, "There's something else to consider."

"What?"

"Admiral Jones asked Isaac to look into this," Gray said. "You and I both know Isaac Shepherd will *never* refuse Admiral Jones. Isaac's going to get into this whether we like it or not."

"You don't think *we* can stop one rogue chief petty officer from interfering in official business?" Cremer sneered.

Gray looked at Cremer, "Shey, tell me *one* time in the last 20 years *any* of us were *ever* successful in stopping Isaac from doing exactly what *he* wanted to do? Hmmm? Well? No? I rest my case."

Gray looked back to Webb, "Charlotte, stopping Isaac has been one of the few failures of my career. He's going to do this. Wouldn't it be therefore prudent to have me work *with* him instead of us unsuccessfully trying to work *against* him? After all, as Shey frequently points out, Isaac *is* a public affairs specialist. He's cultivated numerous media contacts in the local area alone. Do you want to risk him getting the media onto the angle that we're railroading an innocent sailor?"

"You believe he would?" Webb asked, folding her hands again.

"I *know* he would," Gray said. "What better weapon could he use against the Navy if no one listens to him and he believes—or even proves—Cline is innocent? Isaac'll never allow false accusations or convictions to go unchallenged. If he believes an innocent life is at stake, he'll use any means necessary to help that person."

"If Shepherd defies us *and* his own chain of command, he'll get his fag...his ass brought up on charges and thrown out of the Navy!" Cremer barked, barely stopping himself from using the slur. His neck muscles were bulging; always a sign of anger. "He'll lose his precious career!"

"Shey," Gray looked sanguinely at Cremer, "Isaac is a *chief's* chief. He *believes* in what those chief's anchors symbolize. He will protect his sailors and the Navy, even at his own expense. He won't hesitate to sacrifice his career if he believes he's protecting an innocent man. Yes, we could destroy him professionally, but we *have* to consider the damage *he* can inflict if we do."

Webb narrowed her eyes, letting the cool Gray and the spluttering Cremer sit in silence for a moment as she thought.

"I'll let you know what I decide. Please excuse me, gentlemen," She finally said, still looking thoughtfully at Gray.

"You can't be serious?!" Cremer blew up, jumping to his feet. "You're going to jeopardize my case *and* let some fruitcake stick his nose into *our* business *again?!*"

"I said, *please excuse me, gentlemen,*" Webb looked at Cremer, her quiet voice steely.

Cremer's powerful arms quivered with rage, but he turned on the ball of his feet and stomped out.

Gray followed Cremer out of the office, but with a much more relaxed gait. He gave no hint of the elation he felt. For all her outward reserve, Webb had long ago recognized the unique value Shepherd brought to the table. Gray was certain she'd decide in his favor.

Besides, Gray *had* told Webb the truth: stopping Shepherd from playing detective had been one of the few failures of his career. He'd accepted the defeat years ago. Changing his approach to their relationship he instead, made use of Shepherd's vast talents while acting as a mentor, guide, and friend to the brilliant and partially unstable younger man. Gray considered it a mark of success that Shepherd was finally ready to hang up his deerstalker hat when he hung up his Navy uniform.

The Yellow Duck, Shepherd's humorously named yellow-sided house, stood on the corner of Tennant Avenue and Baker Street in Suffolk, one of the seven cities making up Hampton Road. Suffolk was a major peanut producer, and had been home to the first mass production facility of the Planters company in 1913. Even further back, Suffolk held the dubious distinction of being burned to the ground by British forces in 1779 during the American Revolution.

Shepherd and Jennifer, his now ex-wife, purchased the Yellow Duck in 2013, closing on it only six months before Jennifer filed for divorce (she would forever ruefully joke about her atrocious timing on that score). She waived all rights to it, preferring to move with their daughter to a small apartment in Virginia Beach, leaving Shepherd the house so he could start his life over.

The naming of the house was both a way of asserting himself into the void left by losing his family and an irreverent nod to history. George Washington had Mount Vernon, Thomas Jefferson had Monticello, and Alexander Hamilton had the Grange.

What was so wrong with Shepherd having the Yellow Duck?

Gray's blue hatchback pulled into the driveway next to *Sarah Jane*. Three large Bradford pear trees stood in the front yard, sentinels of leafy greenery. Shepherd was standing under them, a long pole in his hands as he sawed at a branch high overhead. There was a pile of branches on the curb that Shepherd had already pruned into submission.

In another act of sheer whimsy, Shepherd named the three trees after the three basic tenants of journalism: Accuracy, Brevity, and Clarity.

Accuracy and Brevity were clearly freshly trimmed. Shepherd was going to town on Clarity as Gray pulled up.

Gray shut down the car and got out, noting that his car was in the shade as it sat under Clarity's leafy branches, but *Sarah Jane* was on the far side of the driveway in the sunlight.

Shepherd was glistening with sweat that rolled off his arms and face, blotching his sleeveless shirt. A bandanna was tied around his head, soaking up the sweat that would have otherwise blinded him.

"Why don't you park under your trees?" Gray asked as he shut his car door. "Your car would be a hell of a lot cooler!"

"You speak as a man who parks inside a two-car garage," Shepherd said, not taking his eyes off the branch he was sawing. Dirt and small chips of wood covered his skin, adhering to his sweat.

"Well, this place *had* a two-car garage until the previous owner turned it into a gigantic master bedroom," Gray said. "But that still doesn't answer my question. Why park in the sun and not under the trees?"

Snap!

The branch cracked loose and twirled downward, leaves and twigs showering Shepherd as he stepped back, allowing the branch to make its way to the ground.

He wore cargo shorts with a pair of pruning sheers stuck into the belt. His hands were protected by thick leather gloves. He pulled the branch away from the tree and picked up a handsaw from the ground by his feet.

"I'll give you a clue, Sherlock," Shepherd grinned. He pointed to the Yellow Duck's roof where a lone pigeon perched, looking down on them curiously.

"Ahh!" Gray said, cottoning on and looking down at the pavement under his car. It was stained and splotched with bird droppings. "So, you keep your car clean by parking away from the trees, but leave your guests to the mercy of the birds in the branches."

"Got it in one!" Shepherd began sawing. He broke up the branch in short order and added it to the pile on the curb. "Charlotte agreed, huh?"

"How'd you guess?"

"Behavioral patterns seldom change," Shepherd said, wiping his face with the back of his glove and leaving a dirty smudge on his cheek. "If she'd canned the effort, you'd have called. Instead, you drove 45 minutes to get here, which you only do when the answer is in the affirmative. So, I'm guessing this is the part where you caution me I'm only a special consultant with no legal powers at all?"

"Not bad," Gray said. "Assuming you're nearly finished out here for the afternoon, I would recommend you clean up before we talk. Frankly, you smell *really* bad, and this is actually the part where you go take a shower!"

Chapter 3
Monday, September 12; 13:00 hours
Naval Station Norfolk, Virginia

"...the court-martial of Navy Petty Officer Jarvis Cline continues this week at Norfolk Naval Station in Virginia. Cline is accused of murdering his roommate, Navy Petty Officer Carl Bacon, in a dispute over a bet..."

"...Well, Sean, the speed with which this case has come to trial is astonishing given the usual deliberate pace seen even in high-profile trials. It can only be assumed the Navy is eager to prosecute Cline as a reaction to the spike in reports of sexual assault cases over the past few years. In fact, Cline's attorney has lodged numerous protests, saying the prosecution has withheld exculpatory evidence..."

An exquisitely made up woman was speaking on TV, her bright eyeliner giving her eyes a lovely glow while expensive lip gloss from New York transformed her mouth into a runway model's lips. A dangerously low-cut, spaghetti-strap blouse revealed a bosom that, if not augmented by skillful surgery, was a rare genetic blessing of mammary proportions. "The culture of toxic masculinity that pervades the military is to blame for this tragedy, Don. The objectification of women is encouraged by the culture of rape. Unfortunately, we have generations of young women who buy into this need to turn themselves into sex objects to attract attention..."

"...traffic on the Hampton Roads Bridge Tunnel will be heavier than usual this afternoon as emergency maintenance shuts down one northbound lane during the lunchtime time rush. In local news, the prosecutors continued their arguments in the trial of Petty Officer Jeffrey Cline by recounting the numerous times he attempted to murder Kyle Sniffer while they were stationed on the submarine *Ponce* off the coast of Africa, and the failure of the Navy to prosecute him for those acts..."

"...today, Florida Senator Diego Alejandro criticized the Navy for rushing to issue a statement declaring the guilt of a sailor on trial for murder. Alejandro said the rush to judgment by Navy leadership was incompatible with protecting the rights of the accused sailor to a fair trial..."

"...the CNO is in a precarious position, Harris. One has to wonder if the Navy's rush to convict Petty Officer Cline is a way for Admiral Donovan to deflect attention from the cost overruns and delays in delivery of the new *Gerald R. Ford* aircraft carrier, as well as the growing scandal in the Pacific over that Singapore-based maritime contractor accused of bribing everyone from low-ranking sailors to a few admirals..."

The creases on Shepherd's khaki uniform were sharp enough to slice bread as opened the passenger door and hopped into Gray's burgundy government sedan outside NEPAC East.

"Sorry about pushing back our meeting; we had some trouble with one of our sailors in Europe," Shepherd apologized as he tossed his cover on the dash board and belted himself in. "I had to do some fast-talking on the phone to get this turkey's ID card expiration date temporarily extended. I also told Dionne to add *another* item to the pre-deployment checklist. From now on we're going to require our sailors verify their ID cards *won't* expire while deployed with NATO forces in the middle of Croatia."

"No problem," Gray said, shaking his head in sympathy. "We weren't expected on board until this afternoon, anyway. We'd have just sat around the waterfront McDonald's going *back* over case files we already spent the whole weekend reading. You have any trouble with your chain of command?"

"Well, the CO and my OIC aren't happy about this," Shepherd said. "However, Admiral Jones talked with them both personally over the weekend, and they *are* both aware of my...my occasional assistance to y'all since that flight line murder last year."

"That was a fun case," Gray said sarcastically.

"So, they're not thrilled, but I'm g-2-g," Shepherd said, using an old aviation term for "good to go."

"In that case, we're off to Pier 1, Sherlock," Gray shifted the car into drive.

"Personally, I've always thought I channeled Agatha Christie's 'Hercule Poirot' more, what, with my focus on behavior and psychology."

"You say that," Gray smirked, sliding the car into traffic, "And then you go and solve how many cases by seeing some obscure point of logic or evidence no one else would pick up on?"

Shepherd laughed, "True. But, what can I say? My brothers and I are geniuses."

"You three certainly don't suffer from an excess of humility," Gray said, grinning, "Just an excess of personality."

"I've never believed in false humility."

"Or any humility," Gray muttered, deliberately loud enough for Shepherd to hear.

Shepherd saw the half-smile playing on the NCIS agent's face.

"Not true, Abe," Shepherd said, a puckish expression breaking over his own face. "I'm the most humble man you've ever met. Hell, I'm so nauseatingly humble that I make *myself* sick!"

Gray burst into laughter. Funny how such an old joke still made him laugh.

"Ok, Genius," Gray brought the conversation back around to the matter at hand. "I think we should start in *Ponce's* well deck, and then go from there. Agreed?"

"Nope."

"Excuse me?" Gray said, startled. It wasn't very often Shepherd outright disagreed with him.

"I said 'no,'" Shepherd asserted. "I want to start on *Mesa Verde*. She's still tied up aft of *Ponce*. Something occurred to me last night, and I want to check it out."

Gray glanced at him as they drove past the base marina.

"Care to share?" Gray inquired.

"Not until we're aboard *Mesa Verde*," Shepherd said. "I just need to verify something personally and not make assumptions."

"That's was an...interesting statement," Gray said, his eyes on the road.

"Abe, look, I'm honest enough to admit I have it in for Cremer just as it much as he has it in for me," Shepherd said with a tired sigh. "I'd like nothing better than to find some way to humiliate him for all the crap he's put me through. However, this isn't about my vendettas. Jarvis Cline's *life* is at stake. I want to make sure Cremer did everything by the numbers...until we have physical evidence he didn't. The best place to start is on *Mesa Verde.*"

"I respect your feelings," Gray admitted. "Hell, I never liked him, even before he crapped all over you in Spain. However, to be fair, he generally *is* a top-flight agent. If he weren't, he wouldn't have lasted this long."

Shepherd was quiet for a moment. Glancing thoughtfully out the window, he watched as they passed the *Iowa* Point Memorial honoring the sailors who died in the 1989 explosion aboard the battleship.

"I'll just say this," Shepherd finally answered, turning back to Gray, "Something in how the *Mesa Verde* sailors phrased their responses to Cremer's questions caught my eye. If I'm right, then we have a *huge* break already. If I'm wrong...well, then I'm wrong. Either way, I want to start on *Mesa Verde,* and then work inward to *Ponce.*"

Gray nodded. "Ok. We'll play it your way, but don't take too long to spill the beans!"

The southern-most pier on base, Pier 1 is in close proximity to the civilian Port of Norfolk. The heavy industrial cranes of the civilian port clacked and clamored as they unloaded a giant container ship. A locomotive chugged its way along the port's tracks, hauling containers to a staging area where they would be connected to a cross-continental freight train.

The sounds of a needle gun chipping away rust rattled on a ship tied up at Pier 2. A jackhammer banged at the road surface in the waterfront's vast parking lot. The buzzing of hand tools lazily rolled out of a nearby maintenance building.

Somewhere in the distance, a dog barked.

The afternoon was warm. Local thermometers registered a solid 81 degrees as partly cloudy sky over the Tidewater area gave limited relief from the sun's incessant rays. The humidity, not quite as bad as in August, was still sultry 67%.

Shepherd and Gray's timing couldn't have been more perfect as *Mesa Verde* was scheduled to get underway the following day.

Mesa Verde's ventilation system hummed loudly enough to create a constant background noise masking the sound of water lapping against her hull. *Ponce* was still tied up just forward of *Mesa Verde* with her stern gate lowered, allowing sunlight to stream into that ship's well deck. Voices drifted across the distance from workers inside *Ponce's* well deck.

Shepherd was holding up his smart phone, filming and photographing *Ponce*. Gray was talking to the three young sailors who had been painting on *Mesa Verde's* fo'c'sle the day of the murder.

Accompanying the was an impatient Cmdr. Andrew Boelin, *Mesa Verde's* executive officer. Standing with Shepherd, he watched him taking photos. The four *Mesa Verde* sailors all wore the heavy-duty blue coveralls that were currently the standard underway uniform.

"Chief, what exactly are you photographing?" Boelin asked as Shepherd again flipped his smart phone to video mode and filmed *Ponce* in front of them. A desultory gull overhead complained about the lack of fish. Boelin went on, "Agent Cremer was here last month. According to him, none of my sailors could contribute anything to the investigation and that none of them need stay behind when we get underway tomorrow."

Shepherd turned off his phone, laying a hand on the gunwale before immediately jerking it away again. The steel was hot.

"I'm not at liberty to say more than what we've already told you, sir," Shepherd said, looking at the commander, his face all sympathy. "Special Agent Gray and I have been tasked with doing a review of the case."

"So, NCIS thinks there's something wrong with the case against Cline?" Boelin asked pointedly.

"What makes you say that, sir?"

Boelin, a heavy-set man in his late 30s, shoved his hands into his pockets (a very non-regulation move). "The court-martial is underway...but *now* NCIS decides to do a case review? You can't tell me somebody high up isn't expecting something to fall apart and wants to get ahead of the problem."

Shepherd was impressed by Boelin's perspicacity, but refused to give him anything.

"Commander, if I could give you any more information, I would. Unfortunately, at this time, I don't have anything to share," Shepherd returned his phone to his pocket.

Boelin drilled Shepherd with his gaze, a sly smile quirking his mouth, "Meaning, you *do* know more, but you're just not going to admit it. Don't worry, Chief, I understand."

Gray finished his conversation with the three sailors. Shepherd watched him shake hands with them and dismiss them. Gray started forward, but momentarily stopped by *Mesa Verde's* capstan to jot in his notebook. Not paying attention, he brushed his leg against an anchor chain link, leaving a dark greasy smudge marring his otherwise impeccable gray suit.

"Dammit!" Gray said, annoyed. "I've *got* to start wearing dark clothes when I'm aboard ship!"

Boelin nodded, looking at his own dark blue coveralls, "It does help to hide the grime, Mr. Gray! Well, is there anything else you need? Do we have to leave anyone behind tomorrow?"

Gray shook his head, "Unnecessary, but thank you, Commander. None of your sailors need to miss ship's movement tomorrow. I've got what I needed. I appreciate your time...and appreciate you clearing the fo'c'sle for us. I know there's a lot to get done before you get underway."

"There damn well is. I'd like to get my Deck Department back to work, if I can," Boelin said.

"Certainly," Gray said. "If I could have a few minutes with Chief Shepherd while you pass the word, I'd be grateful."

"So why is an MCC helping NCIS?" Boelin asked, pointing to Shepherd's name tag. Its two lines read "MCC Isaac Shepherd / NEPAC East."

Gray, accustomed to the question, smiled disarmingly, "Chief Shepherd has a specialized level of training that's proven a critical asset to NCIS on several occasions."

Boelin nodded. Shepherd saluted, and Boelin returned the salute before stepping away and pulling out his hydra, the generic name radios that link a ship's leadership.

"You learn anything new?" Shepherd asked as Gray joined him at the very point of *Mesa Verde's* bow. The Navy Jack hung limply on the jackstaff above their heads, its yellow rattlesnake proclaiming "Don't Tread on Me."

"Actually, yes," Gray said. "Their stories are all consistent with what they told Cremer last month, but I got some new details. Those three *did* see something while they were painting up here, but it wasn't much. One of them glanced up and saw a white male dumping what they thought was one of those dummies used for 'man overboard' drills into the well deck...what are those things called? 'Olivers?'"

Shepherd chuckled, "'Oscars.' The international signal flag for a man overboard is the 'O,' or 'Oscar,' flag, so that's what we call them. Poor old 'Oscar.'"

Gray nodded, "Nice. Anyway, the *Mesa Verde* sailors only realized something was up on *Ponce* when they saw the ambulance coming down the pier. That's when they started rubbernecking and saw Bacon on the floor of *Ponce's* well deck and realized he wasn't an Oscar dummy."

"Interesting." Shepherd said. "And why wasn't *that* little factoid in Cremer's paperwork? After all, the 'white male' angle alone is hard evidence fitting the case against Cline."

"I don't know," Gray said. "But, before we jump to conclusions, it's possible that *I* missed something when I grabbed the paperwork to bring to your house. To borrow *your* joke, 'once in a while even I make a mistake.'"

Shepherd smiled again, amused. "Ok, that question will keep. As to why I wanted to come aboard *Mesa Verde* first...Abe, OS2 Brandy Sniffer is a liar."

"Please give me some facts to support your logic, Mr. Spock."

Shepherd pointed to the busy crew in *Ponce's* well deck, "I can hear them."

"So can I," Gray said, squinting slightly in the sun. He felt sweat beginning to trickle down his back. "Your point being...?"

Shepherd looked at Gray as if he were a bit dim. "We have three sailors up here on *Mesa Verde's* fo'c'sle painting the evening of the murder. Not scrapping, not chipping, just painting. The murder happened around...what, nearly 20:00 hours, right?"

"Right."

"Well, all the heavy work on a ship is usually done by that time of day. Right now, it's middle of the afternoon. *Mesa Verde's* ventilation is humming. I can hear a needle gun going aboard *Jason Dunham* over on Pier 2. There's road work being done in the parking lot, and equipment going at Port Norfolk. Hell, there's even a dog barking somewhere. Despite all this activity, I can *clearly* hear the workers inside *Ponce's* well deck."

"Ok...?" Gray asked.

"Sniffer testified they were yelling at each other so loudly it 'echoed' around *Ponce's* well deck," Shepherd's eyes were steely. "Well, if I can hear *Ponce's* crew casually calling directions back and forth during the height of a normal workday, then how come three sailors painting with soft rollers and brushes heard *nothing* from a fight that was 'echoing' on a *quiet night from the same place?*"

Gray's eyebrows went up as he realized Shepherd's implications. "Good point! Granted, the three sailors did see the body being dumped...but, nothing seemed *so* out of the ordinary that they were alarmed. They just assumed it as an Oscar dummy. You're right; had there been a level of noise like Sniffer said, they would have stopped work and watched."

"Oh, yeah," Shepherd said with finality. "Surprise and curiosity alone would have commanded their attention if Cline and Bacon had been yelling that loudly."

Gray nodded, laying a hand on the gunwale...and then just as quickly jerking it away again. The steel was hot. "Ok, let's assume, just you and I, that Cline is innocent, but that Sniffer's hiding something relevant. Why would she lie under oath? What did she really see...if anything at all? I'm starting to think that's a much more practical set of questions to focus our limited time on."

"In other words, you don't want to review Cremer's case," Shepherd grinned, looking at Gray. "You want to start over from the scratch."

"Yes," Gray said, his face grim. "Your point about what the *Mesa Verde* sailors *should* have heard, combined with the lack of forensic evidence, creates an entirely new canvas."

Memories crowded Shepherd's head like inebriated spiders as he followed Gray up the steep brow towards *Ponce's* Quarterdeck. When *Ponce* was tied up, the Quarterdeck was set up at the forward end of the flight deck. The podium, flags, and sailors standing watch were protected from the sun by a heavy purple canopy emblazoned with the ship's crest and nickname.

Shepherd forcibly pushed all the memories back into the past as he stepped aboard *Ponce* for the first time in four years.

Hello, old girl, He thought to the ship. *It's good to see you again.*

Somewhere in his mind, he *swore* he could hear the ship greet him just as fondly.

Feeling the steel deck solidly beneath his brown leather shoes, Shepherd turned, saluting the national ensign hanging from the staff set up on *Ponce's* fantail. He then joined Gray under the Quarterdeck canopy. Gray showed his badge, and Shepherd saluted and showed his ID card to the officer of the deck, who called the ship's captain on his hydra. Shepherd couldn't help himself; he began looking around and mentally cataloging the changes to the ship that had occurred since he transferred in 2012.

Absently, he turned and examined the Quarterdeck flags— the American flag and the Navy flag set up just behind the podium. Both hung quiet and limp in the still, damp air. Checking them, he found tiny ink marks on the top of each flag's hoist. He smiled; he had quietly put those marks there in 2010 when he'd used the flags as studio backdrops.

Guess the Quartermasters never noticed I marked up their flags!

"Isaac?"

Shepherd turned, snapping out of his nostalgia as he realized Gray was speaking to him. Two Masters-at-Arms had joined the party at the Quarterdeck. Everyone was staring at him bemusedly.

"Huh? What? I'm sorry—I was…I was thinking about something." Shepherd said, shaking his head a bit to refocus.

Gray cocked his head, "Well, once your train of thought reaches the station, MA1 Luke Fredriksen here will escort you to the well deck while MA2 Smith takes me up to speak with the captain. I've explained your role and the scope of your authority here, so if you need to speak with anyone or see anything, just tell MA1 and he'll help you out."

Shepherd glanced over at the big, burly Fredriksen. Fredriksen and Smith both wore the green digital camouflage version of the Navy Working Uniform, but the uniformity ended there. Smith's head bore a peach fuzz of fine blonde hair shaved close. He was small, thin, and looked like he might be starting high school in a few years. Fredriksen's head was covered with vibrant red hair that was quite noticeable despite being trimmed nearly to the skin. He was a big, muscular man who could could easily pass for a Viking.

A puckish expression lit up Shepherd's face as he looked at Gray. "So we're splitting up and looking for clues, Fred? I assume you want Scooby and I to go that way while you and Daphne go the other way? Unfortunately, we seem to be short a Velma in this scenario."

I'll short you a Velma! Gray thought in resigned exhaustion. "Something like that."

Gray and Smith headed forward. Shepherd held out his hand to the Nordic-looking Fredriksen.

"Isaac Shepherd, MA1. Glad to meet you!"

Fredriksen shook his hand. His grip was rather like being caught in a hydraulic press.

"I know who you are, Chief," Fredriksen said, a warm smile crinkling the skin around his striking blue eyes. "I'm familiar with the Ratner case back in 2011. I'm also one of Security's suicide prevention coordinators. I heard you speak at the regional suicide prevention symposium the Naval Hospital held earlier this year. If you'll follow me, I'll take you down to the well deck."

Fredriksen turned and started to head into the ship's superstructure.

"Petty Officer Fredriksen!" Shepherd called as he began to stride in the other direction across the flight deck.

Fredriksen turned, surprised. "Chief?"

"It's actually quicker this way," Shepherd said, striding in the opposite direction along the flight deck towards the catwalk that ran the length of *Ponce's* aft end.

Fredriksen hustled to catch up with Shepherd.

Shepherd's crisp khaki uniform clashed noticeably with the active duty sailors' camouflage working uniforms, and the civilian mariners' grungy industrial clothes. His brown leather shoes, a statement of his time in naval aviation, hit the catwalk floor with a clunk as he hopped down from the flight deck.

"Chief!" Fredriksen looked rather put out as he caught up.

Shepherd looked up and smiled.

"I'm a Proud Lion too, remember? This is the quickest way to the actual crime scene."

Shepherd ducked into a hatch. Fredriksen hopped down and followed.

The smell of a ship was always the first thing to hit Shepherd. The aroma, an odd combination he could only describe as "Band-Aids mixed with hydraulic fluid," always gave him the feeling of coming home.

The compartment's layout had changed slightly, but Shepherd knew the space. During his time aboard it had been a Marine berthing space. More importantly, across the compartment from where he entered, was one of the two hatches leading to the catwalk inside the well deck.

"Chief," Fredriksen thought he could not have heard Shepherd correctly, "Chief, what did you mean about the 'actual' crime scene?"

"I'll tell you in a minute," Shepherd said vaguely, his eyes scanning the area. "This used to be berthing for the Marines when I was on the ship. I remember one rather epic rasslin' match in here between these two huge hulking brutes. It only ended after one of them gave the other an equally epic wedgie."

Fredriksen's eyebrows went up, amused at Shepherd's slip into a Southern accent. "Is that a regular thing? The Marines horsing around like that?"

"Oh, yeah," Shepherd smiled. "But this particular match was brought on by a dispute over a book."

"A book?"

"A book," Shepherd said. "Those two characters were arguing over the interpretation of a book they'd been reading, and decided to decide the issue by rasslin.'"

"What book?"

"*Jane Eyre,* by Charlotte Bronte," Shepherd answered.

Fredriksen's mouth dropped open.

Shepherd smiled and clapped him on the shoulder, and then turned to the task at hand, "Ok, let's go to work."

He ducked his tall head under a low-hanging gray water pipe and headed inboard to the hatch that led to the catwalk.

The well deck was a large, cavernous, wood-lined space. The smell of hydraulic fluid, oil, and diesel fumes mingled with the smell of damp wood.

Shepherd leaned over the catwalk railing and stared down at the well deck floor over 20 feet below. Scanning to his right, he looked forward at the "beach," the metal ramp leading up from the deep well deck floor to the upper level.

"Chief?" Fredriksen asked again, stepping into the musty, humid space.

Shepherd didn't answer, holding up a hand to silence Fredriksen. He was staring down again at an area marked by a thick stain. His mouth quirked as he spun on his heel, looking back into the compartment, then back down to the well deck floor.

Fredriksen had the oddest feeling Shepherd was seeing something in his mind, almost as if he were watching an instant replay at a football game.

Without warning Shepherd plopped his cover on his head (by custom it was worn in the well deck while the ship was in port), and strode to the forward end of the catwalk where the ladder descended to the well deck's upper level. He was already down before Fredriksen even made it to the top of the ladder.

Shepherd scanned the packing crates and pallets jumbled along the upper level near the ladder. Although it would take nearly a year to complete, the stripping of *Ponce* for any usable part or fitting was well underway. Several crates were marked with shipping labels covered in the arcane language of the Navy supply system. Others bore labels indicating they were being sent to such industry giants as Raytheon, Boeing, General Electric, and GDI Tech.

A number of sailors and civilian mariners stopped to watch as the chief and the MA1 executed a swift march down the beach to the well deck's floor.

Shepherd came to the dark stain. His heart sank into his stomach as he looked at the mark of a young life violently ended before its time. Blood had seeped too deep into the wood to be easily cleaned, and it was impractical to replace the planking since *Ponce was* scheduled for decommissioning in a year. Shepherd studied the ugly splotch for a moment before stepping right into the middle of it.

"Chief!" Fredriksen exclaimed, horrified. "That's...that's the bloodstain from Petty Officer Bacon!"

"I know," Shepherd said nonchalantly, staring back up at the catwalk.

"I don't think its' right for you to be standing right...there." Fredriksen was clearly wrong-footed. "Isn't it...disrespectful?"

"Whoever murdered Bacon was disrespectful. I need to see things as Carl Bacon would have seen them if he'd still been alive," Shepherd said. "Still, if you're concerned, you can complain to Special Agent Gray in about one minute when he and an officer I assume to be the ship's captain get down here."

Fredriksen glanced backwards almost by instinct. Abraham Gray, the ship's captain, and two other men in work clothes were indeed starting down the beach.

"Isaac!" Gray called.

"Sir," Fredriksen said while saluting the ship's captain, "Special Agent Gray, I'm sorry, but the chief insists on standing...right there."

Gray shrugged, "MA1, I've learned to trust the chief, even when he seems unconventional."

Shepherd turned, saluting the ship's captain. "Sir!"

Capt. Benjamin Smith, wearing the blue Aquaflage uniform, saluted back, and then shook Shepherd's hand. "Chief Shepherd. Mr. Gray told me you were engaged by NCIS to assist on this case?"

"Yes, sir."

"This is Dr. Tyler Drummin. He was with us the last two years in the Middle East as we tested some new systems GDI Tech and our allies in Singapore are jointly developing with us," Smith introduced.

"Dr. Drummin," Shepherd shook the man's hand.

"And this is Aaron Seeley," Smith said. "He's an electrical engineer with Smith-Table Electronics. He's been on board a little over a year now."

"Mr. Seeley," Shepherd said. "Glad to know you!"

"Chief," Seeley said. He wore jeans and a denim shirt under a nondescript gray jacket with a patch bearing the logo of Smith-Table in bright yellow threads over a black background.

"Dr. Drummin, I'm guessing your PhD. is in physics or electrical engineering?" Shepherd asked.

Drummin laughed. He was a pleasant, average-built man with a vaguely Asian shape to his eyes. He had on gray coveralls and a blue jacket bearing the logo of GDI Tech embroidered in red and yellow thread. "Nice try, Chief. Dual dissertations in chemical and mechanical engineering." "Impressive!" Shepherd said genially. "What brings you to the party? Were either of you a witness to the event?"

"I was not," Seeley said. "I was down in the berthing packing my things. I worked with both of them, well, all three, if you want to add in Petty Officer Sniffer. But I was below when it happened."

Drummin stuffed his hands in his pockets. His glasses slipped down his nose a bit, but he didn't bother to push them back up. He paused before answering to let a couple of sailors walk by.

"I knew the sailors involved, of course," Drummin continued after they had a spot of privacy again. "Unfortunately, like Aaron, I wasn't here to actually see anything, so I'm not much help."

"I was just wondering since y'all came down with the captain," Shepherd said.

"We were in the captain's stateroom discussing some of the equipment transfers when Mr. Gray came in," Drummin said.

"Basically, we're being nosy right now," said Seeley.

Shepherd got the distinct impression Seeley was studying him.

"So what *are* you doing standing in the middle of the crime scene, Chief?" Smith asked, his voice casual, but his eyes narrowed in a look that clearly said Shepherd better have a *damned* good reason for standing where he was.

"I don't think *this* is the crime scene at all, Captain." Shepherd announced.

Drummin, Seeley, and Smith all cocked their heads, but it was Drummin who spoke first. "This is where Petty Officer Bacon died when he was pushed over the railing by Cline. I mean, I guess you could say the catwalk was the 'crime scene' since that's where Cline pushed him over, but he...died...right here."

Shepherd addressed his next remarks to the Smith. "Captain, back in late 2011 we had a guy fall off the catwalk right up there, and he hit the deck floor, well, pretty much right here where Petty Officer Bacon went 'splat' last month."

"'Splat?!'" Smith was aghast.

The captain, Drummin, Seeley, and Fredriksen all turned to Gray, as if he could explain Shepherd's turn of phrase. Gray just shrugged; he was used to Shepherd's irreverent wit.

Shepherd looked at Smith the way a teacher looks at a student unable to grasp the concept of 2 + 2.

"Yes, sir. 'Splat.' 'Crash.' 'Bang.' Right here where I'm standing. Jack Dovey did the same swan dive off that catwalk and went 'splat' right here. He was horsing around when he lost his balance and fell over the railing."

Smith looked extremely irritated. Fredriksen still looked uncomfortable. Drummin and Seeley looked confused. Only Gray seemed to be following Shepherd.

"Isaac," Gray said, "I'm assuming you're bringing up Dovey's accident because he fell at the same place, but he *wasn't* killed by the impact?"

"Exactly," Shepherd said. "He broke both legs and an arm, and was medivaced off the ship, but he survived to be the butt of a thousand jokes among Proud Lion veterans to this day. It's only about 20 feet from up there to down here. Yes, it could be a fatal fall if you landed wrong. Didn't the medical examiner say Bacon's *ankle* was shattered?"

"Yes," Gray said, cottoning on, his eyes widening a bit.

"So what?" Smith interjected, his anger increasing. "Obviously, he broke an ankle in the same fall that smashed his skull."

Gray's eyes widened as he picked up Shepherd's line of thought. He began to speak, but then decided to hold his silence while Shepherd went on.

"Sir, the fatal injury was caused by blunt force trauma to the *top rear* of Petty Officer Bacon's skull," Shepherd explained.

"The top…?" Smith asked. "So what?"

Fredriksen caught his breath as he too now realized where Shepherd was going, "If Petty Officer Bacon broke an ankle in the fall, that means he landed *on his feet*. An impact from that direction couldn't result in catastrophic damage to the *upper* area of his skull!"

Shepherd smiled, his sea-green eyes twinkling. "Top marks, MA1! Based on that information alone, we can safely conclude Carl Bacon was *already dead* when he went landed here, meaning —"

"—He was killed up there and his body dumped to throw us off," Gray finished the sentence so smoothly the other four men wondered if Gray and Shepherd were married.

"You got your kit in the car?" Shepherd asked Gray.

"Of course."

"I'll go up and guard the compartment to keep everyone out. Abe, go get your kit; we need to search it again. MA1 Fredriksen, can you accompany me?"

Smith held up a hand, "Wait! What kit? What are you two talking about?"

"My crime scene kit," Gray explained. "You know, gloves, tweezers, bags, evidence labels, the works. I'd like Chief Shepherd and MA1 Fredriksen to ensure that compartment stays empty until I get back, if you don't mind, Captain. The chief and I are going to search that compartment from top to bottom."

"Sir, since I'm part of the force assigned by the base to augment ship's security, I'll be happy to stay in case they need further assistance," Fredriksen spoke up.

Smith looked exceptionally put out, but his eyes lingered on Gray's badge. He finally nodded. "Ok. MA1 will be your liaison."

"You can't!" Drummin said. "That's a highly classified area! I'm afraid I can't let you just waltz in there and look around. It's secured for a reason. I understand you have a murder to investigate, but we have national security issues to consider here. Besides, what would you find? Cline's already on trial. What difference does it make if he killed Bacon up there and then threw him over, or if he killed him *by* throwing him over?"

Gray pushed his coat back, lowering his head to hide his frustration as he slid his hands into his pockets. His face had regained its professional impassivity when he looked back up.

"Dr. Drummin, it matters because the *form* matters in law as much as the *substance*. If the Navy is charging Cline with murdering Bacon by *throwing him off the catwalk*, but that was *not* the cause of death, then Cline'll walk due to a mistrial," Gray explained.

"Mistrials can happen in a court-martial?" Seeley asked, surprised.

"They can, Mr. Seeley," Gray said heavily. "If we've screwed up the *form* of the charge, then we just forfeited the entire case. It'd be one of those legal technicalities that drive people up the wall, but it would happen. We need to make sure we're charging Cline *correctly*, or else a possibly guilty man will walk and Bacon's family will not see justice done."

Smith's obvious annoyance softened slightly as he considered Gray's statement.

"Besides, Dr. Drummin," Shepherd spoke up, his voice casual. "I think your people are faster than you realize. MA1 Fredriksen and I were already *in* that compartment. It's not locked down anymore. Whatever classified equipment you had in there must have been pulled out because the space is open to regular traffic."

Drummin looked shocked. "Oh. Uh...ok. In that case, I guess I can't have any objections. Captain Smith?"

"Captain?" Gray asked courteously.

Smith nodded, "Dr. Drummin, Aaron, come on back to my stateroom and we can continue our conversation. Mr. Gray, Chief Shepherd, do what you need to do. I'll have the command duty officer pass the word that compartment is secured for now. MA1, give them any cooperation they need."

"Aye, aye, sir," Fredriksen replied.

"Thank you, Captain!" Shepherd said as he and Fredriksen both saluted. "Would you like us to check in with the XO so he knows what we're up to?"

"He's on leave," Smith said, returning their salutes, "So you don't need to worry about that."

Smith, Seeley, and Drummin headed back up the beach, already deep in conversation about logistics.

"Give me 15 minutes to go get my kit, Isaac," Gray said. "MA1 Fredriksen, you've been officially drafted. You two secure that area until I'm back, and then we can give it a proper look."

Chapter 4

The three men were tired, sweaty, and dirty.

Gray's gray suit was wrecked badly enough that even the world's best dry-cleaning service would be hard-pressed to get it looking like new. Shepherd's khaki uniform was equally a disaster area, especially the knees. Only Fredriksen's green "digicam" uniform appeared to have weathered the storm with no major ill-effects.

"It's been over a month since the murder," Fredriksen said as the three sat at a Formica table with a pre-printed chess board on it in the compartment. The table held the scattered parts of Gray's crime scene kit. "What did you two really expect to find?"

"Not much," Gray admitted, enjoying the feeling of a light breeze from the ship's humming ventilation system on the back of his neck. He had abandoned his coat and tie hours ago. "Still, the blood flecks we found on the overhead pipes and on the electrical box near the hatch to the catwalk might be extremely relevant. We just won't know they're analyzed."

Shepherd's glasses were off. He was holding several small plastic evidence bags, each filled with paint chips dotted with a dark substance that Gray's field kit had identified as human blood. Shepherd had one bag nearly to his nose as he examined at it.

Fredriksen looked skeptical, "Mr. Gray, forgive me, but the chance of those blood flecks being related to the murder are...well...come on. How do you know it has anything to do with the murder?"

Before Gray could answer, Aaron Seeley poked his head in, several small boxes in his hands. "Excuse me, gentlemen! I'm sorry to bother you, but I need to go aft. Are you done with your search? Can I cut through here, or do you need me to go up and over the flight deck?"

"Come on through," Gray said, rolling his neck to loosen a kink. "We're done."

Seeley started through the space. Shepherd watched him out of the corner of his eye. Once gain he had the oddest feeling Seeley was surreptitiously checking him out, and not in an amorous fashion. He kept his own gaze indirect, not wanting to alert Seeley as to his suspicions. *Something* was just "off" about how the man looked at him.

Seeley had taken about three steps when his elbow hit a fitting and knocked one of the boxes out of his hands. It hit the deck, bursting open and splashing small screws, nuts, and bolts around the compartment.

"Dammit!" Seeley cursed. He set the other boxes on a nearby table and dropped to his knees to begin scooping up the errant items. "Sorry!"

Seeley looked thoroughly embarrassed as he finished gathering up his things and hurried out of the compartment.

"Terrible when you run into a man you can't help," Shepherd said, exhaustion in his voice.

"What you mean?" Gray asked.

"I'm no psychiatrist, but that man clearly has a screw loose!"

Gray's head fell into his hands, abject exasperation driving a groan from him. Fredriksen just stared at Shepherd, clearly unsure if he'd heard correctly.

"Anyway," Gray said, looking up and trying to steer the conversation back to saner waters, "At least we've got some potential evidence to analyze."

"Again," Fredriksen said, "How *do* you know that blood comes from anyone we're interested in? This is a Navy ship; a lot of sailors probably split their heads open over the past 40 years."

"Absolutely right, MA1," Shepherd answered. "We just don't know right now. DNA sequencing will tell us if this is Bacon or Cline's blood…or someone else's. If it *does* belong to Bacon or Cline, then it's the more hard evidence that Bacon was killed in here and then dumped into the well deck. If not, then it's some poor sap who, like you said, hit their head on that box sometime in the not-so-distant past."

Gray held up another bag with more paint flecks dotted with dark splotches of dried blood. "That still doesn't do anything to change the map of Cline being our prime suspect at the moment."

"No, it doesn't," Shepherd conceded, "But it would further unravel Sniffer's testimony. That alone will hopefully gum up the prosecution's case enough to slow things down and give us more time."

Fredriksen glanced down and picked up a small screw. "Looks like Mr. Seeley missed a piece or two."

"Told you he has a screw loose," Shepherd said.

Before either Gray or Fredriksen could groan, a commotion made all three men look up. Dr. Drummin and two other men were entering the compartment. The three wore HAZMAT suits and gloves, their faces protected by respirators under their hoods. They were struggling to carry a plastic vat that was evidently pretty heavy.

"Sorry, gentlemen!" Drummin called in a muffled voice. "We have to move this through here to the HAZMAT staging area in the starboard aft line handling room. Could I ask you to move outside for your own safety? It'll just take a moment."

"Sure thing, Doc!" Gray said.

The three stood and moved out to the catwalk over the well deck.

Gray looked at Shepherd, "I want you to go to the Portsmouth Naval Hospital and talk to the medical examiner tomorrow. I'll see about talking to Cline and his lawyer during a recess in the court-martial."

"I'd like to talk to Cline with you," Shepherd said.

"Not a good idea, Isaac," Gray said. "I don't want that lawyer of his knowing we have you working on the case with me."

"Good point," Shepherd nodded.

"What's wrong with his lawyer knowing you're reviewing the case, Chief?" Fredriksen asked.

Drummin and his helpers grunted as they stepped carefully through the space, maneuvering the large vat with care. Shepherd glanced in at them, and then returned his attention to Fredriksen.

"Cline's got a good lawyer. And, by 'good,' I mean *very good*. The man's got a terrific success record in court. He's also a genius when it comes to messaging and publicity," Shepherd said. "If this guy gets wind of the fact the Navy has a public affairs guy working on the case, he'll blast it all over the news to discredit the prosecution and the Navy."

Gray looked down at the spot where Bacon's body had been found the month prior. "Agreed. From an outsider's perspective who has no context to understand Isaac's unique skill set and experience, the Navy would look like a bunch of clods."

Shepherd heard the clink of metal on metal behind them. Glancing over his shoulder, he was just in time to see Drummin's foot shoot out from under him. The scientist fell backwards, upending the vat of hazardous chemicals his team was carrying. The vat crashed onto the table holding Gray's field kit and evidence, fairly exploding around the compartment.

"MOVE!" Shepherd yelled, launching himself into Gray and Fredriksen, knocking them away from of the hatch.

Shepherd's tackle prevented the caustic liquid from splashing any of them. A small wave of the stuff landed on the catwalk right where the three men had been standing. Smoke rose as the liquid began reacting with the metal.

"Oh, *hell!*" Gray cursed, jumping to his feet. *"Dr. Drummin!! Are you alright?!"*

"We're...oof...we're fine. Dammit! We're ok, but we made one hell of a goddamned mess!" Drummin replied in his still-muffled voice. "You can't come back this way, not until we've got this contained and cleaned up! It's extremely corrosive and the vapors are poisonous! We're protected, but you three need to find another way to get out of there!"

"We're on our way!" Shepherd called. "Come on, you two. There's another hatch further aft. We can get up to the flight deck from there."

The HAZMAT accident kept Fredriksen, Gray and Shepherd aboard *Ponce* for another few hours.

Shepherd led them out to the ship's flight deck where they were met by a corpsman who took them down to medical.

Located on the second deck along the ship's port side, the medical space was a long corridor, housing a small operating room, dental areas, and not a few video game boxes hooked into various TVs. At Shepherd's insistence, Fredriksen was checked out first before Shepherd and Gray took their turns.

"Well, that's all three of us free from inhalation injuries," Gray said, "Shall we go talk to the captain?"

Located on the starboard side of Ponce, the captain's stateroom was a stately compartment where the CO lived and entertained distinguished visitors to the ship. Entering, they found the ship's captain and safety officer already in conversation, the smell of coffee wafted in from the small galley just outside the stateroom. A beautiful oil painting of *Ponce* hung on one wall while a long wooden table dominated the stateroom's public space.

The interview about the HAZMAT spill didn't take long. Shepherd was the only witness to the spill, and he only had a quick view of Drummin losing his balance before knocking the others out of harm's way.

Finally, well after 19:30 hours, the three descended the brow to the pier and trudged back to the parking lot.

"Well, *that* was an experience," Fredriksen said. "Mr. Gray, Chief, it's been...well, *interesting*. If either of you need anything else, you can get me through base security if I'm not on the ship."

"Thanks for your help today, MA1," Gray shook his hand. "I'm sorry you got stuck with us so late on a Monday."

"Me too," Shepherd said, extending his own hand.

"Oh, it wasn't so bad, Chief," Fredriksen replied, smiling as he clasped Shepherd's hand. "The company was pretty good, at least!"

Fredriksen headed off to a patrol car that was waiting at the pier's entry control point.

Gray and Shepherd exited the security check point and strolled over to the edge of the pier. Gray leaned on a light post as the falling sunlight warmed them both. The scent of refuse wafted from some nearby dumpsters, joining with the smell of salt in the air.

"Goddammit!" Gray cursed, banging his fist on the light post angrily. "Stupid accident! I'll bet you all that damned blood evidence we found was destroyed!"

Shepherd chuckled as he began rummaging in the pockets of his ravaged khakis.

Gray looked at Shepherd, genuinely annoyed. "Really? You think this is funny, Isaac?! We lose my field kit *and* all the potential evidence, and you think it's *funny?!*"

"No, you dimwitted jackalope!" Shepherd laughed aloud, "Hold your horses a bit. I've got an early Hanukkah present for you!"

"What?!" Gray snapped as Shepherd finally pulled his hands out of his pockets.

"Oh, just these," Shepherd said, holding up three evidence bags full of paint chips with blood flecks on them, Gray's small digital camera, and notebook.

Gray's eyes popped open as his face lit up like a child being given the world's greatest toy.

"You son of bitch!" Gray laughed delightedly, snatching the bags, camera, and notebook from Shepherd. "How the *hell* did you pull this off?!"

"Call it a hunch," Shepherd said. "I just had this feeling something was going to go wrong. I expect you're in a slightly better mood now?"

"I am, you beautiful, conceited, paranoid ape!" Gray laughed. "Nicely done, Isaac! Only *you* would think absconding with evidence would be a good idea...and be right!"

By 10:00 the next morning the temperature was already 80 degrees, and it hovered there all afternoon.

Shepherd headed into Portsmouth and made for the Naval Hospital. The visit was not successful. Despite his (admittedly somewhat unorthodox) credentials, he made no headway getting in to the see the medical examiner.

Cutting his losses, Shepherd decided to head back to the naval station and play an ace he hoped was up his sleeve.

Unfortunately, his trip back was delayed when an accident in the Midtown Tunnel across the Elizabeth River stopped traffic cold. Due to his position in traffic, Shepherd was trapped. There was no way for him to get off Highway 58, so he did the only thing he could: he opened the windows, turned off the engine, and spent the next few hours listening to WNIS talk radio while he sweated and wished for a breeze.

Finally rolling through Naval Station Norfolk's gates at 15:00, Shepherd made a beeline for the Subway restaurant in the mini-Navy Exchange building that sat near NEPAC East. He briefly considered stopping at the main "NEX" just outside the base, but decided he wasn't in the mood for large crowds.

His body was feeling human again following a 6-inch sub and unsweetened iced tea. He started up *Sarah Jane* and merged into traffic, arriving at the AFSC building in a few minutes. Glancing into the "Force Master Chief" parking spot, he spied Stiles' car, so he parked and headed in. Putting his combo cover under his arm and showing his ID card to the sailor manning the building's Quarterdeck, Shepherd was admitted and headed to Stiles' office.

"Good afternoon, Chief Shepherd! How can I help you?" Yeoman 1st Class Gordon Grey looked up from his desk in Stiles' outer office.

"Good to see you again, YN1! Is the master chief available?"

"One second," Grey smiled and got up. He knocked on the inner door, cracking it open just enough to pop his head in. "Master Chief? Chief Shepherd's here to see you."

Shepherd couldn't hear the reply, but Grey stepped back, holding the door open. "Go on in."

"Thanks, YN1," said Shepherd, stepping past him. "John! I'm sorry to bug you, but I need some help."

YN1 Grey quietly stepped out, shutting the door.

Stiles' office was spacious, white, and covered in the kind of photos, mementos, and trophies one would expect to occupy the office of a long-serving master chief petty officer.

Stiles sat behind a desk littered with neat piles of papers and folders, his khaki uniform as crisp as a brand-new $1 bill. His computer occupied a credenza behind him, its screen saver showing the AFSC logo swimming around the monitor.

Stiles stood and shook Shepherd's hand before motioning for the junior chief to sit. "I'm assuming this has to do with the Bacon investigation?"

Shepherd smiled, "It does. Aside from getting stuck the Midtown Tunnel for a few hours, my morning was spent trying to get into the see the medical examiner at Portsmouth. No joy. If my memory is accurate, however, I believe you know the hospital's command master chief personally. If you don't mind making a phone call, I think you might be able to get me in."

"You couldn't get in with your NCIS letter?" Stiles was surprised.

"They're pretty serious about not risking any HIPAA violations," Shepherd said. "I can't say I blame them. A letter naming me as a 'special consultant' is a far cry from a badge."

Stiles nodded. "Makes sense. Hang on."

Stiles picked up the phone, his face falling after a couple of moments when he had to leave a voice mail. "Damn. Well, I've got a meeting here in 20 minutes. I'll have to try later, but I be able won't get you that introduction until tomorrow at the earliest. Will that be alright?"

Shepherd nodded. "That's fine. I appreciate it. I need to go back to NEPAC East and shower anyway. Sitting in a car for a couple of hours will leave anyone smelling rather funny."

Shepherd rose, but Stiles held up a hand to stop him.

"John?" Shepherd asked, sitting back down.

"Isaac," Stiles was looking as uncomfortable as a long-tailed cat in a room full of rocking chairs. "Look, I've been thinking about what you said last week. You were right...and I was wrong."

Shepherd looked puzzled, "I love being right as much as the next guy, but what was I right about?"

Stiles sighed and looked anywhere but at Shepherd. He was clearly forcing himself to address something very unpleasant. "Four years ago on the IKE...the gay slurs. I shouldn't...I shouldn't have ever done that bullshit. It was goddamned unprofessional of me to make fun of...well, anyone. I'm sorry I did that, and I'm sorry I did that to *you.*"

Shepherd cocked his head slightly, waiting quietly as Stiles continued to search for the words he needed to say.

"I obviously caused you a lot of pain," Stiles admitted, his eyes still looking away. "Hell, I probably caused a lot of people a lot of pain. I can't change that, and I can't go back and apologize to everyone I ever screwed over. All I can do is admit I *did* act like an ass, and I'm sorry for that. I should have been a better chief."

Stiles finally looked at Shepherd, who was smiling.

"Thank you, John. I know that wasn't easy for you," Shepherd said, standing and holding out his hand. "Don't be too hard on yourself. The measure of a man is not determined by what he was, but by what he becomes."

Stiles rose and clasped Shepherd's hand. "That's profound. Who said that?"

"I did," Shepherd winked, "Made it up just now!"

NEPAC East was largely empty when Shepherd arrived. A few sailors were tying up some projects, and Shepherd spent a few minutes chatting with them. He offered some technical suggestions on the special effects in one video, and did some copy-editing on another sailor's story.

"Thanks, Chief!" The young sailor said when Shepherd was done with his edits.

Shepherd was a good actor; none of the sailors guessed he was a raging tempest of turmoil inside. Stiles' apology had meant a great deal, but it also forced open a wound he tried to pretend didn't exist. Unfortunately, the wound was always there, seeping spiritual blood.

Shepherd kept a couple sets of civilian clothes in his office 'just in case.' Checking the traffic reports online, he groaned when he learned both the Hampton Roads Bridge-Tunnel across the James River and the Downtown Tunnel across the Elizabeth River were snarled with wrecks. That meant the Midtown Tunnel and the

James River Bridge would both be clogged with extra heavy loads of rush-hour traffic. He decided to wait at NEPAC East instead of spending several hours sitting in traffic.

Hauling out a set of civvies, Shepherd headed into the men's locker room.

I must remind the first classes to get this place cleaned up! Shepherd thought irritably, noting a number of towels hanging off odd corners and stray socks that were making a beeline for safety under the benches.

Shepherd took a long shower, letting the sound and feel of the water create a 'white noise' barrier that eclipsed much of the emotional noise rattling around his head. The emotional whirlwind never stopped, but now it was rendered worse by the guilt of his own past actions. Shaking his head to clear it, he focused back on the Bacon murder, hoping Gray had been more successful than he was.

It was beginning to feel like a seriously wasted day.

By the time Shepherd emerged in jeans, sneakers, a T-shirt, and an old green field jacket, everyone had gone. Most of the lights were out. Heading into the production room on autopilot, he wanted to see how well it had been cleaned up considering the male locker room was a mess.

The production area was dark, but ambient light from the hallway revealed a very neat and tidy facility.

Good! He smiled.

Suddenly feeling despondent, he walked into the darkened space and flopped down in a chair. Yesterday marked the official first anniversary of his divorce. Although he and Jenn had separated in early 2014, Virginia law required them to wait a year before filing for divorce. They were all set to finalize everything in July of 2015, but a death in Jenn's family delayed the proceedings.

So, as of yesterday, he'd been legally divorced for a year.

He pulled out his phone and pulled up a photo of his daughter, Martha. She'd recently bobbed her hair and dyed it a bright blue.

Great job, numb nuts, He mentally castigated himself. *Stupid faggot thinking you could live like a normal man.*

Shepherd felt like a fraud and a failure, which furthered enraged him because he felt his emotional problems were skewing his instincts in the Bacon case.

"Chief? What are you doing here in the dark?"

Shepherd's head jerked up as his heart simulated cardiac arrest. Robertson was standing in the doorway. She was dressed in soccer shorts and a T-shirt, but showed no signs of sweat or exertion.

"MC1?" Shepherd asked, regaining his breath. "What are *you* doing here? Shouldn't you be at Cross Fit?"

"I pulled a couple of muscles pretty bad last Saturday working out with Jacob during our Cape Charles weekend," She said, massaging her right shoulder. "I'm taking a few days off to let my body recover. I saw your car in the parking lot while I was driving by. What's up?"

"Well, the men's locker room needs a heavy field day," Shepherd said, deflecting the topic to safer grounds.

"Noted," Robertson said, looking at his phone. "Is that why you're sitting in the dark looking at a picture of your daughter?"

"Hmm?" Shepherd glanced down. "Oh, no. I was just—"

"You're feeling like a bag of crap because yesterday was the first anniversary of your divorce?" Robertson probed.

Shepherd's jaw dropped in pure astonishment. "How…?! Well, you're right, but why did *you* remember something like that?"

She shrugged and sat down next to him. "I've got a good memory, and I remember you being...well...I remember how messed up you were when it all went down. You hid it from most everyone here, but I could tell. So, what's bothering you? Missing your daughter?"

"Yeah," Shepherd said vaguely.

"May I ask you a personal question, Chief?"

"Shoot fire," Shepherd said, too tired and too angry at himself to really care.

"Are you blaming yourself for the divorce and everything?" Robertson asked, her voice gentle.

Shepherd held up his phone, "A little girl's life was upended because *I* was too stupid to realize I couldn't be a normal husband.

So was Jenn's, for that matter. I screwed up *both* Martha and Jennifer's lives in one epic feat of stupidity."

Why the hell am I telling her *this?!*

"You told me last month Jennifer knew you were gay when you two started dating, right?" Robertson asked.

"Yeah. So?"

"So why are you blaming yourself like this?" Robertson asked. "Ok, yes, you made a mistake. A big one. But, you know what? *So did Jennifer.* Chief, she wasn't forced to marry you. You gambled *together,* and you lost *together*. I mean, come on, it wasn't like she was forced into an arranged marriage, was it?"

Shepherd gawped at her.

Robertson looked away for a moment, thinking. "If I understand what you told me, Jennifer's first husband—Martha's dad—died when Martha was two, right? Jenn's also runs a business, right?"

Shepherd nodded, "A glass-making business in Virginia Beach she started with her first husband."

Robertson nodded, "Even I can tell you what happened. I was raised by a single mom. Mama's an amazing woman and I love her very much for all she did, but it was hard on her to do everything alone. Jenn's a widow trying to hold a business together while raising a daughter. Finding a man willing to be a partner in a situation like that is a temptation I'm not sure many single parents could resist. Like Mama says, 'it takes two to tango,' and you two were in a tango, not a couple of solo numbers. "

Shepherd quietly considered her words as she went on.

"There's another thing you did right," Robertson said. "I grew up without a father. *You* didn't just become a dad while you were married to Jenn, you're *still* being a dad even though you've got *no* legal obligations to do so since you never formally adopted Martha. I'm actually kind of jealous. Martha's got a *dad* in her life. I never did."

In a truly rare moment, Shepherd was speechless. His jaw dropped open as he stared at her.

"So, you're sitting here in the dark hating yourself because you can't act out against 'society' or the Navy. Therefore, you're doing the only thing you know to do and blame yourself," Robertson continued, "Am I close?"

He nodded. He'd always known she was smart, but this was damned *unnerving!*

"I should never have done that to either of them," Shepherd said, wiping away a stray tear.

"No, you shouldn't have," Robertson agreed, "But you're not *listening* to me. Think it through, as you always say. You shouldn't have done that to them, but *Jennifer should not have done it to you either!*"

His head snapped up.

"You're *both* guilty of trying to live a lie," Robertson said. "That *doesn't* make you or Jenn 'bad,' or 'evil,' or whatever. To quote something I've heard you say, what it makes you is *human,* Isaac."

Her words hit him hard right across the heart. "You've never called me 'Isaac' before, Dionne."

She smiled, "Like you've often said, sometimes we need to be human first and sailors second."

Shepherd laughed out loud, "Will you *please* stop quoting me, already?!"

Robertson smiled, but didn't let it go. "Stop tormenting yourself for things you had no control over, and stop punishing yourself for past mistakes, however big they were."

"It's hard to...to let go of guilt when you've carried it so long it's really all you've ever known," Shepherd said.

"Guilt for what?"

"For not being what I was supposed to be," Shepherd answered, feeling the emotional turmoil roiling in his chest. "I was in the closet for decades. All I've known is how to hide everything I am. It's terrifying to suddenly have those walls fall at once and be exposed for something I've spent my life seeing condemned.'"

Robertson smiled gently, "Mama says only God knows who's going to heaven and hell, not anyone around here."

Shepherd raised his eyebrows, conceding her point. "Your mama's a smart woman."

Robertson smiled, "I think I'll amend Mama's quote and say, 'Only God knows who any of us are *supposed* to be.' Well, set me an example here, *Chief:* give yourself some grace. Hell, it ain't like you need to *earn* absolution, what with all the monsters you've stopped."

Shepherd tried to wipe his eyes without looking like he was wiping his eyes, "What do you mean?"

Robertson folded her hands in her lap, "You've done pretty well keeping your...your 'second career' quiet, but I know about it. It doesn't take a rocket scientist to figure out you're working on the Bacon murder with your NCIS buddy. From what I've learned, you've solved quite a few murders in the past."

"How did you...?! Where did you...?!" Shepherd's eyes widened with abject shock.

"You need to be more careful," Robertson said. "I overheard you talking to Chief Foltz last Friday. I started digging after that. I've spent quite a few hours stalking you, and I've turned up a lot of your interesting history."

Shepherd was too amazed to speak.

"Go on, Chief. Tell me I'm wrong," Robertson grinned. She clearly enjoyed outfoxing him.

"You're not wrong, Dionne," Shepherd said, chuckling as the shock faded. "Let me get this straight: you only overheard Ben and I last Friday afternoon, and yet you managed to find all this out while on a romantic getaway? I'm impressed, but I hope you didn't piss off your boyfriend."

Robertson looked pleased, "Thank you! It helps to have some friends in security and my own contact at NCIS—Carla Tenbold."

"I know her," Shepherd nodded.

"I got to know her last year when I was deployed on *Theodore Roosevelt,*" Robertson said. "She was the agent assigned to the strike group. She and I paired up several times as a team during video game tournaments. I talked to her yesterday to confirm what my own research indicated. She filled in a lot of gaps, and also told me she was surprised by your decision to retire,

.

even though a bunch of people at NCIS were throwing a party at the news."

Shepherd laughed a deep, booming, genuine laugh. "That sounds about right!"

"If you don't mind me asking, why did you drop your retirement papers? You really seem to love the Navy."

Shepherd straightened up a bit. Slouching too long hurt his lower back. "I do love the Navy, but that's not a reason to stay in uniform when it's time to move on."

"I don't understand."

Shepherd tried again, "I realized I wasn't excited about any of the potential assignments for me when I was talking to my detailer about orders back in July. I talked to my folks about it, and Pop told me he felt something similar when he realized he was ready to retire from the Air Force. I've outgrown the Navy, if that makes sense?"

"It does," Robertson nodded, "But, I have to ask, does any of this have to do with killing that guy back in August?"

Shepherd's temper snapped, *"I didn't kill him!"*

"You didn't?" Robertson flinched, but held her ground, though it wasn't easy facing down Shepherd.

Shepherd forced himself to calm down, "No, I didn't, and I don't give a damn what the news reports said! He *fell* while I was chasing him."

"You didn't push him?" Robertson asked again. "Didn't he try to kill your friends?"

Shepherd again forced himself to relax. "No. I mean, yes— he did try to kill my friends, but I didn't push him off that scaffold. The stinking bastard slipped and fell. I'll admit I probably could've saved him if I had tried to, and I'd be a liar if I said I wasn't happy he's finally gone. But, I *did not* kill him."

"Ok," Robertson said, waiting for him to go on, but Shepherd was clearly intent on shutting down that line of conversation.

Taking a deep breath to steady himself, Shepherd started over. "To answer your original question: no, that has *nothing* to do with my decision to retire. I do admit I want to stop playing detective, but, more importantly, I'm just ready to move on."

Robertson was eager to pump Shepherd for more information about the incident, but wisely decided against it. The hardened look on his face was warning enough to steer clear of the topic...for now.

"Right now, you *are* here and you're still in the game," Robertson said, shifting gears. "So, Chief Accidental Detective, what can I do to help?"

"This is *not* some game, Dionne," Shepherd said sharply. His voice was cold with warning as he tensed up again. "I thought it was for a very long time. My immaturity led me to take some really stupid chances. I treated the whole thing like some great adventure, like something you'd see in the movies where the unlikely hero swings into action saving the day and never gets *really* hurt."

"Obviously, you've changed your mind."

Shepherd nodded. "The stakes are real, Dionne. People *do* get hurt and people die. I've got a partially crippled left knee and some burn scars above my right ear to prove it."

"I know it ain't a game, Chief," Robertson said, a serious tone in her voice. "But, I can't just stand by and let a possibly innocent sailor get screwed. What can I do to help?"

Shepherd looked into her eyes, seeking her measure. Something in her steadiness told him that she *did* understand the nature of what she was offering.

And, truth be told, he could use her help.

"Ok," Shepherd nodded, finally relaxing. "You're in. We need to keep the OIC and CO off your tail, so you *damned* well better maintain a low profile."

"Understood," Robertson said, a devious smirk the only evidence of her enthusiasm.

Shepherd smiled grimly, "Alright, my dear Watson, let's talk murder."

"...in business news, Raytheon and General Dynamics today announced they plan to file an appeal of Department of Defense's decision to award a new contract for a next-generation missile defense system to Gae Dokkaebi Industries Technology on grounds that the bidding process violated federal law because GDI Tech's home office is in South Korea and not the United States..."

"...Admiral David Jones, commander of the Navy's Atlantic Command, issued a statement yesterday reiterating Petty Officer Jarvis Cline remains innocent unless proven guilty in a court-martial. Jones further said any statements declaring Cline's guilt are subverting the bedrock American principle of 'innocent until proven guilty'...."

"...the Chief of Naval Operation's office had no comment when pressed to confirm whether Admiral Donovan quietly ordered the relief of Admiral David Jones in Norfolk..."

"...a spokesman for Admiral Jones said any rumors about his imminent relief are simply that—rumors..."

Founded in 1752, Portsmouth, Virginia, sits on the west side of the winding Elizabeth River across from Norfolk. The Portsmouth Naval Hospital, one of the Navy's major regional medical centers, is the oldest continuously operating U.S. Navy hospital. The hospital's silhouette dominates the Portsmouth skyline because of the Tower, a 17-story tall wing that was the only thing resembling a skyscraper in the immediate vicinity.

Shepherd's parked *Sarah Jane* and strode off across the hospital's campus. Unknowingly, he walked with a spring in his step that had been missing for a long time. Cheerfully greeting the sailors he passed, he headed to a temporary morgue facility made up of prefabricated buildings on the grounds between the hospital and river. The temporary morgue was in use while the hospital's morgue was undergoing long-needed renovations.

John Stiles' call to the hospital's command master chief paid off. Late the night before, Stiles texted Shepherd, telling him to be at the temporary morgue area by 11:00. He'd be talking to Cmdr. Dylan Scott, the medical examiner who had performed Bacon's autopsy.

So, dressed in his blue 'Aquaflage' uniform, Shepherd popped through a prefabricated door at precisely 11:00. He entered a prefabricated administration area and approached a prefabricated sailor sitting behind a prefabricated desk.

"Morning!" Shepherd said, holding out his ID card. "I'm Chief Shepherd. I'm here to see Cmdr. Scott."

The sailor took his card, did a quick check on the computer calendar, and punched a number into her desk phone.

"Sir? This is Petty Officer Heart. I have a Chief Shepherd here to see you."

Heart handed Shepherd back his ID card as she hung up the phone. "Chief, Please go through that door to your right. You'll be met by a corpsman and they'll escort you back."

"Thanks!" Shepherd smiled and headed through the indicated door.

The corpsman escorting Shepherd led him through a maze of corridors until they came to the type of examination room one might find at a forward hospital in a war zone (which, Shepherd reminded himself, was precisely what these prefabricated structures were built for). Three tables graced the room, but only the table farthest from him was occupied by a body. A physician was standing next to the table, his attention on a sheaf of papers.

"Cmdr. Scott, this is Chief Shepherd," The corpsman said.

Scott just grunted and continued reading the paperwork in his hands.

The corpsman looked uncertain, but Shepherd smiled. "It's ok, I'm sure you have work you need to get to."

The corpsman nodded and then headed out, leaving Shepherd alone with Scott, who continued ignoring him.

Shepherd slowly closed the distance, studying Scott. He figured Scott was either furious with everything having to do with the investigation, or else Scott was just a jerk.

"Commander Scott?"

Scott looked up. He was of medium build and a head shorter than Shepherd. The height difference made no difference to Scott as he glared at Shepherd with a hot intensity that could melt steel. "Chief Shepherd, is it? I understand you're here about the Cline prosecution?"

"Nothing quite so grandiose," Shepherd said with a disarming smile. "Just helping do an evidence review."

"Well, you JAG idiots are barking up the wrong goddamned tree for running the prosecution like your doing!" Scott snapped.

Ok, he's angry, Shepherd understood. Realizing Scott obviously thought he was working for the JAG office, Shepherd decided to play *that* role to the hilt. "What do you mean, sir?"

"Well, this unfortunate fellow here is Carl Bacon," Scott gestured to the body. "I had him taken out of storage in the hopes that maybe...just maybe...someone from your damned office would actually *listen* to me this time!"

Shepherd was shocked and looked at Bacon's body in surprise, "He's still here?! He hasn't been buried yet? But he died over a month ago!"

"Chief, you're not very well informed," Scott said angrily. "The JAG office ordered his body held during the court-martial. His family is tearing up the hospital phone lines something fierce and has even initiated a lawsuit, but all I can do is just keep referring them to your office. I can't release this poor kid's body until you people lift the goddamned legal hold you have on me!"

Shepherd was deeply disturbed, but still played the part of a loyal JAG chief for the moment. Quite unintentionally, Scott had given him the perfect opening for what he needed to find out. "Ok, Cmdr. Scott. Tell you what, I have obviously *not* been properly briefed—and I *will* be taking that up when I get back this afternoon —let's just start over from the beginning. That'll avoid me asking any asinine questions and let you present your findings at the same time."

"In other words, repeat every goddamned thing I've already said that no one listened to?!" Scott exploded in a frustrated rage.

"Sir, I know you're angry, and I understand why," Shepherd said, holding up a hand in an apologetic gesture. "I'd be pissed off too if I'd been treated like you have. I am asking you to please bear with me. Unlike the personnel you've already dealt with, I'm here to *actually* listen to *everything* you have to say. I know it's aggravating—and I respect that—but, please, help me do this right."

Scott grudgingly considered Shepherd for the moment, "Ok, Chief. I'll give you a try."

There was slight sneer in Scott's voice, but Shepherd let it go. He couldn't blame Scott for being so angry. He was beginning to feel rather hot under the collar himself at the JAG office's behavior.

Scott reached down and pulled the sheet clean off Bacon's naked, bruised, and battered body. If he was trying to shock Shepherd, he failed miserably. Shepherd was quite accustomed to seeing dead people.

"As you can see, the deceased is a white male in his mid-twenties," Scott began circling the body as if he were a tour guide. "He was in relatively good shape. Decent musculature and his heart muscle was strong. His liver indicates a formerly high level of alcohol consumption, but it was still within healthy parameters."

Shepherd quietly followed Scott, listening carefully.

"As you can see the left ankle is broken in at least three places. I know the news has been reporting the cause of death was blunt force trauma due to his impact with the well deck floor, but this man was already dead before he hit that deck. Come here, Chief."

Shepherd gave no indication that Scott had just handed him what he and Gray needed. Instead, he went to Scott's side as the medical examiner tenderly lifted and turned Bacon's blue-green face to the side. He drew Shepherd's attention to a very large wound smashed into the upper portion of the back of Bacon's head.

"Jeez…!" Shepherd said quietly, not realizing he spoke aloud.

"Pretty gross, huh?" Scott asked, pointing into the wound with his gloved hand. "Chief, *that* is the cause of death, not the fall. The fall caused enough damage to the surrounding bone and tissue that I can't be 100% certain, but I'd stake my retirement on that wound being caused by the impact of a three-sided weapon. Something like the corner of a box, or...I just don't know how to describe it. However, you can clearly see three pieces of the skull fractured inward from the fatal impact."

*A box...*The thought flashed through Shepherd's mind as his memory threw an image from on board *Ponce* onto his mental screen. He pushed the thought aside, filing it away for the moment before and returning his attention to Scott.

"Interesting," Shepherd said, his powerful mind still recording details. "I see your point. What else you got, Commander?"

Scott studied Shepherd for a moment. He began to visibly relax, evidently satisfied Shepherd was actually listening to him.

"Face and torso," Scott said in an easier voice as he tenderly laid Bacon's head back on the table. He began pointing at discolorations in the skin of Bacon's face and abdominal area. "These bruises are consistent with the general shape of a fist. They were only beginning to form a the time of death when blood circulation stopped. His arms show defensive wounds; the kind you'd get by putting up your arms to block someone hitting you." Scott emphasized the point by holding his own arms up in a defensive pose.

"You're saying he was beaten before he was killed?" Shepherd asked.

"Exactly," Scott said. "The wounds on his body and arms tell me he was being beaten, but he *wasn't* fighting back. He was holding his arms up to protect himself. His hands are uninjured. If he'd been punching back at an attacker, his hands *would* show some evidence of injury. Whatever your idiot JAG bosses are charging Cline with, they're wrong. Cline might have killed Bacon, but he sure as *hell* did *not* do it the way the prosecution is saying!"

Shepherd let that sink in for a moment before speaking. "Ok, sir, let me make sure I'm tracking with you. You're telling me

Bacon was *not* fighting back? He was assaulted and beaten, but the only wounds you've found on him are *defensive* wounds?"

"You do a lot better at listening than that Special Agent Cremer ass!" Scott fairly spat out, pointing out the bruises on Bacon's body. "That is *exactly* what I'm saying. Bacon was assaulted, but he was *not fighting back*. Cline might still be your killer, but this line that the two of them were in a fight is just bullsh —"

"What about DNA?" Shepherd cut in, redirecting the conversation. "We have plenty of samples of Cline's DNA. Have you found *any* DNA from Cline on Bacon's body, or did the forensics lab alert you to any of Cline's DNA on Bacon's uniform? Or, can I go out on a limb here and guess that Cline's DNA is *completely* missing from this picture?"

"You really *are* smarter than that assho...than Cremer, Chief," Scott was clearly impressed, and looked at Shepherd with a very satisfied expression on his face. "That jerk never let me finish a sentence and even somehow got me dropped from the witness pool for the court-martial. Never seen a murder case where the *medical examiner* was blocked from testifying at trial! Anyway, I found no DNA here that belonged to Cline."

Shepherd's eyebrows ascended almost into his hairline, "So you *did* find DNA on the body? Other than Bacon's own DNA, I mean?"

Scott looked up, his craggy face twisted into an ugly scowl. "I damn well *did*. The DNA of an unknown male is present in several of these wounds, likely from abraded skin on the attacker's knuckles, or even from spit flying. However, the DNA sample from Cline *does not* match the male DNA found on Bacon."

"What about the forensics lab? Did they find anything else they sent over to you?"

"No. They're not likely to share non-biological data with me at all," said Scott. "You'll need to talk to them directly."

"I've got that covered, sir," Shepherd said. "Commander, I sincerely thank you for your time, and I apologize for how you have been treated. Oh! One last question—do you confirm the time of death was between 19:00 and 21:00?"

"Correct," Scott answered.

Scott tenderly covered Bacon's ravaged body with the sheet, gesturing Shepherd ahead of him as the two began to leave the examining room. Scott removed his gloves before opening the door.

"How much longer until y'all are located back in the hospital proper?" Shepherd asked as they stepped into the field staging area.

"They tell us next year," Scott said gruffly, "But this is the Navy. They could easily decide to leave us out here and give our spaces to some admiral who wants an office."

"Wouldn't surprise me at all, sir," Shepherd said with complete empathy.

Shepherd was startled to find Gray waiting for him in the temporary morgue's lobby. The two men left the building and began strolling along the Elizabeth River. The Norfolk skyline dazzled them as the sun glittered on its many glass buildings.

"What did you learn?" Gray asked. He wore a blue suit with a yellow tie and the usual American flag lapel pin.

"I learned Cremer is more of a headstrong, egotistical twit than even I thought. Hell, I know *I* can succumb to tunnel vision if I get fixated on an idea, but Cremer makes me look like a junior varsity wannabe." Despite the angry words, there was a startling lightness to Shepherd's manner.

Gray stopped in the shade of a tree, his hands in his pockets. He hadn't seen Shepherd this upbeat in well over a year. "Ok, that was a rather colorful response, and, while every answer is a response, not every response is an answer. What did you *learn?*"

Shepherd smiled under his cover. "Cmdr. Scott is pissed off that neither Cremer or the JAG office listened to a word he said… and Cremer apparently got him blocked from testifying. Since when do y'all NCIS agents get to dictate who testifies at a trial?"

Gray rolled his eyes. "Oy gevalt! We're *don't* have that kind of power! Well, at least not officially. Cremer's pretty well connected politically, so I can only guess he used that to sway the situation. Great; there's another problem I get to hand Charlotte! Anyway, what *didn't* he want to hear from Cmdr. Scott?"

Shepherd sat down on a bench under the tree, Gray plopping down beside him. The Elizabeth River burbled to itself.

"Well, Abe, he confirmed that Bacon was dead *before* he was thrown over the catwalk into the well deck," Shepherd said, crossing his legs.

"Just like you called it on the ship," Gray nodded. "Nice one!"

"Thank you," Shepherd said. "Anyway, Bacon had the proverbial tobacco juice beaten out of him immediately before death. His head, arms, and torso were covered with *defensive* wounds, but his hands showed zero evidence of *offensive* wounds."

"Wow," Gray said. "That right there demolishes the last shred of Sniffer's testimony. Go on."

"The fatal wound was a blow from a semi-sharp, apparently three-sided weapon in the upper back of the skull"

"DNA?" Gray pulled out his notebook and began jotting it in.

"Big one there. Absolutely *none* of the DNA found on Bacon was from Cline, but rather from an *unknown* male," Shepherd said.

Gray's head jerked up at that revelation. "Wait—DNA from an *unknown* male was found on the body?"

Shepherd nodded.

Gray took a breath and gazed out over the river, his brain evidently racing. "Isaac, you just earned your pay for the week. Commander Scott just proved the assailant is *still* at large. That doesn't completely clear Cline yet. After all, it *is* possible he was an accessory, so we still have work to do. Please continue."

"As I said, according to Cmdr. Scott, there's *not* one shred of *biological* evidence placing Cline at the scene of the crime," Shepherd repeated. "Unless there's other forensic evidence, like a fingerprint or clothing fibers or something else, then Cline can't be tied to Bacon's death no matter how much the Navy wishes to do so."

"I'm working that angle right now," Gray mused, closing his notebook and putting it back inside his jacket. "You said a blow from a three-sided object killed him?" "Interesting. Unfortunately, that's going to be a complication. It's been over a month; long enough for the killer to dispose of the weapon. It would be easy enough to just toss it over the side. Even if we get divers in the water under *Ponce,* the murder weapon would likely be dismissed as just another piece of junk littering the harbor floor."

Shepherd smiled, recalling the memory his mind unearthed while he was talking to Scott.

"Actually, old friend, *Ponce* already scored one for the good guys there. The murder weapon is still on board, and she showed it to us. You and I looked right at it the other day, and even took some blood samples off of it."

Gray raised his eyebrows as the soft breeze off the river fluffed his white hair. "Come again?"

"That electrical box by the hatch to the catwalk, the one that was about five feet off the deck. That's where we found most of the blood spatter," Shepherd said.

Gray's eyes widened, "Of course! Good call, Isaac! Wasn't it near a corner of the box?"

"Exactly!" Shepherd said. "The *corner* of a box…a *three-sided* weapon if the victim is shoved into it with enough force."

"Well, *that* cinches it," Gray said. "That's the kind of concrete evidence we need to prove that Sniffer is lying. Don't get me wrong, Isaac. Your observation about what the guys on *Mesa Verde* should have heard is significant enough to hold up in court, but what you learned today is a complete game-changer."

"What did you learn from Cline?" Shepherd asked.

Gray leaned back and crossed his own legs. "Well, both he and his mom hate NCIS and the Navy. Can't say I blame them."

"Understandable," Shepherd agreed sadly.

"He's sticking to his story, and I have to hand it to him for courage under fire," Gray replied.

"What about the other forensics?" Shepherd asked. "I mean, we've determined there's no biological evidence placing

Cline at the scene. What about any other physical evidence? Have the forensics wizards found anything on Bacon's uniform?"

"That's what I'm working on," Gray said. "I'll talk to them tomorrow morning. I still have three other cases I have to work on, so this afternoon will be dominated by those. Still, we need to talk to the *Ponce* crew, active duty and civilian alike. We have to get our own picture of what they know unfiltered by Cremer's case reports. We also need to talk to Sniffer. What's she hiding, and why is she hiding it? Is she scared for her own safety, or is she complicit in the murder? Is she covering for someone else out of loyalty? We need to get a good read about her before we talk to her."

"I've…got some of that that taken care of already," Shepherd said.

"Excuse me?" Gray asked as a pair of sailors in Navy PT gear jogged by. A seagull cried out over the water.

"I've got an ally that's working on the *Ponce* crew angle right now," Shepherd said. "Just…just trust me and give me a day or two."

Gray looked quizzically at Shepherd. This was the second time this week Shepherd had gone 'off script' from his former pattern. Shepherd had always been one to dive into a situation, but he had never enlisted allies without talking to Gray first. The realization that Shepherd was becoming more independent in his actions flashed across Gray's mind.

"Ok…" Gray said uncertainly. "Isaac, is there anything I *should* know about?"

"No. Well, not yet. Just trust me."

"Ok," Gray said again, but he obviously was not happy about it. "As it is, between your information and mine, I think I nearly have enough to go back to Charlotte and get her to tell the prosecution their case is officially a bunch of bullshit. Still, I want to wait for another day or two. I hate leaving Cline to be run through the wringer, but we need to build a bigger case if we're going to guarantee stopping this trial. The controversy the CNO lit off has backed the Navy into a corner. The Navy's at a point now that it has to push the case just to keep from being embarrassed, and that's *always* a dangerous place for a defendant to be."

"Agreed. So, the big questions for us now are who the hell killed Carl Bacon, and why?" Shepherd asked, reaching into his pocket. His phone was buzzing.

"Same questions we started with," Gray said. "Well, we can reasonably rule out Cline. I just hope his career can be salvaged and not…wrecked…by…Isaac?"

Shepherd was staring at his phone, a very odd expression on his face. "I've got a text."

"Yeah, those happen these days on those things called 'smart phones,'" Gray said, laughing.

"No, you galactic dork," Shepherd shot him a look, but still smiling. "It's from an unknown number marked 'Private' by my caller ID. Look."

Shepherd handed Gray the phone, and Gray glanced down, his own face growing darker with confusion as he read it.

Hello, Isaac. Been a long time. The investigation on the Ponce *potentially intersects with something I'm working on. Forgive me for being rather cryptic. I know it comes off like a cliché from a low-budget TV spy series, but I have to be discreet.*

The Cline prosecution struck me as rushed. When I found out it was Cremer leading the investigation, I wondered if Cline was being railroaded the way you were 20 years ago.

Do some market research. You're good at zeroing in on your target with laser-like accuracy.

Good luck. Please greet Mr. Gray for me. You both were instrumental in saving my life and giving me a second chance.

-L

"What in the hell…?" Gray asked.

"Whomever this Mr. 'L' is, he just gave us a lot of information while telling us absolutely nothing," Shepherd said, taking back his phone. "He's obviously in the federal government, and likely in one of the intelligence services."

"He certainly knows Shey Cremer," Gray said, just as unnerved by the text as Shepherd had been. "The *reasons* Cremer leaked your name back in Spain were never made public, so Mr. 'L' is clearly someone with access to a lot of *very* confidential information."

"Well, we didn't need Mr. 'L' here to tell us Cline is being wrongly prosecuted," Shepherd said. "Between our observations on *Mesa Verde* and *Ponce,* and what I learned from Cmdr. Scott, we had pretty much surrounded that angle already. What I find interesting is that Mr. 'L' speaks of motives."

"How so?" Gray asked. He thought he knew, but he wanted to be sure.

"One of the first things you taught me to codify in my thinking was to consider who benefits from a crime, and how they benefit." Shepherd said. "Mr. 'L' is making a reference to markets, as if we need to look at buying and selling."

"Well, *Ponce* is going to be decommissioned and put in the bone yard," Gray said. "She'll probably be sold for scrap in ten or twenty years...but that doesn't feel right. I have a hunch Mr. 'L' is referring to something more immediate."

"Me too, Abe," Shepherd said, "But nothing on *Ponce* is ready for prime time in the fleet. At least, nothing that was taken aboard her during this past four-year period. Unless..."

"Unless that's the point," Gray picked up the line of thought. "There was a ton of experimental tech on that ship these past few years. 'Market research,' our Mr. 'L' said. I wonder if he's alluding to an illegal transfer of technology?"

Shepherd gazed across the river at the Norfolk Waterside center. "Now *that* is a motive for murder. What espionage cases have you guys got going on?"

"Nothing you need to know about," Gray said, also looking across the river to Norfolk. "But, there are a few threads I can pull on and see if we get another lead."

"Jeez, are we idiots?!" Shepherd burst out, standing up in frustration and shoving his phone in his pocket as another pair of sailors in Navy PT gear jogged by.

"Isaac?" Gray rose as well.

"Here we are, trusting someone who anonymously texts me," Shepherd said, irritated. "Obviously Mr. 'L' knows of us, but anyone in the law enforcement or intelligence communities could conceivably find out the backstory of *why* my name was leaked in Spain. Are we so bad we need to rely on some unknown texter to give us clues?!"

"No, we are *not* 'so bad' at anything, Isaac," Gray said, stepping up next to Shepherd. "I know we're taking a big leap of faith here, but you know we were already about to start heading in the direction 'L' indicated. I don't trust this 'L' at all, but he might be right, even if his motives are suspect."

"Another point that strikes me is that our Mr. 'L' says Cline is being railroaded for the same reason I was," Shepherd said.

"I noticed that too."

Shepherd looked across the Elizabeth River for a moment. "Cremer got all hot and bothered about nailing me to the wall 20 years ago after he found out I was gay and struggling with mental health issues."

"Interesting observation," Gray said. "If Cline falls into one of those two categories, it would explain a great deal about Cremer's, well, I won't say 'jihad' or 'vendetta,' but—"

"*I* will!" Shepherd snapped. "The bastard went after me on prejudice alone! You know that. If even *one* of his prejudices was triggered by Cline, it would explain his myopically religious zeal in shoving Cline through a blender!"

Gray sighed. "I'm not going to argue that. But, we're still speculating, you and I. We still have work to do if *we're* going to do this correctly."

"Agreed," Shepherd said, clearly agitated about more than just Cremer's bad attitude. "I just feel...I feel we're being played, pranked, if you will. All of this feels like a trope right out of *The X Files,* or even *Scooby Doo: Mystery Incorporated.* A highly placed unknown contact pops up and gives us *just enough* cryptic clues to guide us, but that's it? Isn't that sort of thing kind of old hat by now?"

"In fiction, yes," Gray said. "This is real life, Isaac, and you know better than most that real life does *not* adhere to the rules of fiction!"

Shepherd sighed, nodding, "Good point. Ok, let's tackle this angle. At worst, we just eliminate another line of reasoning we'd have to consider anyway."

"Do you mind if I do some digging through your phone records?" Gray asked. "I want to find out if we can trace Mr. 'L.'"

"Knock yourself out," Shepherd said. "I'm going back to *Ponce* myself tomorrow to see if I can get some information out of the chiefs mess. Can we meet at your house Friday night? Will you and Sarah mind a me bringing an extra guest?"

"An *extra* guest?" Gray's eyebrows lifted again, "Would this 'extra guest' be the ally I don't need to know about right now?"

"I'm not saying that at all," Shepherd grinned.

"So what *are* you saying?"

"To steal a line from a great TV show," Shepherd laughed, "I'm not saying anything. I didn't say anything then, and I'm not saying anything now."

"Well, in that case," Gray began laughing as well, "I'm saying even less than you!"

Chapter 6
Thursday, September 15; 12:30 hours
Naval Station Norfolk, Virginia

"...the Bureau of Labor Statistics said unemployment is still hovering at 5% with no change expected. Moving on to military news, the apparent stand off between the Chief of Naval Operations and the Commander of the Navy's Atlantic Command continued last night when the CNO released a statement saying any sailor, enlisted or officer, will be held accountable under the UCMJ if they engage in criminal acts or disobey direct orders of senior personnel. This is seen as a threat to Admiral David Jones, who, according to unnamed sources, has far repeatedly refused orders from the CNO to issue a statement condemning Petty Officer Jarvis Cline, who is currently on trial for murder in Norfolk. Jones' office released a statement this morning saying the admiral is committed to cheerfully obeying all lawful, legal and morally sound orders in accordance with UCMJ and Navy requirements..."

PTSD is a BITCH!

The thought kept repeating itself like a broken record as Shepherd sat with the other chiefs in *Ponce's* chiefs mess.

High strung when he was a kid, Shepherd sometimes wondered if his anxiety disorder actually began with his two brothers repeatedly scaring the bejeezus out of him when they were young. In more sober moments, however, he knew his own life-long fight with PTSD and its subsequent anxieties began only two decades earlier. He had *not* been kidding when he warned Robertson the detective's life had very real consequences.

Some days he just got up on the wrong side of the bed no matter how good his overall mood. Today was such a day and, as usual, the hurricane of free-floating anxieties fell on him at a most breathtakingly inconvenient moment. Feeling the unrest in his soul during breakfast, he made the decision to go ahead and take his panic-attack meds early. They never fully calmed him down on days like this, but they did 'lower the volume' enough for his own acting skills to cover the rest.

"I remember Sparky here getting ordered *not to* answer questions during our initiation season on the IKE!" Laughed Chief Boatswain's Mate Kelly Tate, picking up her glass and taking a drink. Tate, a stout woman with fiery red hair, was a hard drinker during a port call and a holy terror on the deck if her sailors failed to uphold her exacting standards.

Shepherd was glad to see her again, but personally cursed his doubled bad luck. First he was in the middle of a PTSD bout, and now he'd run into someone he already knew. Finding Tate on board *Ponce* blew his and Robertson's carefully crafted cover story completely out of the water. He fervently prayed he'd get a private moment to alert Robertson before she had to use the story and inadvertently revealed the deception. He had purposely left his actual rate a mystery, but with Tate on board, him being a Mass Communication Specialist had been revealed when they sat down to lunch.

"Why were you ordered not to talk, Isaac?" Chief Boatswain's Mate Thomas Shifter asked. He was burly and had a thick gut and even thicker forearms. He was the epitome of the stereotypical crusty old chief.

"I knew everything," Shepherd said, pushing his plate and the remains of his demolished lunch away. He hitched a very convincing smile on his face. "There wasn't a heritage or procedural or legal question the chiefs could throw at us selectees that I didn't know. John Stiles thought the rest of our class was depending on me too much, so he ordered me to shut up."

Tate laughed again and went on, "John said Sparky was smart enough to figure out other ways to support our selectee class without speaking. I'm sure the sailors in IKE's media center paid the price for *that* one. I mean, Sparky's never really ever been able to shut up!"

Genuine laughter welled up in Shepherd's chest, quieting the emotional storm for a moment. He had to admit, however much it upended his plans, it was good to see Tate again. She had been one of his better buddies on IKE.

"I tried not to burn their ears up too much," Shepherd said through his laughter, "But it wasn't easy!"

"So why are you helping NCIS, Isaac?" Chief Yeoman Jacob Hank asked, his timing uncanny considering Shepherd had just been pondering that very issue.

"I had training in forensics, particularly the photography side of the house, as well as in evidentiary procedures before I joined the Navy," Shepherd said, hoping the vagueness of his response was not noticed. "I've assisted NCIS with a few case reviews in the past, so when they began this one, they called NEPAC East and asked if I could go TAD to them for a few weeks."

"Still seems weird," Hank said guardedly. "Why *you?* There must be outside 'objective' experts they could bring in. Your previous assignment on *Ponce* can't be a factor. Everyone you served with on board is long gone."

"True," Shepherd said, wishing the feeling of a steel band around his chest would go away. "I was immediately available. Cline's court-martial is ongoing, so this review has to be conducted fast. NCIS didn't want to wait for their normal consultants to fly in because there just wasn't time."

The last was a flat out lie, but Shepherd was not about to let on he had been commissioned by Admiral Jones to take up the case.

"When were you stationed on board?" Shifter asked.

"2010 through 2012," Shepherd said.

"Waaait…." Shifter said, cocking his head to one side. "2010 – 2012? You were on board when Ratner killed that Marine and then killed himself, weren't you?"

Shepherd *really* didn't want to get into that whole situation right now.

"I was," Shepherd answered, but then deflected by aiming a question back at Shifter. "You were on duty the night of the murder, weren't you, Thomas?"

"I was Officer of the Deck, yes," Shifter nodded.

"So what all happened?" Shepherd asked. "I've read all the reports, but, they're just reports. I'd rather hear it from you since you witnessed a lot of those awful events."

Shifter shrugged, "It all happened the way I told your NCIS pal, that Special Agent Cremer. Bacon was late to watch, so I sent Cline to find him."

"How long was Cline gone?" Shepherd looked for all the world like a man just making conversation out of nosy curiosity.

Shifter leaned back, looking at the overhead for a moment. Somewhere above them, a needle gun began rat-tat-tatting against the ship's steel.

"It was just before 20:00 hours," Shifter said. "Bacon was supposed to have reported for watch at 19:45, but I gave it nearly ten minutes before sending Cline to find him. It wasn't very long before Cline came running back up here, sweating and bruised all to hell from knocking into equipment as he ran back up here. At least, that's what he said happened to him."

"So what's up with those two getting a house together if they always fought?" Shepherd asked, pretending he didn't already know. "I mean, both used to be first classes, and their fighting with each other got them busted down together, but then they go a get a house together?"

"They only fought when they were drunk," Shifter said. "They actually *were* friends, but were both angry drunks. Frankly, I think they had a thing going for each other. Oh, once they both got sober they were professional as hell, but I'm pretty sure they were dating each other."

Shepherd's eyebrows went up as Shifter inadvertently detoured the conversation right where Shepherd wanted to go. "What about you two? Do you think they were gay?"

"Tom, you should have asked me," Tate said to Shifter, exasperation in her voice. "They *were* a couple, yes. I saw them out in town quite a few times holding hands and being rather lovey-dovey."

"Doesn't mean they didn't also like girls, too," Shifter said. "They hung out with Sniffer all the time. I think they were competing for her, whatever might have been going on between them."

"That girl is just a fruit fly!" Tate said furiously, using a relatively new term for a woman who enjoyed friendships with gay men. "She's also gives female sailors a bad name!"

"How so, Kelly?" Shepherd asked, red flags jumping up inside his brain like whack-a-mole targets in some demented carnival game.

"She's a mattress," Tate said with dripping disgust. "Good women have to work *twice* as hard as it is to get half the respect men get in the Navy, and then some little bitch like Sniffer comes along and sets us all back 50 years by *sleeping* her way around. I wrote several counseling chits on her for flirting with the civilian mariners while we were on duty, and I *know* her own chief had taken her to task for the same thing when we were underway!"

"Who's her chief?" Shepherd leaned back and crossed his legs.

"Brenda Chukwuma," Tate said.

"I know her," Shepherd said, surprised. "I met her a long time ago on Guam. Can I talk to her?"

"She's already in Japan," Tate said. "They're starting to rotate us off the ship now; only a handful of active duty personnel will be left on board by the decommissioning ceremony next October."

"Are y'all sure Cline and Bacon were a gay couple?" Shepherd asked to see their reactions.

"*Everyone* knew they were gay!" Hank said, earning a deprecating look from Shifter. "As if we needed *that* aboard ship!"

"Needed what?" Shepherd asked innocently, hoping Hank was *not* going where he thought he was going.

"Shipboard romances!" Hank snapped, pleasantly surprising Shepherd by not going where Shepherd had been afraid he was going. "We don't need sailors dating sailors on the same ship! Invariably those romances fail, and then you have two people who hate each other stuck together for months on end. Best way to kill morale and discipline!"

"I can't help but agree," Shepherd nodded, recalling the number of shipboard romances that he himself witnessed explode. "Can any of you, or anyone on this ship, state under oath if necessary that Cline and Bacon were a couple and were *not* jealous rivals?" Shepherd asked, still fishing for reactions.

"I can," Tate said, "Considering I saw them kissing out in town!"

"Same here," Hank said with finality.

Shifter looked put-out. Apparently, he wasn't happy he hadn't picked up on the romance between the two men as clearly as the other chiefs had.

Well, that's something very interesting to learn, and very tragic, Shepherd thought. He suddenly realized another aspect of Cline's silence—the man was grieving while being falsely accused of murdering his own boyfriend.

"You have some sailors on board, don't you, Sparky?" Tate asked. "That crew filming some videos?"

"They are indeed, Kelly," Shepherd smiled outwardly. Inwardly he groaned again; he *really* needed a private moment to quietly alert Robertson to the change in cover story Tate's presence necessitated. The team had been ordered to pretend they didn't know him (he'd even chosen to wear his 'Aquaflage; uniform because its name tape made no mention of his rate). He had told the team he wanted to see how the ship treated them when their own chief wasn't around. It was a very thin story, but the junior sailors accepted it without question while gathering their camera equipment earlier that morning.

Still, it was irrelevant now. The whole attempt at subterfuge was shot, and he needed to talk to Robertson. He was tempted to excuse himself for a head break, but decided the conversational momentum was too important to interrupt. He decided to risk it and stay in the chiefs mess.

Shepherd got up and poured cup of coffee from the tiny urn in the corner. Even with cream and sugar, it was strong enough to dissolve the paint off his stomach.

"*Ponce* is currently the third-oldest active duty ship in the Navy," Shepherd sat back down. "My sailors thought a look at the decommissioning process would be interesting, so they pitched the idea for a series of short videos and stories following the process along over the next year. I liked it, so I told MC1 Robertson to get the project moving today."

"Well, she is one *hell* of a spitfire!" Hank said, clearly impressed. "She has that production crew hopping!"

"That girl's also got some guns on her!" Tate declared. "I saw her win an arm-wrestling contest with one of the Masters-at-Arms on the mess deck earlier. She flattened him."

Shepherd nodded. "MC1 Robertson's a two-time middle-weight mixed martial arts champion, including an Olympic silver medal before joining the Navy."

The whole room went quiet.

"You're kidding!" Shifter finally said. "Why the hell did she enlist in the Navy?!"

"She got bored," Shepherd said. "At least, that's what she says."

Shifter cocked his head as Shepherd took another sip of chief-approved coffee, "How much different was *Ponce* back in your day? I know there's been a lot of changes."

"Not that many externally," Shepherd said. "The most obvious external difference was the laser weapon you guys had mounted over the bridge on the 04 Level. Funny enough, it was mounted right where I used to go read in the evenings when we were underway. Now, below decks—that's a different story. Several changes down here!"

"Such as?" Hank asked.

"Well, *this* space was the first class mess when I was on board. The chiefs mess was forward just past the galley. My old office space on the 2ⁿᵈ Deck is now female civilian berthing."

"I understand you and that NCIS agent you're working with nearly got hit with some HAZMAT the other day," Tate asked, swinging the conversation around yet again.

"We nearly did. Fortunately, no one got hurt," Shepherd sipped his coffee.

"That was all just freaking *weird,*" Shifter said, confusion on his face. "The HAZMAT staging area was on the port side of the flight deck until that afternoon. The XO abruptly shifted it to the starboard side aft line handling room, and then switched it back after that accident."

"The executive officer did *what?!*" Shepherd asked. He nearly upended his coffee in his surprise.

"He switched the HAZMAT staging area, and then switched it back. I guess that accident made everyone realize trying to take HAZMAT through that narrow p-way was just too dangerous."

"That's....that's weird," Shepherd said, red flags going off like fireworks in his head.

The other three chiefs shrugged.

"It is," Tate agreed, "But everything and everyone have been a bit...a bit 'off' since the murder."

"I can imagine," Shepherd replied, genuine compassion in his voice. Like all sailors, he knew the pain of losing a shipmate.

"Damn!" Hank said, looking at his watch. "I need to be getting my ass in gear. Still got a few months before we turn the lights out on this old bucket!"

Tate and Hank also rose.

"I've got to get moving too," Tate said. "You need an escort back to the Quarterdeck, Sparky?"

"Technically, yes," Shepherd said. "But I'm not quite done increasing my caffeine level." He held up his coffee cup; it being still a quarter full. "Besides, if my timing is right, my film crew should be on the mess deck right now. I'll fall in with them to see how they're doing."

"Ok, well, it was good to meet you!" Shifter said, holding out a hand as he rose. "You're a *Ponce* vet; once a Proud Lion, always a Proud Lion! Come back anytime, and make sure you get up with one of us so we can get you an invitation to the decommissioning ceremony!"

"Thanks!" Shepherd rose and began happily shaking everyone's hands. "I will!"

The three chiefs then did exactly what Shepherd was desperately hoping they would do—they left him alone as they carried their trays and cups out of the mess to the scullery. It was actually a violation of security protocols, especially since he had a badge hanging from his pocket that clearly read "Escort Required," but long experience had taught him how to use the natural cohesion among Navy chiefs to his advantage.

He took a moment to finish his coffee, organizing his thoughts. He had an idea to pursue, and now was best opportunity for him to take a calculated risk...

...As soon as he got his breathing under control.

So far, he'd successfully managed to hide the raging storm of insecurity and fear jangling his nerves. He now relaxed that iron control for a moment, his hands shaking as he put the coffee cup down hard and fell back in his seat. Breathing became more difficult as his chest muscles tightened. He was glad he wasn't in khakis today; the sweat stains spreading under his arms would have been ugly.

Oddly enough, coffee sometimes helped. He'd never figured out why, but often a cup of high-octane coffee helped calm him down. He closed his eyes and let his mind day dream of a peaceful beach with a tall, silent lighthouse reaching for the sky. Sliding a hand into the right cargo pocket of his trousers, he pulled out a small, toy stuffed crab.

"Well, Albert," Shepherd pressed his forehead to the fuzzy toy, "I don't know how much more of this I can take! I need to hurry up and retire."

Albert the Crab was one of Shepherd's *very* secret weapons against PTSD. The toy had been given to him as a joke by his ex-wife long ago. Then, one day shortly after their separation, Shepherd found himself too panic-ridden to leave the house alone.

Desperately searching for a way to get himself out the door so he could go to work, he had been two minutes from stuffing his old, red teddy bear into his backpack when Albert caught his eye. The plush toy's flat profile fit perfectly into Shepherd's cargo pocket. He had shoved Albert in and got to work.

Every day since, Albert the Crab had been hidden in a pocket or in his backpack. Albert was so secret that Shepherd was confident even Abraham Gray didn't know about the security object Shepherd now pressed to his forehead.

Shepherd lowered the crab and looked at it. Albert's beady little eyes looked back at Shepherd. Smiling and feeling just a *little* better, Shepherd slid Albert back in his pocket. Taking a deep breath, he clenched his fists and tightened every muscle in his body for a moment. The wave of anxiety seemed to crack a bit, and he exhaled. Unfortunately, he now had to deal with two new problems: exhaustion and a very sharp need to find a head.

The latter problem would actually provide him the opportunity he needed, but he had to send a text first.

Privately thanking the stars above he had a moment alone, he texted Robertson, telling her to pass the word to the NEPAC East team that they could drop the pretense of not knowing him.

Robertson texted back within seconds, acknowledging his instructions.

Picking up his tray, he stepped out of the chiefs mess, entering the spacious mess decks where the junior crew ate. Despite the emotional storm he was weathering, he couldn't help but smile fondly. The main serving line was still topped by the heavy purple 'Herculite' awning featuring the *Ponce's* crest and the words "Proud Lion" emblazoned in gold letters. The mess deck floor was still covered in that wonderful old blue clearcoat surface. The smell of the dinner being prepared snuck out of the galley just forward of the mess deck.

Several of the mess deck tables had been pushed aside and he saw Robertson hovering like a cloud over a small crew of NEPAC East sailors. They were putting a lavalier microphone on a civilian mariner's shirt. Clearly, they were about to do an interview.

"Watch your shadows!" He heard Robertson say as he carried his tray to the scullery. "This gentleman is taller than our last subject was. You need to get the main and fill lights adjusted for his height, or you're going to throw half his face into shadow!"

Shepherd pretended to cough, surreptitiously pulling his "Escort Required" badge off and hiding it in his pocket.

"Chief!" Robertson looked up and smiled as Shepherd walked over. "Where were you hiding?"

"Had lunch with the chiefs mess," Shepherd said casually. "They were pumping me for sea stories from the days of yore!"

"We're getting some *great* footage and interviews!" Robertson said, laughing. "Everyone here is eager to work with us all the way through the 'decom' ceremony in October, so I think we're going to really have a great series!"

"Where's your escort?" Shepherd asked Robertson as the rest of the NEPAC crew adjusted the portable studio lights.

"He had to take a call in private," Robertson said. "It's an MA1 named Fredriksen. Great guy; said he met you the other day."

"We did meet. He *is* a good guy," Shepherd said, once again cursing his bad luck. He needed to get out of there before Fredriksen came back. "Well, I need to find a head, then I'll swing back to hang out with you guys for bit. Back soon!"

Shepherd gave her a warning look, and she winked back her understanding.

He turned and headed towards the port side where a ladderwell pierced the main deck, giving access to *Ponce* lower spaces. Shepherd paused and glanced through a locked glass door by the ladder well. This was...or, rather, had been, the ship's store. Clearly empty and unused now, the shelves inside were bare, as was the counter where he and thousands of other sailors and Marines had once paid for various snacks, uniform items, and even the occasional "swag" with the ship's crest on it (lighters, hats, coffee mugs, etc.).

Dropping down the ladder to the 2nd Deck, Shepherd stepped into the head. The head was sandwiched forward of the entrance to the medical spaces and immediately aft of Shepherd's old berthing. Many a morning had been spent in here brushing, shaving, and otherwise doing what groggy people do in the morning.

"Chief Shepherd!" Dr. Drummin looked up from the sink as Shepherd stepped inside. Drummin, Aaron Seeley in his Smith-Table jacket, and another man in a blue jacket with the GDI logo on it, were all scrubbing their hands, clearly having just finished using the facilities.

"Dr. Drummin," Shepherd smiled. "How are you?"

"Not too bad. We're nearly done on board. The GDI team will be disembarking in a few more days," Drummin said, turning off the water.

Seeley pulled a few paper towels to dry his own hands, "How goes the review?"

"It's going," Shepherd said, "Today I had lunch with the chiefs mess since I'm a *Ponce* vet, so it's been a social visit this time."

"Oh, Chief, this is Buck Sherman, one of GDI Tech's electrical engineers," Drummin nodded towards the other man.

Sherman held up his wet hands to show he couldn't shake hands at the moment. He was of average height, but had forearms that made Shepherd think of Popeye.

"Mr. Sherman," Shepherd nodded.

Drummin turned to Sherman, "This is one of the men Aaron and I told you about who're looking into the Navy's case against Jarvis."

"Ah," Sherman said in a voice so gravelly it could have surfaced a driveway quite nicely. "Any luck?"

Shepherd chuckled. "Luck's not really too much a part of this, but events are moving forward."

"Well, good luck to you, anyway!" Drummin said. "Personally, I hope you and Mr. Gray succeed. I liked Jarvis a lot, and I can't see him murdering anyone. Assuming he really is innocent, I hope you two can prove it."

"Thanks!" Shepherd said as Drummin, Seeley and Sherman left, the metal door swinging shut with a bang.

Shepherd took a moment to use the facilities himself before beginning his skulduggery. After washing and drying his hands, he cautiously stepped out of the head, ensuring no one was in his immediate vicinity. Forward of the head was his old berthing. Undogging the hatch, he stepped inside and closed it behind him, maintaining the air conditioning boundary. He made a very brief stop to glance at his old rack before moving on. Ahead of his old berthing were two more berthing spaces. He didn't know who occupied them now, but the spaces were still configured as they had been back in his day. He thanked his stars this part of the ship had not been altered.

Passing through the open hatches forward-most berthing, he entered another head, allowing him to cut over to the starboard side of the ship without the risk of running into MA1 Fredriksen on the deck above.

The only hatch that was closed was the one into his old berthing. All the berthing compartments he was sneaking through shared the air conditioning, so the "boundary" was maintained further aft. He was grateful; the fewer hatches he had to open and shut, the quieter he could move.

Ponce's forward berthing spaces were quiet, still, and empty. Shepherd could hear distant thumps and pounding and general sounds of heavy manual labor happening further aft, but he met no one. The ship's work had obviously pulled everyone, active duty and civilian alike, away from this area. Navigating on memory, he swiftly ascended to the 02 Level. The XO's stateroom was located on the starboard side, aft of the captain's stateroom.

He was grateful the p-way was empty as he emerged from the ladder and quick-marched to the XO's stateroom, ready to play a hunch. He knocked on the door, but no one answered.

"Excuse me, Chief."

Shepherd looked over his shoulder; a civilian carrying a large box was trying to get by him.

"Oh, sorry!" Shepherd flattened himself against the bulkhead (as much as he could with his 230 lbs. frame), and let the man pass.

As soon the passageway was clear, Shepherd acted. During his time aboard *Ponce* he had been given the combination to the XO's stateroom, which also doubled as the XO's office. Clicking the buttons on the mechanical cypher lock, Shepherd was elated when the door clicked and opened, grateful the combination had never been changed. He slipped inside, shut the door, pulled a pair of nitrile gloves out of one of his pant leg's cargo pocket, and started to snoop.

He had to be quick. The unexpected always seems to happen at the most inconvenient moment in real life, so Shepherd was quite keen to avoid the unexpected.

Shepherd scanned the space quickly, noting the thick layer of dust that lay over most everything. He then began to move with studied practice and rigidly controlled urgency.

He had no idea what he was looking for, but he looked nonetheless. The XO's clothes and uniforms were neat in the closet; nothing there. The XO's clothing drawers only contained neatly folded piles of socks, underwear, undershirts, and the like. The hanging uniforms—khakis, dress blues and dress whites, were all pressed and snuggled closely with a scattering of polo shirts and blue jeans.

Sitting under the clothes was a hamper. Shepherd pulled the dirty laundry out, searching rapidly.

An old, fuzzy yellow windbreaker was buried at the bottom of the XO's dirty laundry, underneath a heap of uniforms and civilian clothes. Shepherd pulled a pair of tweezers and an evidence bag from his pocket and collected some fibers from it, and then returned the bag and tweezers to his pocket. Piling the laundry back into the hamper, he took a second to check all the pockets in each pair of pants. Snooping through the pockets of one pair of khaki trousers resulted in a tiny, petite pink thong falling out on the deck.

Shepherd was taken aback. He was certainly not one to look down his nose at other people's sexual interests...as long as everyone involved was a consenting adult! However, nothing he'd found in the XO's stateroom indicated even a mild interest in cross-dressing...

Shepherd's logical brain kicked back in to operation and smacked him upside the head. The thong was *way* too small for the XO anyway. Obviously, the man had entertained a young woman here.

He piled the laundry back into the hamper and moved on.

The small nightstand next to the XO's rack contained nothing of real interest. A couple back-issues of *Monster Truck Monthly* were stored inside the nightstand, but nothing else. A quick lift of the mattress revealed nothing.

Smoothing the sheets after he reset the mattress, Shepherd headed back into the office area and sat down behind the XO's desk. A few family portraits were placed where they could be easily seen. Neat piles of folders occupied neat spaces on the desk's surface.

The desk was not locked. Shepherd only had time for the most cursory of glances in the drawers, but they yielded nothing more earth-shattering than a revelation the XO liked spearmint gum.

A lot.

Beyond the boxes of gum, there was only routine ship's business in the desk. The XO's computer was locked; Shepherd ignored it. Without the XO's ID card *and* six-digit PIN number, there was no way he could access the machine. A sticky note pad contained a neatly written note that looked liked a DoD form number. A few other sticky notes clinging to the computer monitor contained minor notes like 'complete crew awards by Sept. 15th, min what Shepherd guessed was the XO's smoothly fluid handwriting due being in green ink. Green ink was traditionally used by executive officers for ship's business.

He scanned the desk itself. The dust on it was scattered and disturbed, as if someone else had been sitting here working not too long ago. Nothing really weird jumped out at him until he spotted the corner of a piece of paper sticking out from under the old-fashioned blotter pad the XO had in the middle of the writing area.

Pulling the paper out, Shepherd's eyes narrowed as he read the hasty scrawl:

25G 4 ANQ45 161017

He used his phone to photograph the odd note, and then stuck it back where he had found it.

Standing back up, he carefully replaced the chair, and did a fast sweep to make sure he'd returned the space to the condition he had found it in.

Standing by the door, he eased it open a crack. Seeing nobody, he quickly stepped back into the passageway and shut the door behind him. Pulling off his gloves, he stashed them back in his left-leg cargo pocket.

Shepherd started back the way he had come, dropping back to the 2rd deck and cutting forward so he could circle back around to the ship's port side.

Underneath his boots, the ship hummed with the tiny vibrations imparted by the sea, ventilation system, and heavy equipment moving in the well deck and on the flight deck.

Exiting the head after swinging back to the ship's port side, he hurried aft through the berthing compartments towards his old berthing. Reaching it, he undogged and opened the hatch, entering the space. Securing the hatch behind him, he continued aft through the berthing towards hatch the leading to the head right below the mess decks.

The lights abruptly clicked out and the compartment, with both hatches closed, was plunged into darkness. The emergency battle lanterns cut in, but their feeble light wouldn't be picked up by his eyes for several moments.

Still, this wasn't Shepherd's first rodeo.

The lights hadn't completely faded when his body, trained by long experience, began folding in half and rolling to the right of its own accord, his arms coming up to shield his head in case he collided with a locker as he jumped to the side out of reflex.

A powerful blow crashed down onto his left arm just below the elbow. The impact knocked his arm into his head, causing him to see stars as his rightward defensive lurch was suddenly transformed into a rightward crash landing. Instinctively, he pulled his head further downward just before feeling his right arm smash into a locker. His head plowed into his right arm, the impact causing a brief clanging to echo in his brain

Footfalls began to rush away, heading forward. Shepherd heard a smash and a man's voice cursing in pain as the assailant collided with the closed forward hatch. The hatch squeaked open, and the footfalls faded away.

Shepherd was alone. Feeling like the fourth day of a three-day hangover, he gingerly got to his feet. Both of his arms were badly bruised and would hurt for days. His bad left knee had taken a hit on the deck, and he could feel an ice pack in his very near future.

However, his quick reflexes had probably saved his life. Running what he could remember through his head, he realized the blow that landed on his left arm would have crushed his skull had he not already been in motion. Feeling his left forearm, he wondered if he had a fracture, and knew he he needed to go to the ER and have it x-rayed.

Shepherd's eyes finished adjusting to the dim light of the battle lanterns. Slowly moving forward (meaning he was still heading aft), he found the other light switch. Flipping it, he flooded the space with light, and conducted fast scan of the compartment before heading back to the forward hatch through which the assailant had fled.

Idiot. That hatch was open *when you first went through heading up the XO's stateroom,* Shepherd castigated himself. *Brilliant, Sherlock—not even noticing it was closed and dogged the second time you came through.*

On a hunch, he dropped to the deck and, ignoring the pain in his arms, looked for anything. A few yellow fibers caught his eye near the hatch.

Reaching again into his left cargo pocket, he pulled the tweezers and evidence bag along with a tiny ruler. Using his phone, he photographed the area and the fibers, using the ruler to provide scale. Employing the tweezers, he collected some fibers and put them in the evidence bag. He thought briefly about jury-rigging a fingerprint kit to examine the hatch's dogging handle, but dismissed the idea. The assailant's fingerprints were likely on it along with about a hundred other sets of fingerprints.

Pocketing the evidence and his phone, he turned aft again, grunting through his bruises.

Shepherd took a breath, focused, and went back into full-on 'acting mode.'

Stepping back into the space aft of his old berthing, he entered the head again to wash his face.

"Chief!" Aaron Seeley was there, washing his hands again.

A flush came from a commode, and Buck Sherman stepped out of a stall. "Chief."

"Mr. Seeley, Mr. Sherman," Shepherd smiled genially, "We *must* stopping meeting like this! People will talk!"

The three men chuckled.

"Too much coffee with lunch," Sherman said. "What's your excuse?"

Shepherd laughed, "Same as yours, actually! What about you, Aaron?"

"I just wash my hands a lot aboard ship," Seeley said. "Best way to keep from getting sick since this is a closed environment."

"Can't argue with that," Shepherd said.

Climbing back up to the mess decks, Shepherd quickly clipped his 'Escort Required' badge back onto his uniform. Joining the NEPAC film crew and MA1 Fredriksen, he was all smiles. No one there guessed that he had been sneaking around a U.S. Navy warship, breaking into high-ranking officers' staterooms, and getting assaulted in the dark. He looked for all the world like a happy chief who enjoyed watching his sailors excel.

The rush of adrenaline and elevated heart rate had created a catharsis that relaxed him back to normal. Shepherd almost laughed when he realized the assault had kicked him out of the lingering anxiety attack he'd been fighting all day. A mental health benefit was probably *not* the outcome the assailant intended, but Shepherd enjoyed the irony.

Still, man oh man, did Shepherd's arm *hurt!*

Chapter 7
Friday, September 16; 18:00 hours
Chesapeake, Virginia

"...This kind of insubordination from a flag officer is unacceptable and must be punished!" The retired general was screeching on the late afternoon broadcast. "For Admiral Jones to defy the CNO—in public, no less—sets a terrible example for the rank and file soldiers manning these ships! He should be immediately relieved of his command and brought up on charges! Officers do *not* have the privilege of picking and choosing what orders they feel like obeying!"

"Senator, could you comment on the general's statement?" The anchor asked, looking at another talking head on the split-screen.

"Certainly, Harris," Responded Florida Senator Diego Alejandro, smiling pleasantly. "First, I must respectfully correct the general. 'Sailors' man our warships, not soldiers. Second, while I understand the general's point, the fact is the CNO has made repeated public statements prejudicial to an on-going court-martial. The UCMJ requires our uniformed service members to obey the orders of those appointed over them, but the caveat here is that such orders must be legal and moral. I think *Jones* set the proper example because he's insisting on upholding the rights of *all* sailors to due process and a *fair* trial. Speaking as a current member of the Senate Armed Services Committee, I can tell you there are discussions on Capitol Hill about whether the *CNO* should be made to answer for his apparent attempt to improperly influence legal proceedings against one of the very sailors whose welfare he's responsible for..."

Abraham and Sarah Gray's house was a pleasant two-story structure on Stony Brook Landing in Chesapeake, another of the seven cities making up the Tidewater area. Gray himself had a pretty good commute getting to Naval Station Norfolk, but he and Sarah valued the privacy and quiet of the neighborhood.

The view from the Grays' back yard had once been of a meandering, man-made lake, some small shrubs, a narrow Greenbrier Parkway, and rustic farmland. Abraham and Sarah had often been required to recall their daughters after the girls climbed the fence to go play among the crops.

A lot changed during the intervening 15 years. The Grays' daughters were grown and living their own lives now. The shrubs had reached for the sky, which was just as well because the rolling farmland was long gone and Greenbrier Parkway had been enlarged to a four-lane highway. What had once been pastoral land now featured a Fazoli's restaurant and a Wells Fargo Bank. A Men's Wearhouse could be seen peeking out peeking out from behind the Wells Fargo building (ironically, the same Men's Wearhouse where Gray got most of his politician-like suits made these days). Even so, the Grays had long ago decided to retire here and considered the house as their 'forever home.'

Sarah Jane turned into the Grays' drive at precisely 18:00 hours and shut down. She settled herself for a pleasant evening chatting with the Grays' two-car garage door as Shepherd walked up to the front door, pressing the bell.

"Isaac, you're an idiot!" Sarah Gray laughed as she opened the door and hugging him. "Why do you always ring the bell? You *know* you can just come on in! You've had a key forever!"

Sarah was a tall, slender black woman with a degree in cybersecurity. While her husband had spent his career solving crimes, she had spent hers largely at home, homeschooling their daughters and slowly developing her credentials. Now Sarah and Abraham laughed that they both chased bad guys: Abraham chased them on the streets and Sarah chased them in cyberspace. Once the girls were off to college and she could go full-time, Sarah had quickly become a highly sought-after cybersecurity consultant.

"I know," Shepherd said, stepping inside and returning her hug, "I just never think about it. My mom raised me to never just walk into someone's house."

"We're not 'someone,' we're *family*," Sarah admonished him as Shepherd kicked off his sneakers and reached into the coat closet for the cross-strap flipfops he kept there to wear around the house when visiting. He shucked his beat-up looking green field jacket and hung it up before snapping the door shut.

"Isaac!" Abraham said, sitting behind the grand piano that took up a good chunk of what was intended to be a dining room (the Grays had, instead, turned the breakfast nook into the formal dining area).

"New piece?" Shepherd asked as Abraham continued to play.

"Yes," Abraham said, his unseen hands still floating over the keys, producing a wistful, gentle melody. "Something I'm writing to play at synagogue next April when we have our springtime social."

"You *really* need to get your music out on YouTube or something!" Shepherd said. "Hell, you could probably pick up work with an orchestra. You're certainly good enough!"

"I keep telling him, but I'm just the little old Jewish wife," Sarah said, rolling her eyes with exaggerated frustration, pretending to be annoyed as she her own Southern accent slipped out. "Why should the Big Man of the House listen to lil' 'ole me, after all?"

Shepherd smiled, leaning on the grand piano. "There was a time when a comment like that would have made me think your marriage was on the rocks."

Sarah leaned in and kissed Shepherd lightly on the cheek, "There was a time when you didn't know us nearly as well as you do now. By the way, you're in a better mood than I've seen you in a while. You get some good news or something?"

Shepherd shrugged noncommittally. "Things are just going generally good for me."

"I'm glad! Anyway, would you like some coffee? Tea? Bloodthirsty revenge?"

"Tea, thank you," Shepherd said, chuckling at the old joke Sarah had employed for nearly 20 years.

She headed off to the kitchen as Abraham stopped playing, picked up a pencil, and made a note on the sheet music in front of him.

"Tell me," Abraham said, "Which of these two phrases do you like better?"

He played a piece, paused, and then played a similar piece.

"The second one," Shepherd said. "Assuming I've learned enough about music terminology to say this correctly, the emphasis on the minor chord generates greater feelings of mystery, suggesting the topic is open to a dream-like interpretation. The first version was good, but it felt like it was telling me what to feel instead of letting me ponder my feelings."

Abraham nodded, making another note, "My thoughts exactly."

"Dr. Goldberg would be proud," Shepherd said. "I wish I'd met him."

Abraham stopped playing and lowered the keyboard cover. Standing up, he pushed the stool in and nodded sadly, "He would have liked you. He was as much a historian as a musician, and was very disappointed I didn't study music formally."

Abraham unhitched the piano's lid from its support and gently lowered both. "Did you hear from your friend in D.C. yet about the background information on the company with reps on *Ponce?*"

"Not yet. Stephanie texted me earlier that she's behind on a lot since she's new to the bench. She told me she'll call me tomorrow night with the information I asked her for, but it might be pretty late."

"Well, whatever time she calls you, call me," Abraham said. "Wake me if you have to. So, what time is your mysterious ally going to get here?"

Shepherd glanced at his watch, wincing as his injured arm reminded him it was there. "Any time now, actually."

"Hurt your arm?" Abraham asked as Sarah returned with a mug full of hot tea.

"I did, but I'll tell you about it when we start the official meeting. Thanks for the tea, Sarah."

The doorbell sounded.

"That'll be her," Shepherd said, setting his tea down on a side table with 'Virginia Beach' coasters stacked on it. "I'll get it."

A few minutes later, he returned to the living room with Dionne Robertson. Her eyes were bright and she wore a jean jacket over a T-shirt emblazoned with 'Pac-Man' characters. The denim jacket had a shiny DC Comics 'Wonder Woman' badge over the right breast, and a patch of Marvel Comic's 'Black Widow' character on the left shoulder.

"Abe, Sarah, this is MC1 Dionne Robertson, my Production and Operations LPO, and my ace-up-the-sleeve. Dionne, these are my rather secret friends that I don't tell anyone about."

"Dionne, hello! I'm Sarah," Sarah came forward, extending her hand.

"A pleasure to meet you," Robertson said, taking Sarah's hand.

Abraham was staring at Shepherd, a look of anger flashing across his face. Shepherd gave him a "what's up?" look. Abraham shook his head, and mouthed, "Later."

"Dionne," Shepherd, slightly confused, gestured towards Abraham, "This is NCIS Special Agent Abraham Gray, my unintentionally accidental partner."

"Mr. Gray," Robertson held out her hand.

"Dionne," Sarah admonished, "Don't start that. I'm Sarah and he's Abraham, or Abe. If Isaac thinks so highly of you that he enlisted you, then you've already earned first-name rights."

Shepherd saw Abraham flick an annoyed look at Sarah.

"Abe," Robertson said, holding out her hand. Abraham shook it and smiled at her.

"Dionne, a pleasure!" Abraham glanced at Shepherd. "Isaac, can I see you in the kitchen for a moment? There's something I need to discuss with you privately before we have dinner."

"Sure," Shepherd nodded and headed to the kitchen. He racked his brain, but could think of no reason why Abraham would be angry with him.

"Ladies, if you'll excuse us men-folk for a moment," Abraham said grandly before heading to the kitchen himself.

"What's up, A—" Shepherd began as Abraham entered the kitchen.

"Isaac, you're an *idiot!*" Abraham Gray snapped venomously as the door shut.

"Come again?" Shepherd said blankly, actually taking a step backwards in surprise.

"What the hell is wrong with you, man?! Why in the *world* would you bring an unqualified, untrained...*amateur* into this investigation?!" Gray demanded angrily. "Forget the risk of jeopardizing everything we're trying to do; you know the dangers she could be facing!"

"Watch your goddamned mouth, Abraham!" Shepherd spat back, his hand snapping up, finger raised in warning. The movement was so unexpected it was Abraham's turn to step back in surprise.

"That woman is no 'wanna be' anything!" Shepherd went on, his voice harsh as gravel. "She's a *damned* capable sailor, she has one of the most incisive minds I've ever run into, and she sees *everything* while missing *nothing!* Dionne can get into places my gender and my current rank *prevent* me from going, so I consider her an extremely valuable asset!"

Shepherd inhaled and sent one final verbal broadside into Abraham's rhetorical flank, his finger still raised.

"Final point, Mr. NCIS Special Agent—I'm an 'amateur' too, *remember?! You* brought *me* aboard back in '99 while *I* was under suspicion of murder myself, or did you forget about *that,* you amnesiac jackalope?!"

Gray's mouth was open and his hand raised to argue back when he froze, a look of shock widening his eyes.

Shepherd glared at him.

Abraham finally dropped his hand. "I...uh...I...."

"Yeah," Shepherd said, his voice gritty with sarcastic irritation, "You...uh...you."

Gray dropped his head for a moment, and then looked back up, his face a nice tomato-sauce red. "I'm sorry. I shouldn't have jumped down your throat like that. By now I know you well enough to know you don't do things without thinking it through… well, most of the time, anyway."

"Damn straight!" Shepherd said tightly, then took a breath and visibly relaxed. "Look, I'm a *chief petty officer.* I just can't go where I used to go and talk to lower-ranking sailors like I used to when I was a junior sailor myself. You've been around the Navy long enough to know how it works. No matter how friendly and disarming a senior-ranking person is, the junior people, and especially the *really* young ones, never see past the rank. They only see 'The Chief,' or 'The Captain,' or whatever, and they behave accordingly."

Shepherd shifted his weight to one foot, his stance back to that of his normal, relaxed self. "Dionne's still a first class. She can get junior folks to talk to her in a way I can't anymore. We need information from the lower ranks that neither your badge nor my anchors will get for us. We need clues and gouge and…and *gossip* from below decks, and that's the kind of information *she* can gather."

Gray raised both hands as if in surrender. "I apologize again. You're right. I just…I think I just stopped thinking of you as an 'amateur' a long time ago. It was jarring to be reminded of that so…so abruptly."

Shepherd took a breath and blew it out, his own anger evaporating as he looked at his old friend.

"Well, hey, relax," Shepherd finally said, a quirky gleam starting to glow in his eyes. "No one's perfect. I mean, hell, even *I* made a mistake once myself, believe it or not."

Gray caught the syntax of the sentence and realized he was being set up for one of Shepherd's (in)famously corny jokes. He knew if he didn't bite now, Shepherd would just keep winding him up until he finally did.

Might as well get it over with!

"You made 'a' mistake 'once?'" Gray asked, bracing himself.

"Well, actually twice," Shepherd apparently corrected himself, his face completely serious. "Back in '89, and then again in 2011. By that pattern, I'm not due to make another mistake for 17 more years...until around 2028."

Gray rolled his eyes as Shepherd started laughing. The booming, staccato laugh that Shepherd worked so hard to keep under control bellowed out as Abraham Gray, defeated, just turned and left the kitchen.

Shepherd remained a moment, processing the surprising lump of emotion that hit him when Gray told him he didn't consider Shepherd an 'amateur.' It suddenly occurred to Shepherd he was actually going to miss working with Gray once he retired.

They ordered pizza and ate while watching a movie about a World War II super soldier who wielded a round, spar-spangled shield with lethal efficiency.

Finally, with the movie and meal finished, and the dishes cleared away, Sarah leaned over and kissed Abraham lightly on the lips.

"Ok, you guys talk shop," Sarah said, getting up. "I'll be in my office; I've got some work to do for a client in Manassas."

She headed upstairs. They heard a door click shut.

"Coffee, Dionne?" Gray asked, getting up from the sofa and turning on the overhead chandelier. The room had grown dark during the movie as the sun faded. Night ruled over Virginia now as the two guests found comfortable seats.

"Thank you!" Robertson said, "One sugar and a lot of cream, please. I take it blonde, the way Chief Shepherd takes his men."

"I—what—*Dionne!?!*" Shepherd spluttered.

Gray stopped cold and did a most impressive double-take. He started laughing; it was a hearty, mellow sound. "I like her! Anyone who can turn *you* in a spluttering boob is ok in my book, Isaac!"

Gray turned to Robertson, "Working with Isaac is enough to make you wonder if you slipped a drug that creates a psychedelic conversational experience."

"You should see him at morning Quarters...*before* he's had coffee!" Robertson said as Shepherd's beat-red face dissolved into silent laughter.

Once the three of them had coffee, Gray settled in a lounge chair, his legs crossed, his pure white hair creating the impression of a professor about to hold forth on some esoteric subject. Shepherd sprawled on the sofa, his long legs strewn about like the lifeless tentacles of an equally lifeless giant squid. Robertson, still feeling the slight insecurity of being the 'new person' in the room, sat on the love seat, her own legs folded under her. She resembled a cat that was chilled out, but ready to spring if necessary.

"Isaac," Gray said, "You start. Then we'll move to Dionne's information before I present."

"Well, the murderer is *still* aboard *Ponce*," Shepherd said. "He or she clocked me a good one while I was sneaking back from breaking into the XO's stateroom."

"You did *what?!*" Robertson choked on her coffee.

Gray didn't look phased. "Start with your lunch. Then move into that story."

Shepherd nodded and recounted the lunchtime conversation with the three chiefs.

"I got an interesting view from the chiefs mess about our old friend, Bandy Sniffer," Shepherd said, moving from the XO's odd behavior to Sniffer.

"Oh, boy, do I have some stories to tell you guys about her!" Robertson said.

"I'll bet you do," Gray said. "Hold fast for a moment, though, please. Let Isaac finish his report, and then the floor is yours. Isaac?"

"Sniffer's been written up several times for inappropriate behavior with both civilian mariners and sailors," Shepherd said. "The chiefs have a very dim view of her. I think that'll be a good angle to hit her over the head with when you speak with her."

Gray nodded, "Agreed. Now, tell us about the snooping you did yesterday."

"When I ostensibly went to the head while Dionne and her crew were filming on the mess decks, I actually sneaked around the ship to the XO's stateroom on the 02 Level. Overall his stateroom was clean—"

"I'm sorry, Chief," Robertson cut in, "But I've got to know how you got *in* if he wasn't there?"

Shepherd smiled, "I had access to his stateroom when I was the ship's PAO. They haven't changed the combination since then."

She laughed, "So much for security."

"I found two things that struck me," Shepherd went on. "The XO had an old yellow jacket buried at the bottom of his laundry. The other was a note on his desk I photographed. It said, and I quote from my magnificent memory, '25G 4 ANQ45 161017.'"

"What the hell does *that* mean?" Robertson and Gray asked at the same time. They looked at each other in surprise and laughed.

"I have no idea," Shepherd said. "Anyway, on my way back to the head, a hatch that had been open was closed. Granted people are moving through the ship all the time, but I should have been clued in because the hatch in question was well *behind* the AC boundary, and had been secured open when I first went through. I'm just so used to dogging hatches behind me aboard ship that I didn't even think about it when I opened it, stepped through, and closed it behind me."

"That's when you were attacked?" Gray asked.

"Yes. Bugger turned off the lights and tried to wallop me in the brain case with something metal and very hard," Shepherd said. Pointing to his left arm, he went on. "The assailant missed my head and hit my arm. I've had it x-rayed; nothing's broken, but it's *badly* bruised. If the assailant *had* hit me in the head, I'd likely be dead. Unfortunately, going to the ER forced me to delay my weekly daddy-daughter night until Sunday."

"What'll you two be doing?" Gray asked.

"Martha wants to go check out that new exhibit at the Virginia Zoo where you can pet goats," Shepherd said. He began laughing, "When I called Jenn last night to bail out of daddy-daughter night and see about doing our daddy-daughter day Sunday at the zoo, Jennifer said Martha squealed with excitement. Oh, and by the way, I'm not supposed to tell you my 'very grown up' nine-year-old daughter *squealed!*"

The three laughed.

"Why Sunday, Chief?" Robertson asked. "Why not get up with Martha tomorrow?"

"Tomorrow Cody Rupp, Ben Foltz and I will be leading an over-night heritage for the chief selects aboard the *Wisconsin*."

"That's pretty late in the season for a selectee event, isn't it?" Robertson asked.

"It is," said Shepherd. "The naval station chiefs mess wanted to do something this weekend since the pinning ceremony got shoved back until next Friday due to Rear Admiral Durham's schedule. So, Cody, Ben, and I—along with some grizzled old retired chiefs who volunteer on the 'Whisky'—are going to have a bit of fun with the selectees."

"You really *are* a good actor," Robertson said, bringing the conversation back to the previous day's skulduggery. "When you came back up to the mess deck, I'd never have guessed you were injured."

"Part of being a good leader is being a good actor," Shepherd said. "You'll learn. Now, the last thing I have to report is that the assailant ran right into the closed forward hatch and hit it pretty hard. I wasn't able to get the lights on fast enough to see who it was before they got out of there, but I found these where they collided with the hatch."

Shepherd pulled the bag of yellow fibers from his pocket and tossed it to Gray, who took it and began studying it.

Shepherd produced a second evidence bag, "And here are the fibers I collected in the XO's stateroom."

"More yellow fibers?" Gray asked, taking the second bag.

"Yep," Shepherd said. "Forensics will need to examine them, but they appear to be similar to the yellow fibers we found at the scene of the murder near the blood evidence, and the fibers Cmdr. Scott found on Bacon's body."

"Forensics found yellow fibers on Bacon's uniform and none on Cline's uniform," Gray said, looking at the fibers through the bag. "I'll go into that later. I presume you used the mini-kit you keep to collect these?"

"I did indeed. Tweezers touched them, not my hands," Shepherd said. "Also, I took photos of the area and the evidence before I collected it. I'll upload those to our shared drive on the cloud later tonight. Ok, that's it for me."

Gray shook his head, "So, Dionne, what was your...assignment?"

Robertson set her own coffee down on a coaster and uncurled her legs. "Chief asked me to start up a long-running series of videos and written stories on *Ponce's* decommissioning process. Three birds with one stone: give my sailors gainful employment, document the decommissioning process for history, and let *me* have a chance to talk with the junior sailors and civilian workers. The big takeaway is that half a dozen people who expected to be interviewed during the original investigation never were, and there's a general feeling on the deck plate that whatever *really* happened is a far cry from what the prosecution is arguing. Everyone I talked to said Cline would never have lifted a finger against Bacon because the two were so obviously in love."

"What about their relationship to Sniffer?" Gray asked.

"No one likes Brandy Sniffer very much," Robertson said flatly. "Cline and Bacon only let her hang out with them because there were limited choices for 'liberty buddies' overseas, and she was not generally well-liked. Most everyone I talked to with any knowledge of that...that 'triangle' said the same thing: Cline and Bacon apparently felt sorry for her, so they let her hang with them, but they didn't like her a whole lot. The chiefs were right. Sniffer is what we girls in the female berthing call a mattress."

"Oh, good grief," Gray rolled his eyes.

Robertson shrugged and went on. "I managed to ease into getting them talking about her by 'innocently' fishing for names they might think would be good on camera. When I mentioned her, the reaction was consistent in one of two ways."

"Which were?" Gray asked.

"Half the guys on that ship indicated they had been inside her pants; the other half of the guys...and the women I talked to...considered her a whore who would sleep with any guy, especially if he had power. Quite a few people were pretty sure she and the XO were banging each other in his stateroom because she was often seen hanging around there. She always said she was bringing the 8 O'clock reports up."

"That might explain the thong..." Shepherd said to himself.

"Thong?" Gray asked.

"Yeah," Shepherd nodded, swinging his feet to the floor and sitting up straight. "I found a small woman's pink thong hidden in the pocket of one of the XO's trousers when I searched his laundry. It was *definitely* too small for him, so he didn't have it for cross-dressing. If the XO and Sniffer were boinking, that would explain how her underpants got into his outer pants."

"'Boinking'?" Robertson looked at Shepherd, not sure she heard him correctly.

"But, then, why does she maintain that Cline and Bacon kept fighting over her?" Gray asked, not hearing Robertson. "Dionne, did you find out anything about that?"

"I did. She was...what did they used to be called? 'Fag hags?'" Robertson asked.

"Accurate, if ugly," Shepherd confirmed. "Go on."

"She told people she liked hanging out with gay guys because they 'understood' her. I don't know why she's maintaining the fiction of a love triangle. Maybe she's just desperate for attention, or maybe she's delusional."

"Or maybe she's lying to cover something else up," Gray speculated. "Thanks, Dionne. That actually helps put a great deal of the puzzle together." Gray said. Loathe as he was to admit it, Shepherd chose well. Robertson had done the job properly.

"Well," Gray went on, "I spent a great deal of time over the last two days at the forensics lab. There is not a hint of *any* forensic material on Bacon's uniform that could be traced to Cline. The lab *did* find several yellow fibers on Bacon's uniform, and they appear to be similar to the ones we found near the blood evidence up in that compartment. I'll be interested to see if the fibers you collected match up to those, Isaac."

"So there was no DNA evidence at all?" Robertson asked,

"I didn't say that," Gray said. "Bacon had some nearly microscopic flecks of blood on his uniform. All type O-positive."

"Terrific," Shepherd said, rolling his eyes. "The most common blood type in the U.S. That just narrowed this search down to about a 100 million people."

"Don't get ahead of yourself, Isaac," Gray said. "Bacon himself was O-positive, but the *DNA* in the blood flecks was *not* Bacon's DNA, so right there we have biological material from the *real* assailant. I'm wagering this new DNA evidence will match the DNA from the unknown male that Cmdr. Scott found on Bacon's body. Oh, before either of you ask, Cline's blood type is A-negative, and *his* DNA does *not* match the DNA found on Bacon's uniform."

Shepherd stretched. "Let's cut to the chase. Do we have enough that you guys can get the charges dropped and release Cline?"

"I'm meeting with Charlotte tomorrow afternoon to present all of our findings," Gray said. "I think the forensics alone are compelling enough to get Cline released. So, to sum it all up, I *do* believe you've fulfilled the commission Admiral Jones gave you, Isaac. We can get the charges dropped."

"The job's not finished, though," Shepherd said.

"Chief?" Robertson inquired as Shepherd's sea green eyes locked onto Gray's blue-gray eyes.

"There's still a murderer loose aboard my old ship, and that's a situation I will *not* stand for," Shepherd said.

"Oh, no you don't!" Gray said, eyeballing Shepherd. "Not this time. Look, Isaac, you've done *more* than has ever been asked of you for 20 years. It's time for you to step back and let me handle the rest of this case. You and Dionne helped save Cline's life. Let it go at that and start focusing on planning for your retirement."

"Abe," Shepherd started, but Gray cut him off.

"I mean it, Isaac," Gray said firmly. "Promise me you'll give it a rest. I know that's asking a lot, but your job was to clear Jarvis Cline, and *that* job *is* finished. Start taking care of yourself, and let me do the rest."

Shepherd looked exceptionally unhappy, and his jaw was clenched so tight Robertson was surprised his teeth didn't crack.

"Ok," Shepherd finally said, his voice a sea of gravel.

Gray looked sympathetic, "Thank you. I mean it; you've earned the retirement. Once you get that information from your friend in D.C. tomorrow night, let it go."

Gray turned to Robertson, "Dionne, you've done a *remarkable* job. If you ever decide to go into law enforcement, give me a call and I'll give you a reference that will get you into any law enforcement academy in the country. Thank you. You've helped to free an innocent man today, and I'm grateful for your efforts!"

Chapter 8
Saturday, September 17; 22:40 hours
Norfolk, Virginia

USS *Wisconsin* (BB 64) was the last battleship built by the United States. Following her final decommissioning in 1991, she spent nearly a decade in mothballs before being towed to downtown Norfolk and put on display as a semi-official museum ship while still on the Navy's inactive roster. Steadily becoming an increasingly popular tourist destination while sitting idle, the 'Whisky' waited for a call back to action that would never come. Norfolk finally became the proud owner of its very own battleship when the Navy struck the old warhorse from the inactive register in 2010.

The setting of choice for ceremonies, such as reenlistments and retirements, *Wisconsin* holds a special place in the heart of many of the visitors who walk her decks. Tourists throng the ship every day, meeting former Navy sailors who volunteer their time as docents, learning history and basking in the ship's lore.

The special heritage event he and his fellow chiefs were running for the selectees was one such golden opportunity. He always appreciated a chance to come aboard and learn something new about the battleship's remarkable service. During the busy day, the small class of selectees looked like a flock of blue and gold flamingos in their Navy PT gear as they darted about the ship, meeting the grizzled veterans who were happily passing on their wisdom and sea stories.

The Moon finally supplanted the raging sun, the night settling at comfortable 73 degrees. A hint of a breeze inflicted only a minor chill as midnight neared.

The selectees, 23 in all, now stood under the shadow of the long-silent giant guns on the ship's fo'c'sle. Tired and worn, they were eager to answer the final question from the *one* chief petty officer who stood between them and a few hours in the rack.

Shepherd stood forward of the tired group in his own PT gear. Always one to get chilled rather quickly, Shepherd wore Navy sweat gear to stay warm. His phone hung off his sid*e, its belt* clip attacked to his waistband. Marveling at how others were comfortable in shorts and T-shirts while he was freezing, Shepherd launched his final *Wisconsin* history question to the group.

"You've had quite a day aboard, and I know y'all are tired. I *did* promise that y'all'd be in the rack before 23:30, so, one final question, and then off you go."

Shepherd leaned back, settling his weight on the huge piece of curved steel jutting from the deck called the cutwater, designed to sluice water off the sides of the ship in case a wave broke over the bow.

"Depending on how you want to look at it, you could say you've been aboard *two* battleships today," Shepherd crossed his arms. "What are they, and why can you make that case?"

"Chief," Said spindly-looking man with a long, reedy face as he raised his hand, "*Wisconsin* collided with the destroyer *Eaton* in 1956 and severely damaged its bow. The ship was repaired when a 68-foot section of the bow from the incomplete battleship *Kentucky* was cut from that hull and welded onto *Wisconsin* at the Norfolk Naval Shipyard. The *Kentucky* and *Illinois* were supposed to be the final two *Iowa*-class battleships, but neither were completed after World War II."

"Very good!" Shepherd said. "You guys paid attention! Ok, that's it for tonight. I know you've all heard this before, but I *will* reiterate it: there is *no* 'honeymoon' period when you make chief. As soon as you have those anchors on your collar, you *are* the chief, so be ready to hit the deck plate running after your pinning ceremony next week."

The collected group of selectees looked like more like tired recruits at boot camp, rather than future Navy leaders.

Shepherd smiled, "Great job today! Strike below and hit the rack. Reveille is at 07:00 tomorrow!"

The selectees vanished with a speed only achievable by tired sailors seeking sleep with religious zeal.

"So, what happened to *Eaton?*" A voice from the darkness asked in the most drawling Oklahoma twang imaginable. "Did she sink?"

138

"*Eaton* was saved when the crew literally tied her bow to the main body of the hull with her anchor chain," Shepherd said as two darkened figures stepped into the wash of *Wisconsin's* floodlights. "She was finally decommissioned in 1969, and sunk as a SINKEX target in 1970."

"Wow," said Chief Aviation Structural Mechanic Cody Rupp.

Walking next to Rupp, Ben Foltz had his hands stuck in the front pocket of his own blue Navy hoodie.

"I'm not sure if there's anything Spark here *doesn't* know," Foltz said, his eyes twinkling. "As he continually likes to remind us."

"I thought you had a screwdriver you needed to go put through your eye, Ben?" Shepherd retorted, laughing.

Rupp also began laughing heartily, even his laugh having a country-western twang. Rupp had grown up on a family cattle ranch in Oklahoma. What made people's head's turn was the fact that this dyed-in-the-wool cowboy was a full-blooded Chinese man. Rupp's parents escaped from Communist China, but both sadly died shortly after Rupp was born in San Diego's Chinatown. Adopted as an infant by an Oklahoma ranch family, Rupp grew up riding horses and wrangling cattle.

"You not rackin' out, Spark Nuts?" Rupp asked, using a highly personalized variation of Shepherd's long-running Navy nickname, "Sparky."

"Not yet, Stud Rupp," Shepherd replied with his own nickname for Rupp. "I'm waiting for a phone call."

"Hot guy?" Foltz asked.

"I wish," Shepherd answered. "What about you, Cody? Still seeing that red-head?"

"Yee-ep," Rupp said, plopping his backside against the cutwater next to Shepherd. "Not sure we're gonna git too serious though. She's active duty too, you know. Neither of us really wants to git tied down followin' someone else around, and she's transferrin' to Japan next year. So, I guess we're just enjoyin' it fer now."

Shepherd sighed, exhaustion creeping over his face, "I wish this call would hurry up and come through."

"How's the *Ponce* investigation goin'?" Rupp asked, all innocence.

Shepherd looked at Rupp, shocked. "How the *hell* do you know about *that?!*"

Rupp looked at Shepherd as though Shepherd were a bit slow. "Come on, Spark Nuts. I've known you since yer first rodeo in Spain. Hell, *I* was part of that one. Never will fergit how you pumped me fer information while I was workin' on that P-3 and I never realized it. It ain't hard for me to guess when yer workin' a case. Ben confirmed it when I asked him earlier tonight."

Shepherd looked at Foltz, who shrugged, "Hey, don't look at me. I didn't know anything about your 'second career' until you drug me along to the naval station flight line two years ago."

"I seem to recall you ease-dropping on my phone call and *demanding* to come along," Shepherd countered, caught between annoyance and amusement.

"Not my fault you had the phone's volume up while we were in the car together," Foltz shot humorously.

"You still insisted on coming," Shepherd pointed out. "Something about 'morbid curiosity,' I think you said? Well, you got your curiosity morbidly satisfied when we were shot at in the hangar!"

Foltz nodded with a sigh, "Yeah...I'll give you that one."

Shepherd chuckled triumphantly, crossing his arms. "Maybe I *am* getting predictable? Yeah, Cody, to answer your question, I'm working on the *Ponce* case."

"I've been wonderin' about that," Rupp said, frustration breaking out over his face. "I've had a lot of my airmen asking me about the CNO's statements about Cline's guilt. What am I supposed to tell them about obeying the chain of command when a four-star admiral apparently diso*beys* the CNO in public?! A lot of them feel like Cline's gettin' railroaded and confused because the press is saying Admiral Jones disobeyed direct orders about *his* public statements. "

"I've got to give it to Jones on this one, Cody," Foltz said, his own lanky frame settling on the cutwater. "Admiral Donovan shot his stinking mouth off and condemned a kid before any *real* evidence was in. Forget what Spark's investigating here. If you watch the trial coverage you can see the prosecution's case is nothing but goddamned weak-sauce. I think Jones got it right when he stood up and said the kid is innocent unless proven guilty."

"We're all used to seeing senior leaders fall prey to political cowardice," Shepherd interjected, his eyes scanning over both Rupp and Foltz. "Donovan's either a political coward, or else he's trying to deflect in order to protect himself. Or both."

"He don't need protection from nothin,'" Rupp said, confused by Shepherd's declaration.

"Oh, hell *yes* he does!" Foltz said angrily. "You don't work in media like we do, so you probably haven't seen the stories from the Pacific yet. I guess they haven't really hit prime time. There's a growing scandal out there. It's ugly, and I think it's going to take out more leaders and sailors than Tailhook did in '91. It might even reach Donovan himself."

"What scandal?" Rupp asked, surprised.

"Ever hear of Oceanic Supply and Service Corporation?" Shepherd asked Rupp.

"Uh...no," Rupp answered after scanning his memory.

"OSSC is a maritime contractor based out of Singapore, and headed by some clown nicknamed 'Big Mitch,'" Shepherd said.

"'Big Mitch?'" Rupp blinked in surprise.

"'Big Mitch,'" Shepherd confirmed. "He's the CEO, an ex-pat British guy who weighs something like 350 lbs. Anyway, back in July, the *Pacific Times Herald* out of Honolulu broke a story about a commander aboard the *Blue Ridge* taking bribes from Big Mitch to influence the ship's port call schedule in order to favor ports where OSSC provides services...and can make millions off the Navy."

"Wow," Rupp said.

Shepherd nodded, "Gets worse. Last month, the *Seattle Daily News* ran a piece that detailed an NCIS investigation into a chief and a petty officer in Bremerton, as well as two captains and one rear admiral in Hawai'i. They're all under suspicion of taking bribes from Big Mitch. Neither of those newspapers are known nationally, but you can bet it's only a matter of time until this story blows up nationally."

Rupp shifted his weight, "That's a shitty situation, but what does it have to do with the Cline court-marital?"

"Hang on. As they say on TV, 'just wait, there's more!'" Shepherd said, wishing his phone would buzz. The thing was being annoyingly silent. "The whole Big Mitch thing got buried by the Bacon murder, but another news outlet—I can't remember which one off the top of my head—anyway, another outlet ran a small piece saying one of the *CNO's aides* is under investigation after she was linked to the *original* commander this all started with on the *Blue Ridge.*"

"It's ugly, and it's going to be embarrassing for the Navy," Foltz said. "It was bad enough that a commander was first implicated, but with the investigation reaching the CNO's office now...well, Donovan's got plenty of reasons to try and deflect attention from the whole thing."

"So he's goin' after Cline just to cover his own ass?!" Rupp was outraged.

"That's my guess," Shepherd said. "I also agree with Ben's assessment of Jones' behavior. Admiral Jones is the only one who's conducting himself like an officer *should*. I think Donovan's just out to protect himself, and he doesn't give a crap who he hurts to do it. Tell your sailors the truth: the CNO *has* made a series of legal and moral mistakes, but they need to focus on obeying their immediate chain of command and let the machinery in Washington do its work."

"I heard on TV the Senate's Armed Services Committee is probably going to be calling Donovan to testify about his statements in the Cline trial," Foltz said.

"Yeah," Shepherd nodded, *really* hoping his phone would finally decide to ring. "I also heard Diego's interview on the radio. He's pissed."

"'Diego?'" Foltz looked surprised. "You know him?"

"We went to high school together," Shepherd said.

"Is there *anyone* you don't know, Isaac?!" Foltz's exasperation burst out of him.

Shepherd's sweat pants buzzed. He eagerly pulled his phone from the belt clip and looked at the caller ID.

"Ah, HA! Guys, this is the call I've been waiting for," Shepherd said apologetically.

Rupp nodded, getting to his feet, "Don't be out here too long. You got to be able to keep up with yer daughter tomorrow, you know?"

"Night, Spark," Foltz said, also standing upright.

Rupp and Foltz chatted amiably as they headed off, vanishing into the shadows.

Hitting 'receive,' Shepherd took the call.

"Good evening, Your Honor!" Shepherd said jovially.

"Don't start that 'Your Honor' crap with me, you sarcastic twit!" Said a merry female voice from the phone. "If you do, I'll 'Chief Petty Officer Shepherd' you all night!"

Shepherd laughed. "How's D.C. treating you, Steph?"

"I miss Chicago, but at least here I'm closer to my son!" Federal Judge Stephanie Limbani said from a couple of hundred miles north of him.

"Well, you *did* agree to move when you accepted the commission as a federal judge," Shepherd pointed out. "I bet you'll be running that court in no time."

"Don't get ahead of yourself, Isaac," Limbani said. "I'm only a junior Circuit Judge right now."

In his mind's eye, Shepherd could see Stephanie Limbani. The two had run with the same misfit gang at Niceville High School back in the day. Tall and spare, thin but deceptively strong, Limbani mainly took after her mother and grandmother, but she got her twinkling eyes from her father.

Limbani's family took a rather circuitous route to the United States. Leaving Nigeria as a young man, her father settled in the U.S. Virgin Islands, meeting her mother shortly thereafter. Little Stephanie had only been a few months old when the family decamped because an engineering firm in northwest Florida hired her father.

"Well, you have to admit you and the other judges the president swore in back in August had the most exciting swearing-in ceremony in living memory!" Shepherd leaned back on the cutwater, crossing his feet and looking skyward.

"Considering you killed that evil old coot who tried to kill *us*, I think it *was* rather memorable!" Limbani said.

"*I didn't kill him!*" Shepherd's temper exploded.

Limbani laughed, "Isaac, chill! I know. I'm just hoisting your anchor chain, as you might say in the Navy!"

"No one says that in the Navy," Shepherd said, still nettled. "But, anyway, how's your boy doing? Is he happy mama moved to his city?"

"He didn't have a say," Limbani said. "Mama does what mama does, particularly when the President of the United States plucks her from being the Chicago District Attorney for the D.C. Circuit's bench!"

Shepherd laughed, "Good point!"

"I'm sorry to be calling so late," Limbani said. "There was a *very* excited four-year-old boy who just *had* to show grandma every one of his new birthday toys...in *excruciating* detail! And then he *still* wouldn't go to bed."

"No worries, Steph," Shepherd said fondly as he watched a brightly lit sailboat slide along the Elizabeth River past *Wisconsin's* stern. "You're doing me the favor. What did find out?"

"Isaac, I'm worried about you," Limbani's voice sounded a note concern. "I thought you said you were planning to retire from the Navy *and* playing detective? Something about *not* getting a bullet in your head?"

"That's the plan, but I have another year until I actually retire," Shepherd shrugged automatically, even though he knew she couldn't see him. "I've dropped my retirement papers, so the wheels are turning and nothing short of World War III can stop it. But, this case was...I was asked by someone I respect very highly to take it up. Once I got a look at it, I became convinced Cline is being court-martialed for a crime he did *not* commit. How can I *not* do something to help?"

"Fair enough, Oh Knight of the Woeful Countenance," Limbani's voice regained a hint of merriment as she used one of the nicknames he carried back in high school. "You never did know when to quit. I guess that's why you're the one who figured out that whole 'Ghost of Niceville High' business back in '87."

"We *all* had a hand in that one," Shepherd reminded her.

"Well, us *and* the ghost. So, what did you learn?"

"I'm not a D.A. on the street anymore, so my resources are a bit limited," Limbani said. "Still, I was able to get a considerable amount of info that might be of interest. I'm going to email you the link to a secure server you can download it. Most seems pretty routine, but there *is* one item I need to flag for you, if you're in a private space."

"I'm alone," Shepherd told her.

"I ran the companies you asked me to," Limbani said. "I even got my contacts to run some of the names of the employees that you met on the ship. Most of the companies are pretty obvious, like Raytheon, General Electric and GDI Tech, the one that's made the news lately. GDI Tech is a South Korean firm, whose founders have acted as joint CEOs for thirty-some-odd years now, but haven't been seen in public since January. Industry speculation says they're retiring and grooming some as-yet unnamed successor. The uncertainty over GDI Tech's status has pulled stocks down a bit, but not much. Beyond that bit of news, almost all of the other companies you asked me to look at came back pretty normal."

"'Almost all?' Meaning someone didn't come back 'pretty normal?'" Shepherd's ears perked up and he rose, striding around the cutwater and walking up the sloping deck towards Whisky's prow. He nearly tripped on the anchor chain in the dark, and was very grateful no one saw him stumble.

"Almost all," Limbani repeated. "There's a problem. Smith-Table Electronics does *not* exist. Aaron Seeley's company is phony. A sham. The ostensible parent company, Dolus Holdings, is real, but they've got a problem too. When I got this data, I contacted Dolus myself and spoke with their chief counsel; you know, their top lawyer?"

"I know what you mean. Go on," Shepherd stood at the very tip of *Wisconsin's* bow, his brow furrowed in shock.

"I didn't let on that I knew Smith-Table is a fake," Limbani said. "I gave him a story that some paperwork errors had crossed my desk, and I just need confirmation of their affiliation so I could correct the mistakes. Their counsel assured me Smith-Table is indeed a subsidiary specializing in government electronics support. However, my contacts uncovered hard evidence proving Smith-Table is a front, and that raises the question of who or what is it fronting for?"

"How could Dolus Holdings get suckered like that?" Shepherd asked. "Do you think their chief counsel is being duped, or do you think he's part of a conspiracy, or something cooky like that?"

"Isaac, you've been around the block as many times as I have," Limbani said. "You know perfectly well conspiracies *do* exist."

"I know," Shepherd said lightly, "I just like saying the word 'cooky.'"

Limbani sighed wearily, "You have *not* changed since we were in the 9th grade. Anyway, the chief counsel at Dolus Holdings has either been bamboozled, or else he's a damned good liar. Either way, your 'Aaron Seeley' is a fraud."

"Did you happen to dig up anything on him personally?" Shepherd asked, already knowing the answer.

"Of course I did," Limbani said. "You know I don't half-ass my work. The 'Aaron Seeley' *you* met on *Ponce* last week died in 1963."

"Say what?" Shepherd blinked, watching a few lonely cars cruise past on Boush Street.

"*Your* 'Aaron Seeley' was born in Iowa in 1942, and died in Vietnam at the age of 21 in 1963," Limbani said.

"Stolen identity. Classic," Shepherd commented, his voice taking on a hard edge. "A bit of digital skulduggery, and you have a false identity that will bear up to all but the closest scrutiny."

"Bingo," Limbani responded. "One of the last cases I prosecuted in Chicago involved a human trafficking ring. The bastards were bringing in underage girls from Asia and Eastern Europe, and then selling them off. They faked American identities for the girls by stealing the names of dead American kids from small towns in out-of-the-way rural areas. It's not that hard to do these days."

The phone went silent for a moment. Shepherd could almost hear Limbani gathering her thoughts.

"This *really* worries me, Isaac" Limbani finally spoke, her voice deep with anxiety. "This is big. I mean *really* big. This 'Aaron Seeley,' in concert with persons unknown, faked an identity and an entire *company* so thoroughly he passed every background check performed by the Navy and Department of Defense. There's only *two* types of organizations big enough to pull something like that off: a government intelligence agency, or a *highly* sophisticated organized crime ring. Either way, you're looking at something far, far bigger than a simple murder...if any murder can be called 'simple,' that is."

"Wow," Shepherd said, his voice slightly vague as he considered Limbani's analysis. "This whole mess is getting *really* interesting now!"

"Isaac, I'm serious!" Limbani snapped, her anxiety evident in her voice. "You be *goddamned careful!* Whatever's happening aboard *Ponce* is big. *Really big.* We're talking international espionage, or major cartel activity here."

"I hear you," Shepherd said earnestly. "Please don't think I'm taking this lightly. Quite the reverse. I've fought international terrorists before. And won."

"*And* nearly got a bullet through your eye," Limbani reminded him.

"Point taken," Shepherd conceded with a sigh.

"What's your next move?" Limbani asked.

"Wake up Abe Gray and tell him," Shepherd said.

"Isaac, it's nearly midnight!"

"I know, but he asked me to call him as soon as I heard from you, no matter what what it was," Shepherd said. "So, I better get off this line and give him a holler."

"Ok. Well, you be careful," Limbani admonished yet again.

"I promise," Shepherd said, and he meant it.

The two parted ways. Shepherd immediately dialed Gray.

"Abe? Sorry to wake you," Shepherd said into the phone as he continued aft along *Wisconsin's* starboard side. "I just got off the phone with Stephanie. You're *not* going to believe this!"

"What's the bad news?" Gray's voice was thick with sleep.

Shepherd quickly relayed Limbani's findings. When Gray spoke again, his voice was no longer thick with sleep, but sharp like a new kitchen knife.

"That *is* an interesting development," Gray said. "I owe your friend in D.C.!"

"What do you want me to do?" Shepherd asked innocently.

"Nothing!" Gray said as sharply as a bear trap snapping shut. "Nice try, but you're done with this, remember? I had a very long talk with Charlotte today. She's going to present our findings to the JAG tomorrow. That *ends* your part in all this. I'll see to the rest."

"Abe, are you sure?" Shepherd reached the end of the Whisky's fantail. Gazing across the river to the Portsmouth city lights, he began to plead his case, "You know I can—"

Gray cut him off. "I know you can. But, don't. Look, you're smart enough to know we just kicked over a *huge* rock. This is *my* job, not yours. *You* focus on getting ready to retire, ok?"

"Ok, ok," Shepherd said, frustration in his voice. "You just...you just be careful."

"Always," Gray's voice said. "Night!"

"Good night," Shepherd said as he hung up, sticking the phone back onto its belt clip.

He was tired. It was late, and he had to be alert for the selectees in the morning, as well as for daddy-daughter day tomorrow at the zoo.

Still, he couldn't stop his mind from racing. Placing a hand in the front pocket of his sweat shirt, he felt Albert the Crab hiding in there, quiet and comforting.

Shepherd stood alone on the battleship's fantail in the quiet night breeze, thinking.

Chapter 9
Tuesday, September 20; 10:30 hours
Naval Station Norfolk, Virginia

"...turning to military news, the Navy's stunning announcement yesterday that all charges against a Norfolk-based sailor accused of murder have been dropped, causing an uproar on Capitol Hill as congressional leaders demanded answers from the Navy's leadership..."

"...the family of Carl Bacon issued a statement from their San Francisco home today condemning the Navy for dropping charges against a man they accuse of preying on their son by luring him into what they characterized as a 'deviant, unnatural, and unhealthy' relationship..."

"I appreciate you having me on today, Harris," Florida Senator Diego Alejandro said to the TV host. "Jarvis Cline suffered a horrible ordeal. First, his boyfriend is murdered and he finds the body, and then Navy leadership deliberately ignores a preponderance of evidence in order to use him as the 'fall guy.' The Armed Services Committee chairman sent a letter to all of us on the committee early this morning announcing preparations to begin immediate hearings. We have to determine why the Navy's leadership acted as they did, and hold anyone who behaved inappropriately accountable..."

"...in a statement issued by their lawyer, the family of Petty Officer Jarvis Cline said they're considering a lawsuit against the Navy for damages due to what they are categorizing as 'malicious prosecution' they say was designed to shield high ranking Navy officers..."

A member of the White House press corps was speaking to a TV camera from the White House lawn during a late morning news show, "The president's press secretary addressed this during the daily briefing. He called attention to the actions of officers like Admiral Jones in Norfolk, who resisted pressure from Admiral Donovan by consistently defending due process for Petty Officer Cline..."

Mass Communication Specialist 1ˢᵗ Class Dionne Robertson stepped into the NEPAC East Operations Office and stopped short.

"Chief?" She asked, incredulously.

Shepherd looked up at her from behind his standing desk, a device he had long adopted to improve his posture. He wore civilian khaki cargo pants, a blue T-shirt and his old green field jacket.

"MC1," Shepherd greeted her, and then continued typing on his computer.

"Uh, shouldn't you be in uniform?" Robertson asked, looking at her watch.

"Nope," Shepherd smiled, clicking his mouse and then pulling his ID card out of the smart card reader, locking the computer. "I'm officially on leave. I just had to finish up a couple of things so our team can start work-ups with the *Kearsarge* ARG."

"That was fast. You taking leave, I mean."

Shepherd put his ID back in his wallet and jammed it into his back pocket. "This is my reward for very quietly helping NCIS. Besides, I maxed out my leave bank. If I don't take leave now, I'll lose six days come the start of the fiscal year, so that's another consideration."

Shepherd snapped shut a binder and slid it back into its place under the platform which raised his computer to standing level, "Unfortunately...or, maybe, fortunately? Anyway, since neither the OIC nor the CO knows you were involved, you're not officially getting any time off as a reward. However, once I get back, I'm giving you some comp time. I just don't want us both gone at the same time."

"Fair enough," She said. "So...what do you think's going to happen now?"

Shepherd walked over to a giant grid-lined board on one wall, pulling a couple of magnetic markers with sailors' names out of the "dwell time" category and snapping them into the "work-ups" category.

"Truth be told? I don't know. Admiral Donovan will be called on the carpet by Congress, and I wouldn't be surprised if he eventually gets his ass fired. You can gauge which way the wind is blowing in the Pentagon just by watching the news. Neither the Secretary of Defense nor the president are very happy with him at the moment."

"Why the *hell* did he do it?" Robertson asked, flopping down on the government-issued sofa along the other wall. "I mean, it's one thing to say 'the Navy will ensure the guilty party is punished,' but to *name* the guy before the court-martial even *starts* is a dumb-ass move! What was he thinking? Why didn't his own public affairs team stop him?!"

Shepherd moved another few magnetic tiles with names from "work-ups" to "deployed."

"It's not that simple, Dionne," He said, stepping back and scanning the board to make sure everything was displayed correctly. "I don't know his public affairs officer, but I met their chief when I attended that symposium at DINFOS last spring. The guy is good; I can't see *him* not raising ten kinds of hell about it. However, in the end, it doesn't really matter what the public affairs staff advises. Admirals sometimes think they can just do whatever the hell they want."

Robertson shook her head, "It's a hell of a media circus. I'm kind of surprised your name hasn't been leaked somehow."

Shepherd turned and walked back over to his desk, hitching a hip on it. "It's not the first time NCIS kept my name out of things. "

"As much as you guys told me about that Cremer dweeb, don't you think he might leak your name to embarrass or harass you?" Robertson asked, concern on her face.

"Not this time," Shepherd smiled gently, touched by her concern. "Abe texted me that he and the rest of the office could hear Charlotte, their boss, ripping Cremer a new one through her office door yesterday. He's under one hell of a microscope right now, so I'm confident he'll be cautious for a while."

"Think he'll get booted out of NCIS?" Robertson asked eagerly.

"I wish! But, no."

Robertson's face fell. "No?"

Shepherd shook his head, "No. He hasn't blown it *that* big, unfortunately. Cremer's cultivated some heavy-duty political connections. His sister's in Congress, and he's golfing buddies with a number of high-ranking leaders in the Navy and Justice departments. Connections like that often make people untouchable, even when they're crap weasels. Cremer *is* on thin ice right now, what with illegally influencing the witness pool at the court-martial and all, but it's not going to take him down. Oh, a few heads *will* roll in the JAG office, mark my words; but, sadly, the crap weasel will survive."

"So, what *are* you going to do with your week off?" Robertson changed the subject. "Chill out?"

"Hell, no!" Shepherd stood and grabbed his backpack, slinging it over his right shoulder. "I'm going to do what I've done best for nearly 20 years now: stick my nose in where it doesn't belong and finish the job."

"I don't understand...?" She asked. "Cline's been released, hasn't he?"

"Correct," Shepherd nodded, "Cline's been acquitted, but the *job* isn't finished. There's still a murderer aboard my old ship, and I'm going to nail their ass to the wall."

Robertson blinked in surprise, suspicion in her eyes, "Does Mr. Gray...uh, I mean, does *Abe* know you're still working the case?"

"Nope."

"Then why?" Robertson demanded. "After all the noise you've made about getting out of the 'detective business,' why keep going when you've finished what you were asked to do?"

"The job is not finished," Shepherd said harshly. "Murder is one of the most heinous acts a person can commit, Dionne. Murder doesn't just end the life of the victim, even though *that's* bad enough. Murder wrecks the lives of the victim's family and friends. Cline lost a boyfriend, the *Ponce* crew lost a shipmate, and Bacon's parents lost their son. The murder of a single person spreads out like the blast of a fragmentation grenade in a crowd, leaving *no one* associated with the victim uninjured."

Robertson was quiet. She had never seen Shepherd exhibit this kind of quiet rage before. She found herself actually a little frightened because he looked like a completely different man.

Is this *what he's been keeping hidden all these years?!*

Taking a breath, she studied him cautiously, leading her to experience a sudden flash of insight about Shepherd's character.

That's right! HE *lost a buddy to murder!*

Robertson's unexpected bout of fear subsided completely, replaced by a sense of wonder. She had always admired Shepherd, but now she realized she was getting her first *real* glimpse of what powered the man's crusade as an amateur detective.

"I lied when I told Abe I'd be a good boy once Cline was acquitted," Shepherd said, his eyes still dark with fury. "Frankly, though, after 20 years, the man *should* know me well enough to know I *won't* stop. Abe ain't dense; I can only guess he succumbed to wishful thinking since I *am* on my way out and he's been after me to quit playing detective for years. But, the job isn't finished, and I'll be *damned* if I just quit."

"Chief!" Lt. Commander Jeanne Clooney, NEPAC East's OIC, walked briskly into the Ops office, a sheaf of papers in her hand. She was a lithe, short woman with her blonde hair pulled back into a bun so tight it made Shepherd wonder how her head kept from hurting. "I thought you were on leave?"

"Yes, ma'am, I am," Shepherd said, smoothly sliding into a casual voice. Robertson was impressed by the abrupt change in Shepherd's demeanor. "Had to tidy up a couple of things so the *Kearsarge* team can start their work-ups next week."

"Are you doing anything special during your leave?" Clooney asked.

"I've got some digging to do," Shepherd said blandly.

Robertson coughed and fought to keep a straight face.

"Digging?" Clooney asked, confused.

"I've got a tree I need to pull up at the Yellow Duck. A young Bradford pear started growing right at the corner of the house. I have to get it out before its roots damage the foundation."

"Chief Li's covering for you this week?" Clooney asked.

"Yes, ma'am," Shepherd nodded. "Even so, MC1 here can pretty much run ops and production by herself, so you're covered, no matter what. Do you need anything from me?"

"No," Clooney said, smiling cheerfully and holding up the papers in her hand. "I'm just dropping these on the lieutenant's desk."

Clooney put the papers on a desk and began to leave the room. "Have a good time!"

"Thanks, ma'am! I'll just keep digging and see what I turn up," Shepherd said innocently.

Robertson nearly fell off the sofa.

The Norfolk NEX boasts that it's the world's largest Navy Exchange for a very good reason: it *is* the world's largest Navy Exchange. The sprawling mall contains the NEX's retail store, coffee shop, barber and beauty shop, travel office, optometrist, and food court. The complex connects directly with the Commissary, making it a convenient, one-stop shopping destination for the area's military population.

His lunch demolished, Shepherd continued sitting alone in the food court. The taco and burrito wrappers were crumpled up on his tray as he looked at his phone. He had been staring at the photo of the cryptic note he'd found in the XO's office on *Ponce* for the last hour.

25G 4 ANQ45 161017

Putting the phone down, Shepherd pulled off his glasses and wiped a spot off the lens before replacing them. Feeling the wistful pull of nostalgia, he glanced at the crowd of service members. How young most of these people looked!

Was I ever that young? He wondered.

Was it only 20 years ago that *he* was the skinny, green-behind-the-ears newbie who didn't quite fit the uniform yet? He had joined late; being 25 when he went to boot camp. Turning 26 at boot camp had been mildly depressing, to say the least.

Unfortunately, the extra age had not helped his confidence or emotional stability when he went overseas to Naval Station Rota, Spain, for his first duty station in early 1998.

Before he could really find his feet, he'd gotten hammered during a barracks cookout, accidentally outing himself as a gay man during a time when being gay in the military wasn't exactly a politically safe situation. Forty-eight hours and five boxes of sleeping pills later, he woke up in the Rota Naval Hospital, his suicide attempt having failed.

Facing the command after all of that was hard, but his commanding officer insisted he resume his duties in a slow, methodical manner *and* be treated as a trusted member of the squadron team. Then-Commander David E. Jones provided the lifeline Shepherd desperately needed.

By March of '99, Shepherd was finally starting to feel normal again when he tripped over the dead body of one of his squadron mates in the barracks. The subsequent whirlwind adventure revealed the depths of strength, cunning, and fire Shepherd never realized he possessed. Unfortunately, the experience of being falsely and publicly accused of murder, and then nearly murdered himself, inaugurated his own life-long battle with PTSD.

I seemed to become a tragedy magnet after that, Shepherd thought with wry humor.

Bringing his attention back to the present, he silently fumed, staring at his phone as though the device were being deliberately obstinate. That damned note was driving him around the twist. He had the unshakable conviction he *knew* what it meant, but couldn't quite get his finger on it. The whole thing just sat there, like a puzzle laughing at him.

Changing his train of thought, he pondered the odd, cryptic text he had received the other day at Portsmouth. Two lines kept bugging him:

Do some market research. You're good at zeroing in on your target with laser-like accuracy.

Granted it was a text, and text-speak was infamous for its truncated words and tortured grammar. Still, Shepherd was certain the bit about 'market research' and the whole 'zeroing in on your target' were connected by more than just convenient placement.

A group of boisterous young sailors fairly crashed into a table across from him. The happy crowd, carrying trays from all the different food vendors, were clearly enjoying a fast lunch before returning to work.

Shepherd set the phone down, plopped his chin in his hand, and sipped his soda. He looked up at the TV monitors around the food court again. There was no way to hear the TV over the bustling crowd. Squinting a bit let him read the closed captioning of what the anchor was saying. A photo of the Chief of Naval Operations was splashed on screen, the anchor talking about the congressional probe of Admiral Donovan.

"With more than $300,000 was spent on the case," Shepherd read as the TV anchor mouthed the words, "Senators today announced the Senate Armed Services Committee will begin hearings tomorrow into Admiral Donovan's actions as public outcry against the Navy grows..."

Shepherd seethed quietly against the photo of the CNO on the television. Shepherd deeply loved the United States Navy, and deeply resented anyone who brought disgrace upon it.

Market research? Shepherd's mind idled like a waiting diesel truck. *Nothing on that ship is for sale, and Abe was right—the ship herself won't be sold for scrap for a decade, at least.*

Glancing over to another monitor above a group of young Marines who might be able to shave in a year or two, Shepherd saw a Navy recruiting commercial playing. Scenes of destroyers plowing through blue seas and a submarine diving into the darkness were interspersed with scenes of corpsmen bringing humanitarian aid to South America and an F/A-18 fighter jet launching off a carrier's flight deck.

Shepherd smiled again. Not that many years ago, it would have been an F-14 Tomcat on that commercial. Shepherd counted himself lucky to have ended up an F-14 Tomcat technician, assigned to the photo reconnaissance shop of the VF-213 "World

Famous Fighting Black Lions" for a couple of years. Carrying a tool pouch and working on the flight deck with the other maintainers, Shepherd's team maintained and loaded the massive recon cameras the old F-14s had operated. He had even gone out of his way to train as a 'final checker,' one of the squadron sailors who walked the jet to the catapult and did a final check to ensure its air worthiness immediately before launch.

Settling his chin back in his hand, Shepherd let his mind wander back to those days. He recalled one particularly trying day aboard USS *Carl Vinson* (CVN 70) when the radar on one of the Tomcats broke right before the launch cycle began. VF-213's Tomcats weren't carrying any reconnaissance gear that day, so Shepherd had been more than willing to help the electronics technicians fix the radar.

What was that damned thing called? He racked his brain. *AQ...AN...AR...AZ...*

Dammit.

Pulling up his internet browser on his phone, he typed in "F-14D Tomcat radar."

A list of articles popped up, and he selected one from an aviation forum he trusted.

That's right! He thought, pleased. *The AN/APG-71.*

Putting the phone back down, he plopped his chin back in his hand.

So...what the hell *was Carl Bacon murdered for?* Shepherd wondered. *The attack was swift and brutal. There doesn't seem to be anything premeditated about it; Bacon was killed by a man in a desperate panic to hide something, or else a man suddenly enraged at being discovered.*

Or both...

Shepherd took another sip from his soda, and then plunked his chin back in his hand yet again.

He tried to create a mental list of who on *Ponce* might benefit from Bacon's murder, but the only two people he could think of who might have a motive were the XO and Sniffer...and that was to hide their apparent affair.

And that's assuming Bacon knew they were boinking, of course...

Shepherd looked back at the monitor that had been showing the Navy recruiting commercial. It was back to its regular programming now: a home improvement show.

Starting to feel like he was staring into a brick wall, Shepherd stretched and prepared to get up. He jammed his phone back into his pocket, setting his now empty cup on the tray. For some reason, that F-14 Tomcat radar was sticking in his brain, a visual ear worm that wouldn't go away. It began twisting around with the mysterious text's line about 'market research' and his skill at finding his suspects with 'laser-like accuracy.'

Goddammit! He was fed up with the whole thing now. None of it made sense!

Glancing back up at the news on the monitor, he saw the chyron still displaying the amount of money the Navy had wasted on the Cline prosecution.

$300G spent on this fiasco so far. Shit! No wonder we don't have the money to actually fix *our ships!*

Shepherd picked up his tray and started to rise when his brain lit off like a fire cracker.

$300G?! AN/APG-71?!

Shepherd dropped his tray back on the table with a resounding '*crack,*' startling everyone in his vicinity. He fell back into his seat as though his legs had suddenly vanished. He didn't register the nearby crowd staring at him in surprise.

My God! My God! I'm an idiot!! AN/APG-71?! $300G?!

He yanked his phone out of his pocket and pulled up the photo of the note.

25G 4 ANQ45 161017

Sucking in a breath, he smiled as he suddenly realized what the note said...and *why* he knew what the note said. A new picture snapped into place with a mental shock wave that echoed down his spine.

Market research!

Laser-life accuracy!

Murder committed in the heat of passion!

An impostor from a fake electronics company on a ship doing top-secret experiments!

My God! My God! Shepherd's brain whirled the thought around like a banner waving at a ticker-tape parade. *That's it! That's freaking IT!!!*

Shepherd pulled up a number out of his contacts and dialed it.

A polished voice spoke in his ear, "423rd Analysis Squadron, Lt. Colonel Stavenger's office, Senior Airman Quintet speaking. Please be aware this is an unsecured line. How may I help you, sir or ma'am?"

"Airman Quintet, this is Isaac Shepherd. Is Lt. Col. Stavenger available?"

"The colonel's in a meeting right now, sir. May I ask, is this Chief Petty Officer Isaac Shepherd in Norfolk, Virginia?"

"It is indeed, Airman," Shepherd said.

"Chief, I have standing orders to take any messages from you and pass them to the colonel immediately. If I can please have your number, I'll take it to him and he'll call you back shortly."

Aidan Stavenger, you proactive son of a beech tree!

"Just tell him I'm on my cell, Airman. He has the number," Shepherd said.

"Very good, Chief. The colonel will call you shortly."

"Thank you very much. You have a good day, Airman."

"You do as well, Chief."

Shepherd broke the connection. Pocketing his phone, Shepherd disposed of his trash and left the food court.

Exiting the NEX, he headed across the vast parking lot to *Sara Jane.* The day was a comfortable 76 degrees with a breeze moving west-south-west. He got in, cracking the windows to let air flow through the car as he did some fast internet research while waiting on Stavenger's call. He had expected to still be searching when Stavenger rang him, but he found what he was looking for in less than 30 seconds.

"Son of a bitch…!" He said, triumph still in his voice.

The phone buzzed, and Aidan Stavenger's name popped up on his caller ID. Shepherd clicked "receive."

"Aidan! How's Ohio?"

"We're still settling in somewhat," The voice of Lt. Colonel Aidan P. Stavenger, his old high school best friend, came back. "But it's not too bad. You need to come visit us sometime; you know the Wright Brothers lived here in Dayton, right?"

Shepherd laughed, "Of course I know that! They used Kitty Hawk as a proving ground until 1904. Then they shifted to Huffman Prairie outside Dayton where they finally perfected the airplane in 1905."

"I should know better than to try and impress you with a historical point," Stavenger said, disgruntled. Shepherd could almost see him shaking his head. "Well, you certainly *sound* more upbeat than I've heard you sound in a long time. It's a nice change. What's up?"

"Aidan, since you're a big, bad Air Force commanding officer now, I wondered if you might be able to help me run something down," Shepherd said. "Can you call me back on the 'bat-phone?' I have a case I need your help on."

The "bat-phone" was an encrypted cell phone very few people knew Shepherd possessed.

"Ok..." Stavenger's voice took on a bit of an edge. "Give me a second."

Shepherd hung up his personal phone and reached into *Sara Jane's* glove compartment. He pulled out the super-secret cell and its headset (wired in, not Bluetooth). He had just settled the headset over his cranium when the phone began to ring with, in true corny fashion, the 1960s *Batman* TV series theme music.

"Hey, old friend," Shepherd said as the connection clicked in.

"Isaac, I thought you were giving up playing the Accidental Detective?" Stavenger's voice was stern. "Come on, buddy. You're already a walking case of nerves."

"I'm not that bad!"

"Isaac, you're so distrustful of humanity you hide in that video collection you don't think I know about and actively dissuade

160

potential boyfriends from getting anywhere near you," Stavenger said tightly. "Don't argue with me on this, or I'll get Linda to chew your ass out later tonight."

Colonel Linda C. Stavenger, Aidan's wife, was also part of their old high school crowd. Being an Air Force intelligence officer, just like Aidan, Linda had been promoted past him the year before. Linda had taken over command of a cyber intelligence squadron at the same time Aidan assumed command of the 423rd Analysis Squadron.

"Hey, I *am* on my way out!" Shepherd barked, slightly stung. "And I *meant* it when I said I wasn't seeking out any new 'adventures.' This one got handed to me by someone I can't say 'no' to, ok?"

"Admiral Jones?"

"As matter of fact, yes."

Stavenger's voice softened. "I'm sorry, Isaac. I shouldn't have jumped to conclusions like that. We both just worry about you, bro. You've been through so much crap since you enlisted. We want to see you get out of the Navy alive *and* sane."

Shepherd smiled, his own voice losing its edge. "Don't sweat it, Aidan. My brothers say the same thing."

"A.J. still in Bremerton studying volcanoes for the University of Washington?"

"Seattle, actually," Shepherd corrected, "But, yes. And, Joshua is on the short list to be named head coach of the Saints. Mom'll be thrilled if that happens, what with her being from Louisiana and all. Anyway, my *other* best friend—"

"Would this 'other best friend' be a certain NCIS agent who's made it his life's mission to keep you in one piece?" Stavenger cut in, laughing.

"Funny you should guess that!" Shepherd said, "He wasn't too thrilled when I knocked on his door either, but, when he found out it was Admiral Jones...well, you know Abe has as much history with the admiral as I do. Anyway, I do need your help. Maybe Linda's too. Can you two run something down for me?"

"Let me guess," Stavenger said. "I'll wager you dinner and a year's pay this is tied up with that murder on the *Ponce.*"

Shepherd's eyes twinkled. "Why, yes! By an *amazing* coincidence it *does* have everything to do with murder aboard *Ponce...*"

Chapter 10

Thursday, September 22; 11:00 hours
Suffolk, Virginia

Consistent with his melodramatic bent, Shepherd christened the Yellow Duck's computer room the "Federal Room" due to the blue paint the room was done in. The Federal Room was one of the two bedrooms off the loft area on the second floor. The loft area, decorated like a Florida beach house, was the informal TV area overlooking the more formal Great Room downstairs.

The stereo, sitting on a shelf below the television, was set to classical radio, but at the moment, the top-of-the-hour headlines were being recited by the announcer.

"...the chairman of the Senate Armed Services Committee opened the hearings today by berating Admiral Thomas Donovan, Chief of Naval Operations, for his public statements declaring the guilt of a Navy sailor before the court-martial had even started..."

"Jerk," Shepherd said under his breath as he read another story about the Proud Lion, cross-referencing it with stories about technology being unsuccessfully developed by a major Asian adversary.

"Bingo!" Shepherd said, sitting back in his plush, executive office chair with a rush of satisfaction. *That's it!* Thank you, Aidan and Linda Stavenger!"

Shepherd was confident he now had the motive, but he still needed the "who."

I have a horrible feeling Bacon just walked into the wrong part of the ship at the wrong time, Shepherd thought. Rubbing his eyes and rolling his neck to stretch it back out, he winced when a muscle complained after being stationary for far too long. He'd been sitting in the same position for a couple of hours by now.

I really need to get a standing desk for home like I do at work!

Rising, he grasped one of the tall book cases next to his desk to steady himself as he grabbed an ankle to begin stretching his quads. The bookshelf was one of four sagging under the weight of his personal library. It creaked unhappily when he added his mass to its load.

His legs stretched and his neck somewhat flexible again, Shepherd put the computer to sleep and headed downstairs to make lunch. The strains of a Mozart piano concerto began playing from the radio. The acoustics from the upstairs loft area caused sound to be reverberated around and down by the house's roof line, resulting in as rich a listening experience downstairs in the kitchen as upstairs by the radio.

The kitchen looked like an old farmhouse had sprouted in the middle of the Yellow Duck. Chickens anchored the country-style decorating scheme, and a small herd of cows and pigs accented the space. A large bay window, bursting with an indoor garden of house plants, looked out over the deck and Shepherd's back yard.

Shepherd spread peanut butter on two pieces of bread. He always put peanut butter on both slices so the jelly wouldn't soak through and turn the bread to mush. It was trick he learned from his mom.

Sitting at the breakfast table in the kitchen, he stared out the window past the deck, watching the birds as he ate. He deliberately pushed all thoughts of murder and mayhem away; he needed to let his mind rest. Chewing happily, he watched the house finches daintily picking out their favorite seeds from the bird feeders. The cute little birds were permanent Virginia residents who would visit his feeders all winter long.

Shepherd swallowed the last of his very light lunch as his pocket buzzed. Fishing out his phone, he saw a text had arrived from Abraham Gray.

Naval Hospital Portsmouth morgue. Come if convenient.

Shepherd's heart was still dropping into his gut as a second text from Gray buzzed in.

If inconvenient, come all the same.

Shepherd was actually sweating. Gray had never—*never—contacted* him like *this;* not in 20 years. Something was wrong, and Shepherd had an ugly idea what it was. Typing a fast reply, he abandoned the dishes. Jumping into street clothes and rushing out the front door, he got *Sara Jane* moving in record time.

Shepherd found Gray in the lobby of the temporary morgue on the Naval Hospital's front lawn. Gray wore his brown suit, his usual American flag lapel pin, and a dark yellow tie that, oddly enough, gave Shepherd the impression someone had spilled mustard down Gray's front.

"I'm sorry to interrupt your leave, Isaac," Gray said heavily, shaking Shepherd's hand and clapping him on the shoulder. "Unfortunately, we now have a double homicide, and I need your help."

Shepherd was in his tan cargo pants, a T-shirt, and his old green field jacket. He pulled a round-rimmed cowboy hat off his head as he shook Gray's hand.

"I guess it was too much to hope that we'd get away with only one dead body for a change," Shepherd said. "I was about to call you anyway. I've got the motive."

Gray froze, his eyes widening in anger.

"I beg your pardon?! You were *still* working on the case?!" Gray asked furiously.

Shrugging, Shepherd was completely unapologetic. "Come on, man; you know me too well to really believe I'd just walked away like that, don't you?"

Shepherd's newly emerging streak of independence startled Gray for the third time in two weeks.

Dropping his head in resigned frustration, Gray cursed his own naivety under his breath in Yiddish, *"Goyisher Putz!"*

Looking back up with a sigh, he led Shepherd to the autopsy room. Cmdr. Scott was there with a partially disassembled body on the table.

"Isaac, I'd like you to meet what's left of OS2 Brandy Sniffer," Gray said, his face twisting furiously as he waved his arm towards the rather full figure of the dead woman on the table. "I was supposed to interview her yesterday, but she never showed. Her body was found this morning in a dumpster."

"Strangled?" Shepherd's face hardened angrily as he approached the table.

"You're fast, Chief," Scott said, his eyes holding respect for Shepherd as he looked up from his examination of Sniffer's brain. He held the non-functioning organ in his left hand while his right made notes on a chart resting on a stand next to him.

"There's a distinct ligature mark around her neck," Shepherd said. "It wasn't hard."

Scott nodded, setting the brain into a metal bowl. "That's what finally killed her, but the murderer *tried* to kill her by bashing her head in first. Look here."

Scott gently rotated Sniffer's head, pointing to its back side under incision where he had removed the upper portion of the skull cap. A horrible dent deformed the bone.

"See the crush injury there? The killer hit her with a blunt object, maybe a pipe or length of wood" Scott said. "She didn't die right away, so the assailant strangled her. Wasn't necessary, though; the blow to her head caused severe cerebral hemorrhaging. She would have been dead within an hour anyway."

"Great," Shepherd said, gritting his teeth, "Our one *known* witness to the Bacon murder is dead."

"She was found in the dumpster near *Ponce's* pier, a little bit away from the ECP," Gray began filling Shepherd in. "At night that area's pretty dark. It's right next to a turn in the waterfront road, and there are no security cameras close by. If you pull up right next to it, the watch at the ECP can't see a thing you're doing. I've already got Carla Tenbold and a few other agents asking around the ships in the area to see if anyone saw anything."

"Time of death?" Shepherd asked Scott.

"Based on the rate of decomposition and the level of insect larvae on the body, I'd say she was killed sometime Tuesday evening, between 18:00 and 22:00 hours," Scott said.

"Her uniform and personal effects are at the forensics lab," Gray said, sliding his hands into his pockets. "I've got agents searching her berthing on the ship and her apartment in Norfolk."

"I've got more work to do, if you gentlemen will excuse me," Scott said, gently. "I still need to swab for possible evidence. DNA, fibers, anything that might help you two. Please, don't hesitate to contact me if you need something before I file my own report."

"Thanks, Commander!" Gray said as he and Shepherd took their leave.

Once back outside in the partly cloudy day, Shepherd set his hat on his head. The two men walked over to the same bench they had relaxed on the previous week, plopping back down on it.

"Maybe I should've been a surgeon instead of going into law enforcement," Gray said. "I'd still get to play detective of a sort, but at least I'd be working with *living* bodies."

"Except for the patients who die," Shepherd said, staring across the river to Norfolk. "No surgeon keeps everyone alive."

"Thanks a lot."

Shepherd shrugged, "Statistically speaking, we *were* overdue for a second dead body. Normally we get the second stiff within the first five days. It's took over five *weeks* before Sniffer got snuffed. I think we just set a record."

"That's ghastly, Isaac!" Gray said, cocking his head in disbelief. Once in while Shepherd still shocked him. "What, have you got a spreadsheet going, or something?!"

"Oh, come on, Abe!" Shepherd said, a bit of puckish mirth returning to his eyes, "Tell me *one* case we've worked on together over the past 20 years that had only *one* dead body!"

Gray opened his mouth to speak, closed it, and gave up. Running a hand through his shock-white hair, he shrugged in defeat. "Touche'! Ok, ok, so you figured out the motive. Hit me."

"First, have there been any developments where 'Aaron Seeley' is concerned?"

Gray nodded, "Yes, but they're not good. I was got a hold of a glass he'd been drinking out of yesterday when I had breakfast aboard *Ponce* with the captain, Dr. Drummin, Buck Sherman, Mr. 'Seeley,' and a few others."

"You swiped his glass?!" Shepherd was clearly impressed by Gray's chutzpah.

"I did indeed," Gray confirmed. "You're not the only person who can sneak around a ship, you know. Oh, by the way, you *do* realize no one in the 21st century says 'swiped' anymore, don't you?"

Shepherd shrugged again, clearly unconcerned.

"Anyway," Gray said, "I've got a friend at the forensics lab who owes me a favor, and she did the fastest DNA analysis I've *ever* seen. She got a profile of 'Seeley's' DNA to me about an hour ago. You're going to *love* this."

"What am I going to love?" Shepherd asked, clearly expecting bad news.

Shaking his head in disbelief, Gray shrugged, "'Seeley's' DNA does *not* match the donor DNA that was found on Bacon's uniform or skin."

Shepherd took a minute to process that.

"Crap," He said simply. "Then who the *hell* is 'Aaron Seeley,' and what's he doing on *Ponce?!*"

"That's a secondary question right now, Isaac," Gray said. "Our *primary* job is finding out who killed Carl Bacon and Brandy Sniffer."

Several hours had passed since the two retreated to Gray's office at NCIS. Night had fallen. Papers floated around them like some insane tide as they read, re-read, and re-re-reread every scrap of information on the Bacon murder. Transcripts of every interview, shipboard diagrams, even *Ponce's* deck logbook that recorded the night of the murder lay scattered across Gray's desk.

Gray sighed, wiping his tired eyes. Long since abandoning his coat and tie, his shirtsleeves were rolled up and his shoulder holster was hung over the back of his chair. A pizza box lay on one cabinet, its contents reduced to a couple of partial crusts.

Shepherd stood at the office window, staring out of the bulletproof glass with its tiny white noise generator attached (to foil external microphones). The beautiful vista of the fleet lit up for the night escaped his attention.

"I'm still drawing a blank," Gray sounded defeated. "You nailed down the motive beautifully; I'll give you that. The theft and sale of the laser weapon *would* be a huge victory for our adversaries, and it's *definitely* motive enough to kill for. The thing is, except for Sniffer, there's no one on that ship I can see benefiting from such a sale...or who we can forensically place in that compartment the night of the murder."

"It's too bad you can't just compel everyone on *Ponce* to submit a DNA sample," Shepherd said.

"I wish," Gray responded wearily. "All active duty members have to give a DNA sample to the DoD upon enlisting for identification of remains. However, those samples are collected *only* for postmortem identification. I'd need a court order to get a hold of them, but that would only cover the active duty folks. There's just *no way* a judge will order everyone on *Ponce* to submit a sample based on what we have so far, especially after the crap show Admiral Donovan caused."

Gray picked up a paper, ignored it, and tossed it down.

"'Aaron Seeley,'" Gray mused. "False identification, false company...he's definitely a player in this, but *how?* What did he get on that ship to *really* do? What's so important that he and persons unknown fabricated a whole company? Your friend Stephanie was right—that kind of cover is *way* too big for anyone except organized crime or a hostile foreign government to pull off. Of course, you do realize right now that we're just *speculating* 'Seeley's' involvement in Bacon's murder. We have to keep in mind it *is* possible he's got nothing to do with the laser or the murder, or else we might go down the wrong rabbit hole."

"I just realized something," Shepherd said, looking back over his shoulder at Gray. "I told you that my friends Aidan and Linda said his contacts had picked up chatter indicating someone on *Ponce* was trying to steal that laser weapon and sell it to the Chinese government, right? Well, I just realized that if Aidan's timeline holds up—and his data is usually pretty damned accurate—then the chatter he picked up seems to have teed off right when our 'Aaron Seeley' went aboard *Ponce* last year. The timing can't be a coincidence. 'Seeley' *is* involved in this case, even if he isn't involved in the murder."

Gray dropped his tired head on the desk for a moment. Lifting it back up, he rubbed his eyes. So far, his 50-year-old eyeballs were holding out. Still, he knew reading glasses were inevitably in his future.

"Perhaps, but then again, perhaps not," Gray said, cautioning Shepherd. "Let's get back to Sniffer for a moment. Our killer was rather clever by dumping Sniffer's body in a dumpster. There's some *possible* DNA material on Sniffer's skin and uniform, but it was too badly degraded by the garbage she was tangled up in to be of any use. The yellow fibers found on Sniffer's uniform are a different story...well, I *hope* they are. Unfortunately, the fiber analysis just started. It'll be a few days before we know if all the yellow fibers we have came from the same garment."

Moving with all the grace of an inebriated cat on roller skates from the window, Shepherd collapsed into a chair opposite Gray's desk. A few loose pages of case file fluttered to the floor in his wake.

"Our killer also likes to bash people's heads in," Shepherd said distantly.

"I noticed that pattern too," Gray said.

"We're looking at him, Abe," Shepherd said vaguely. "The damn thing's right in front of us. I just can't quite see it yet."

"What is it, Isaac? Something's nagging at you."

"There's something I heard...something someone said last week when we were aboard *Ponce* that's bugging me. Can't tell you what it is, but, there's something there."

"I'm going to talk to the XO tomorrow," Gray said. "He's obviously in this too, what with the note, pink underwear, and yellow jacket you found in his stateroom. I just can't see why Cremer didn't interview him in the first place. That was a *glaringly* odd oversight."

"Sniffer's thong..." Shepherd said blankly, his voice tired and sad. "The XO has a family."

"I *really* hate those guys," Gray said. "God knows I've seen too many families destroyed by shipboard affairs, forget the more violent crimes."

"We're still jumbled up too much," Shepherd said suddenly, shaking his head as if to clear out the cobwebs. "I have the creepiest feeling we're being hoodwinked."

"Me too," Gray said. "But I can't see how."

"Sniffer's underwear..." Shepherd said again, staring into nothing and lapsing back into silence.

Gray smiled wanly, arching his back and stretching, "A pink thong, yeah."

"A pink thong..."

"Isaac?" Gray asked, cocking his head, an amused smile on his face. "You seem to be obsessing on a woman's pink thong. Considering your particular interests, why is a small woman's pink thong capturing your attention so much?"

Shepherd's head snapped around, his eyes locking onto Gray's. Gray could almost hear the relays clicking over in Shepherd's brain.

"Isaac?" Gray asked.

"Hang on," Shepherd suddenly straightened up. He rested his elbows on the arms of the chair and steepled his fingers in a gesture Gray was very familiar with. Except for the normal ears, Shepherd's posture and expression made him a dead ringer for Mr. Spock.

"A pink thong..." Shepherd turned inward, talking to himself. An odd light began growing in Shepherd's eyes. "A *small* pink thong…!"

Gray began to slowly uncoil and straighten up in his own chair. He'd seen this behavior way too many times to dismiss it.

Shepherd was on to something.

Shepherd's brain began pulling memories out of storage. He didn't have quite the photographic memory so common in detective stories, but he possessed a steel-trap mind that missed little. The memory he sought was retrieved and played back on his internal screen...

...Piling the laundry back into the hamper, he took a second to check all the pockets in each pair of pants. Snooping through the pockets of one pair of khaki trousers resulted in a tiny, petite pink thong falling to the deck...

"No...it can't be that...that clumsy..." Shepherd said to himself, amazed at the ridiculous nature of what he suddenly perceived.

"Isaac?" Gray probed again.

Shepherd continued muttering to himself, his eyes narrowed as Gray waited patiently.

"Abe," Shepherd finally spoke, "The pink thong I found in the XO's laundry. We're only *assuming* it belonged to Sniffer. It was a pink, petite woman's thong, right?"

"Right. So, what?"

Shepherd looked up, meeting Gray's eyes again.

"We both saw Brandy Sniffer today in person. Would you describe her as 'petite?'"

Gray stiffened, his own energy level jazzing up, "No. Hell, no! She had a full figure. If had to use a word for her, it'd be 'voluptuous.'"

"Therefore, the thong in the XO's stateroom *wasn't hers!*" Shepherd declared.

"And the apparent affair between the XO and Sniffer...?" Gray prompted, waiting. *Here it comes...*

"According to Dionne, the rumors of an affair got started because Sniffer was seen near the XO's stateroom a lot, and because Sniffer kept dropping sly hints. In other words—"

"Sniffer might have staged the whole thing!" Gray finished the thought smoothly. "Assuming your hypothesis is accurate, she and her *real* accomplice, or accomplices, were planning to set up the *XO* as a fall guy. Now, the note you found. Give me your thoughts on that."

"What if it were also planted?" Shepherd asked, looking back out the window. His brain was sliding pieces of information around to find a new and more complete configuration. "It wasn't hidden very well under the desk blotter. Granted, the XO could've hidden it there himself, but if you were an important ship's officer *and* involved in a dirty deal to sell stolen technology, would you hide a note like that so...so carelessly?"

"Depends," Gray said, arguing the point to see where it might or might not lead, "He could just be stupid. We've both seen that. There's also the yellow jacket in his laundry."

"Granted," Shepherd said, his sea-green eyes becoming two lighthouse beacons illuminating the night—always a sure sign he was finally getting the big picture. "But, let's assume it was *all* planted. Abe, what if...what if *I'm* not the only unauthorized person accessing to the XO's stateroom? That yellow jacket is *too* damned obvious, now that I'm thinking about it."

"You're right," Gray agreed. "Ok, let's assume the note, thong, and jacket were all planted to frame the XO. Let's further assume the frame job was being set up *expressly* to protect Sniffer and her accomplice or accomplices. That immediately brings two questions to mind: why was Bacon murdered, and why didn't the XO find any of the items planted in his stateroom? Could he be involved after all?"

Shepherd listened quietly as Gray continued.

"Was Bacon in on the deal, and maybe wanted a bigger cut?" Gray asked. "Perhaps he's the one who spilled enough beans for our intel people to get wind of the illegal deal and begin investigating? That alone would be enough to kill him."

"No, I don't think so," Shepherd disagreed, looking at the ceiling as he thought. "The murder was swift and *brutal*. It doesn't look like a premeditated hit to me. It strikes me as the kind of crime done by someone who's unexpectedly discovered, and enraged they were discovered. Same with the attempt on me; it was fast; a 'spur of the moment' type of attack. I don't have anything concrete to base this on, but the whole pattern violence also strikes me as the work of *one* suspect, not multiple suspects."

"I agree," Gray said, shifting his position in his chair, "But, we still have no theory as to why *Cline* was set up the way he was by Sniffer. They went through all that trouble to implicate the XO, only to abandon it. Why did Sniffer suddenly decide to falsely testify against Cline? That was so damned public she could only have done it with her accomplice's approval."

"She still got killed for it," Shepherd pointed out. "It's no coincidence she got brained and strangled the day before your interview. First rule of good crime: eliminate all witnesses as quickly as possible."

Nodding, Gray tapped his fingers on the desk. "Clearly, our suspect is a highly intelligent man who can think on his feet."

"We've got one *hell* of a weapon in our hands, though," Shepherd said. "Abe, our killer *must* be desperate not to get caught. Two murders and one attempted murder? Attempted theft of government technology? He has to be stressed, on edge, and jumpy. There's got to be a way we can leverage *that* against him."

Gray's eyes narrowed as he considered the point. "We can, but we need to have an idea *who* to leverage it against. We can't just shoot in the dark."

Shepherd took off his glasses, wiping some dust off the lens, "I wonder if...if...*good grief! DUST!*"

Jumping to his feet, Shepherd nearly Gray startled into a heart attack.

"I've got it, Abe! *Give me that damned log book!*" Shepherd ordered, another memory dropping into place.

Picking up the green log book, Gray held it out.

Snatching it with little courtesy, Shepherd fell back into his seat and began flipping pages so fast it sounded as if a miniature tornado was in the room.

"Something the captain said the *first* day we were on the ship, the day we found the blood spatter up on that electrical box! *That's* what I've been trying to recall!" Shepherd feverishly scanned entries in the log book.

"I'm thinking...but I don't recall anything myself," Gray said.

"Gadzooks!" Shepherd declared triumphantly. "The captain told us the XO was on leave, remember?"

"He did?" Gray said, trying to remember.

"He did! Says here he checked out on emergency leave September 5 and has *not* returned. *He's not here!"* Shepherd smacked himself upside the forehead, taking care not to smash his glasses. "I *cannot* believe I forgot a detail like *that!* That's what I meant by 'dust.' When I searched the XO's stateroom, except for the desk where Sniffer hid the fake note, the room was *covered* in dust because no one's been in there for some time!"

"Let me see that," Gray said, taking the logbook from Shepherd. Looking at the log entry, Gray sat back.

"You're right, now that you've reminded me, I *do* remember the captain telling us the XO is on leave!" Gray said, before his own spine snapped straight. Clearly the lightning of inspiration had struck his brain as well. "Wait a minute…!"

It was Shepherd's turn to quietly watch as Gray started flipping pages in the deck log, searching for an earlier entry. Gray would stop, read a page, shake his head, and then flip back farther.

"I've got a hunch..." Gray said somewhat vaguely.

Finding what he was looking for, Gray stabbed an entry with a triumphant finger. *"Ah-ha!* Isaac, you *are* on to something. According to this, the XO *first* checked out on emergency leave August 1ˢᵗ, and did *not* report back aboard until *August 14ᵗʰ*. His current emergency leave period is his *second* time off the ship in the last two months. No wonder Shey never interviewed him; he wasn't even in town! And now he's checked out on leave *again!* Perfect target to frame, even if only for a diversion."

"So he could never have changed the staging area…!" Shepherd started, but cut himself off as his thoughts raced ahead of his mouth.

"Staging area?"

"First things first," Shepherd shook his head, jumbling his tumbling thoughts into some semblance of order. "We still need to find out where the XO actually was, just to properly eliminate him from our new suspect pool."

Gray looked up, surprised, "You *already* have a new suspect list, Isaac?"

"A very short one, yes. Listen to this!" Shepherd became as hyperactive as a cat on a hot tin roof.

Gray sat back, struggling to listen. Shepherd's speech accelerated to blisteringly fast velocities when he was seized with revelations like this. Still, Gray managed to keep up, suffering only a minor headache from the effort. When Shepherd finished and finally took a breath, Gray nodded.

"That makes sense, but how do we *prove* it?" Gray asked. "Your theory tracks with everything we have, but we still don't have enough to convince a judge to issue any warrants."

Smiling wickedly, Shepherd said, "We prove it the old-fashioned way, old friend. To borrow a line from Agatha Christie, we'll use the moving finger!"

Chapter 11
Friday, September 23; 18:30 hours
Naval Station Norfolk, Virginia

"...turning to Capitol Hill, Senate hearings into the Chief of Naval Operation's conduct are still underway at this hour. Senator Diego Alejandro pointedly asked Admiral Thomas Donovan if he had the legal authority to declare the guilt of a sailor prior to a trial. Donovan replied by saying he was dedicated to protecting the integrity of the service, and all the men and women in its ranks. Alejandro repeated, the question, which the CNO again did not directly answer..."

"This sort of toxic masculinity is the hallmark of the jingoistic mindset of the armed forces. Military culture is based on an outdated, patriarchal hierarchy ensuring blind compliance while keeping people of color and women in a second-tier status," declared Rhode Island Congresswoman Dana Cremer on an evening talk show.

"...the president deflected questions about the Senate hearings, insisting he was present to speak in honor of the National Museum of African American History and Culture..."

"...turning to the tech markets, Microsoft and Apple again boasted gains during the last quarter. GDI Tech futures were up in anticipation of it being awarded contracts by the Oregon, Nevada, and North Dakota state governments to provide cybersecurity systems. In other business news, Oceanic Supply and Service Corporation's Honolulu office was raided by the FBI this morning. Federal agents seized computers, smart phones, files, and other potential evidence in the widening 'Big Mitch' scandal engulfing several prominent Navy officials in the Pacific..."

The elegantly geometric form of USS *Ponce* emerged from the quiet waters of the James River, a stately old lady holding herself proud in the early evening light. She was the last of her breed, but she was content…mostly. Only one thing now remained, and that was going to be finished tonight.

The Proud Lion looked down at one of her former sailors who stood under her bow, gazing up in thoughtful silence. Anyone with any degree of poetry in their soul would have been hard-pressed to deny a feeling the ship regarded this particular sailor with special solicitude and affection. *Ponce* seemed to recognize him as a special ally who would jealously guard her honor and the lives of her crew.

Shepherd stood in his khakis, his black "Eisenhower" jacket zipped halfway up. Gazing over the great number "15" on her prow and the 20,000 lbs port side anchor nestled against the hull, he permitted himself a moment to admire her. Despite lacking the sleeker lines of more modern warships, *Ponce* exuded a certain grace and symmetry with her square superstructure rising up forward, and then tapering down to the long flight deck aft.

Shepherd patted his jacket's interior pocket. Albert the Crab was hidden in there, his ever-constant secret companion.

Funny, He thought, *My first sea-going command was the Black Lions. My first time as an actual member of the ship's crew was the Proud Lion. Two lions. Wonder if I ought to look at the lion as a spirit animal?*

"Well, old girl, you and I've done this waltz once before," Shepherd finally spoke. He began rubbing his hands together, showing just a hint of the nervous energy seething inside him (and which would make him have rather uncomfortable bowels for the next few days). "Let's just hope that no one blows their brains out all over your side *this* time. I don't want to have to organize the detail to clean up that kind of a mess again!"

He abruptly realized the sailors standing the evening's watches were staring at him.

They'll be old-timers too, one day, He thought, chuckling. *They'll understand.*

"Well, old girl," He said again, sketching a slight bow to *Ponce*, "Shall we dance?"

Shepherd required only moments to stride half the length of *Ponce* and ascend the brow to the Quarterdeck. He stopped at the top of the brow, turned and saluted the ensign on the ship's fantail, then covered the last few feet, reaching the podium where the Quarterdeck watches stood.

"Chief Petty Officer Isaac Shepherd requesting permission to board. I believe I am expected," He said, holding up his ID card and saluting.

The officer of the deck returned his salute.

"Permission granted, Chief. Please wait here; Mr. Gray wanted to speak with you before you head in," The chief said. He turned to the Messenger of the Watch, but the messenger nodded before he could speak and vanished inside the superstructure. She returned not two minutes later with Abraham Gray in tow, looking as politician-like as always in his favorite dark blue suit.

"Isaac," Gray said, shaking his hand, "A word before we kick off, if you don't mind?"

Gray led him across the flight deck away from the Quarterdeck watches. They huddled under the ship's hangar doors. The *Austin*-class amphibious transport docks had semi-retractable hangars that could telescope out to house larger helicopters. Right now, *Ponce's* hangar was pulled back to its shortest length and the roll-down hangar door was closed.

"What's up, Abe?" Shepherd asked, having to pull his mind away from memories to focus on the present.

"I've briefed MA1 Fredriksen on our suspect's identity," Gray said under his breath. "He and one of his hand-picked MAs will move in when the moment is right. I've also got two MAs on alert to keep 'Seeley' under observation. Still, you need to be careful. I think we've got everything covered, but your position in the compartment tonight could potentially put you in a line of fire."

"I'll be careful," Shepherd promised. "Shall we?"

"We shall."

Ponce had been cleared of nearly all personnel except the security guards, watch standers on the Quarterdeck, and engineering personnel in the MMRs. The mess deck tables had been stacked to one side, opening up space. A circle of folding chairs arced around the deck. Sixteen Navy MAs, all heavily armed, encircled the very confused gathering of people occupying those chairs.

Capt. Smith sat at the forward-most point, the ceremonial "head" of the odd conclave.

Next to him, like the numbers on a clock, were the ship's executive officer, then Chief Yeoman Jacob Hank, Chief Boatswain's Mate Kelly Tate, Dr. Tyler Drummin, Chief Quartermaster Thomas Shifter, Buck Sherman, and Aaron Seeley. At the eleven o'clock position, on Capt. Smith's left, sat a shivering, shrunken Operations Specialist 2nd Class Jarvis Cline and his lawyer, Samuel Holder.

Gray and Shepherd entered. In a set of moves choreographed over long years working together, Gray cut to the starboard side and passed around the circle of chairs until he stood behind the captain and next to the burly form of Fredriksen.

Shepherd, going full-bore into character, strode into the middle of the circle and walked up to the executive officer.

"Commander Franklin Platter!" Shepherd extended a hand, his voice booming around the space, "It is a genuine pleasure to *finally* put a name and face to your title, and to meet you instead of your laundry, sir! Thank you so much for coming off leave for this little party!"

Platter shook Shepherd's hand, a bemused expression on his face. "Uh...my laundry?"

"Tell you later, sir!"

"Chief..." Capt. Smith began, voice dripping with irritation. His face was red, and it was clearly evident he was barely holding back an angry tirade.

"One moment, sir!" Shepherd said jovially. "I have yet to make this young man's acquaintance in person! Petty Officer Cline! It's lovely to finally meet you as well!"

Cline, a slight young man with thin blonde hair and gaunt skin hanging from his bones, pulled his sunken eyes from the deck to look at Shepherd with curiosity. His eyes, dull and empty, were like looking like worn glass eyes of a forgotten doll. "Ch-Chief?"

"Mr. Shepherd! I want to know why you have asked my client here!" Holder started to rise. He was a powerfully built man with olive skin and dark eyes that were constantly evaluating his surroundings.

"Hold your horses, Mr. Holder!" Shepherd used the power of his booming baritone to derail the lawyer's objection. "I just wanted to finally meet your client in person after Mr. Gray and I did so much work to clear his name!"

Holder sank back into his chair, shocked by the revelation of who Shepherd actually was.

Shepherd bent down, placing a gentle hand on Cline's quivering shoulder.

"I'm sorry for your loss, Jarvis," Dropping out of character for a moment, Shepherd whispered so that only Cline and Holder could hear him.

Shepherd's transition from clownish joviality to sympathetic earnestness caused both Cline and Holder to stare at him, mouths agape.

"Please bear with me," Shepherd went on, ensuring only Cline and Holder could hear. "I can't bring Carl back, but I will bring justice to his killer. You have a right to see that happen, especially after what the Navy did to you. You have no reason to trust anyone in the Navy right now, but I'm asking you to trust *me*. Not as a chief, but merely as Issac."

Cline and Holder exchanged very startled glances. Glancing at Holder, Shepherd could tell the lawyer suddenly had no idea what to think of him.

Cline nodded and whispered, "O-Ok."

Shepherd winked conspiratorially at him, and then unfolded back to his full 6'4" height, stepping to the middle of the circle.

"Good evening all!" Shepherd's smiling voice was energetic. One might have thought he was acting as ring master for a particularly slapstick circus. "I suppose you're all wondering why I asked you here tonight!"

"Chief…" Smith growled, his patience about to expire.

The performance was so over-the-top that no one noticed Gray and Shepherd both watching a particular individual for his reactions.

"You see," Shepherd boomed on, ignoring the captain, "I realized that we have never properly been able to settle this sad business about the death of Carl Bacon. I think it's time we let this matter finally rest in peace by telling you we have found our suspect! It took some work, but we've been able to identify the killer with laser-like precision. I must say, the involvement of the laser in this affair really helped shine some light on the case!"

Fredriksen choked into a coughing fit that might have been badly disguised laughter.

Gray stopped his covert observations just long enough to roll his eyes.

Drummin did a double take.

Cline and Holder stared at Shepherd as if he'd just declared he was a talking mouse.

"Chief!" Smith came to his feet, eyes blazing in anger, "That's enough! We were brought here tonight at the request of NCIS! What the *hell* are you doing acting like a drunken ass?!"

"Oh, Captain, I never act like a drunken ass!" Shepherd clasped his hands behind his back, his buffoonish air a calculated ploy. "With my height and lack of coordination, I come off more as a drunken baby giraffe!"

Shepherd continued quietly monitoring the suspect even as he addressed Smith.

"Enough! This shit ends now!" Smith bellowed.

"This gathering is *not* over until *I* say it's over, Captain Smith!" Gray spoke up, his voice so frigidly cold it created a miniature ice age in the space.

Smith spun around furiously, clearly ready for a fight, but Gray outflanked him with stunning speed.

"You're a suspect in the murder of a *Ponce* sailor, as well as two attempted murders, Captain!" Gray's glacial calm hit Smith like a brick wall, stopping the captain cold. Gray spoke in a level voice, but the authority of his tone subsumed all attempts at resistance. "Everyone in this compartment, with the exceptions of Petty Officer Cline and Mr. Holder, are suspects. Sir, I strongly recommend you allow these proceedings to continue, or else I will exercise *my* legal authority to place you and every other suspect here under arrest."

The power of Gray's personality hit Smith like a tsunami. Even Shepherd found himself frozen with frightened awe.

Gray's quiet command of the room forcefully reminded Shepherd once more why Gray was the one man Shepherd never wanted to square off against. The mild-mannered, casually affable persona Gray affected hid a stunningly powerful soul bearing the strength of ages. Suspects, witnesses, lawyers, and angry captains alike crossed him at their peril. All were inevitably were out-classed.

Gray and Smith continued their staring contest, silently competing for control.

Smith blinked first.

"Very well," Smith said, clearly trying to save face, "I will allow this...charade to continue for now, but you better have your chief there stop acting like an ass and do something *useful* before I call his commanding officer about his unprofessional behavior!"

"Chief Shepherd never does anything without a *damned* good reason, Captain," Gray's voice was still soft, but his anger slammed into Smith like a rogue wave. "Now, sir, I *invite* you to have a seat so we can present our findings in the murder of Carl Bacon, the attempted murder of Chief Shepherd here—"

That statement brought a gasp from Tate and Shifter, a shocked expression to Seeley's face, and caused Drummin to nearly jump out of his chair.

"You think someone tried to murder Chief Shepherd?!" Drummin fumbled out the words.

"I *know* someone tried to murder the chief, Doctor," Gray said, still watching Smith. "He was assaulted in one of the berthing spaces, and we've forensically linked his attacker with the same person who killed Bacon *and* tried to kill Brandy Sniffer."

"Brandy's alive?!" Drummin blurted out, shocked. "But I...I...I thought...wait...we were told..."

"She's very much alive, Doctor," Shepherd said. "She's currently under guard at Portsmouth."

"Thank God!" Tate said, color draining from her face in relief. "I couldn't...another sailor murdered would be just too much."

Smith's resistance crumpled as he absorbed this most recent detail. Turning away from Gray, he looked at Shepherd, suddenly perceiving a strategy like a carefully planned chess match being enacted between Gray and Shepherd. He sat, watching the Queen's Gambit unfolding before his eyes.

Between his antics and Gray's quiet authority, everyone was now glued to him with religious devotion, and the suspect was looking increasingly ill at ease. Shepherd dropped his clown act and began in a very formal voice.

"Sniffer has confessed to her part in the murder of Carl Bacon—"

Cline's head snapped up, eyes dripping with disbelief and betrayal. "She did *what?!*"

"She confessed to helping murder Carl?!" Drummin looked like he couldn't handle another shock.

Platter leaned back in his seat, mouth agape. Sherman crossed his arms, clearly confused.

"Sniffer helped kill Bacon?!" Shifter actually reached up and swiped his fingers through his ears, as though a build-up of wax might have affected his hearing.

"She's did, and she's now cooperating with NCIS," Shepherd repeated.

"The...that bitch..." Cline hissed, his fists squeezing shut and a tear of rage escaping his eye. Holder laid a hand on Cline's arm to steady him.

Shepherd glanced at Gray, who gave him the smallest of nods coupled with the ghost of a triumphant smile. Shepherd returned the tiny nod. It was as if they telepathically agreed the suspect was within inches of cracking.

Shepherd raised his arm and pointed at the captain, then began a slow sweep around the circle with the moving finger.

"As Mr. Gray said, with the exceptions of Petty Officer Cline and Mr. Holder, one of you in this circle is a *murderer,*" Shepherd declared. "Carl Bacon's killer is in here with us *right now.* One of you has blood on your hands. Take a look at each other. To paraphrase *Macbeth*, see if you can out the damn spot."

Silence again flooded the room. Drummin was sweating. Seeley glanced to either side. Tate began scanning every face around the room. Hank did the same. Sherman kept his eyes on Shepherd. Shifter just stared at Shepherd, fascinated. Smith's eyes were narrow and focused, and Platter wordlessly shook his head.

"Let's take a trip back to last month," Shepherd said, his hands now clasped behind his back. "August 9th. The evening was partly cloudy, but there was enough sunlight to illuminate *Ponce's* well deck since the stern gate was lowered. Poor Carl Bacon was apparently in trouble as 20:00 hours approached because he was late for watch. Unfortunately, he was late for watch because he had just gone *splat* on the well floor!"

Shepherd stamped his foot on the word "splat," making everyone in the compartment (even Gray) jump.

"*That's* where the misdirection began," Shepherd declared. "It was then stoked by our not-so-poor Petty Officer Sniffer's bogus testimony of Cline and Bacon fighting on the well deck catwalk."

"Brandy Sniffer lied," Gray's quiet interjection was so unexpected that nearly everyone jumped in surprise. "Her 'sworn testimony' fell apart after Chief Shepherd and I interviewed the sailors who had been painting on *Mesa Verde's* fo'c'sle the night of the murder. Not only did those three men *not* see or hear a 'loudly echoing fight,' they actually saw a white male calmly dump what they thought was just an 'Oscar' dummy over the catwalk. Seeing someone drop a 'dummy' down into the well deck seemed perfectly normal since that's where everything's being staged for removal form the ship."

Shepherd kept watching the suspect out of the corner of his eye as Gray went on.

"Chief Shepherd found a note in your stateroom, Commander Platter," Gray said. "He also found a woman's pink thong and a yellow jacket in your laundry."

Platter's thin face twisted into an expression of pure, speechless shock.

"Those pieces of evidence were very compelling," Shepherd said, taking the reigns from Gray. "You see, Sniffer had gotten nearly everyone on this ship thinking you were sleeping with her, sir."

"*WHAT?!*" Platter was on his feet, his deep-set eyes wide with angry indignation. "I have *never* cheated on my wife!!"

"Sit down, Commander," Shepherd said. "Sniffer and her accomplice were trying to frame you."

The blood drained from Platter's face.

Shepherd started to turn, then looked back at Platter, "By the way, sir, I recommend you change the combination of your stateroom's cypher lock. It's hasn't been changed for at least six years."

Platter sat down.

"Of key importance, the note in your stateroom was *not* in your handwriting," Shepherd continued. "Sniffer planted all those items while you were on leave."

"And the motive was...?" Smith prompted. His anger was ebbing fast now as he followed Shepherd's narrative.

"The ANQ45, sir," Shepherd answered casually. "The Chinese are trying to build their own laser weapon...and failing at it. A contact I have in the intelligence community found evidence indicating the attempted sale of *Ponce's* ANQ45 to a Chinese buyer. The sale never happened and the whole thing just went cold."

"You have a contact *where?!*" Seeley blurted, his eyes popping from his head.

"I've got contacts everywhere," Shepherd shrugged causally. "I'm a very popular man."

"Sniffer told us what happened the night of August 9th," Gray took up the story again without missing a beat, his hands folded in front of him. "She and her accomplice were on the phone with their buyer when Bacon accidentally walked in on them. Her accomplice attacked Bacon, smashing the back of his head into an electrical box before dumping his body over the catwalk."

Dozens of eyes blinked as the assembly looked at each other, and then back to Gray. He went on as calmly as if he were lecturing a class on how to tie their shoes.

"Unfortunately for our killer, things immediately began going wrong," Gray said. "First, the killer was seen by the sailors on *Mesa Verde*. Second, Bacon's body landed on its feet at an angle which precluded fatal damage to his head from the fall. That damage therefore had to come from somewhere else. Blood evidence proved the electrical box was used as the murder weapon."

Drummin's face was a study in horror. Tate listened, the expression on her face the same as if she were helplessly watching a horrific train wreck.

Shepherd smoothly took over, "We found an unknown male's DNA on Bacon's body and uniform. We determined the donor DNA did *not* come from OS2 Cline, clearing him from the Bacon's murder."

Cline blinked, the color in his face gone as he listened to the story. Holder now put a comforting arm across Cline's back as Gray began speaking again.

"Sniffer had already been spinning her tale of a 'love triangle' between the three of them. She probably started it just to get attention. The night of Bacon's murder, she and her accomplice realized it was a golden opportunity to set Cline up, so they abandoned the frame job against Cmdr. Platter in favor."

Cline looked as if he was about to throw up.

"Sniffer may be devious woman, but she's a naive amateur," Shepherd said. "By agreeing to testify, she actually set *herself* up as a victim. Our killer is far too smart to leave someone like her alive once her usefulness was over."

Drummin looked like *he* was ready to throw up as well. Smith was leaning forward, clearly beginning to put the pieces together himself. Hank, still silent, shook his head.

Shepherd continued to closely watch the assemblage. The ploy was working. Glancing at Gray, he saw that Gray also noticed the cracks widening in their suspect's innocent facade. Gray gave Shepherd the tiniest of nods. Shepherd flicked his eyebrows slightly in acknowledgment, and then cracked on with his performance.

The pieces were in place. It was now time to play the endgame.

"Last week I took advantage of an opportunity to poke around a bit," Shepherd said as causally as if he were talking about lunch. "I met Dr. Drummin, Aaron Seeley, and Buck Sherman below decks before I conducted my search. On my return, our unnamed male assailant killed the lights and tried to brain me in my old berthing space. The assailant got away, but not before he collided with a hatch in the dark, leaving behind more yellow clothing fibers. And then, after that, I ran into Mr. Seeley and Mr. Sherman in the head again. Odd how they were there before and after that attack..."

Seeley and Sherman shifted uncomfortably.

"So now we have a pattern," Gray declared suddenly, causing Platter to jump in surprise. "Our suspect likes to kill by bashing in skulls with a blunt object. He only tried to strangle Sniffer because he realized the blow to *her* head didn't immediately kill her. Our suspect has a habit of wearing yellow jackets...or, at least, jackets with something on them containing yellow fibers."

Shepherd wheeled around and stared at Buck Sherman...who happened to be wearing a yellow jacket.

"Why are you looking at me?" Sherman was both angry and scared. Realizing what he was wearing, he blurted. "Wait! You can't think—!"

"Yes, I *did* think," Shepherd retorted. "However, it turns out you weren't on the ship the night of August 9th any more than Commander Platter was. He was on leave, and you were at a movie according to the sales records from your credit card and the young lady at the box office who recognized your photo. So, I'm sorry, Mr. Sherman, but you too have just been eliminated from the murder game! We will instead have to rely on Commander Platter's evidence."

"*My* evidence?" Platter was confused.

"What the *hell* are you talking about?!" Drummin demanded, sweat stains spreading profusely from under his arms.

"Commander Platter told us who it is," Shepherd said.

"I did *what?!*" Platter nearly fell out of his seat in confusion.

"You told us exactly who the murderer is by *not* being here, Commander," Gray said. "Your *absence* gave us the evidence we needed."

"I...*what?!*" Platter nearly fell out of his seat for a second time in as many minutes. He looked to Captain Smith for help.

"We'll get to that in a minute, sir," Shepherd said. "However, there is also the fact that Mr. Seeley over here wears jackets with yellow fibers as well, was in the immediate vicinity both before and after the attempt on my life...and is a fraud."

"I'm a what?" Seeley said quizzically, cocking his head.

"A fraud. Fake, poser, impostor, pretender...I can go on if you like," Shepherd said pleasantly.

"How do you figure that?" Seeley asked, crossing his arms. He was not agitated, but instead now had the casual air of a man mildly interested in an esoteric discussion about the breeding habits of sea sponges.

"Smith-Table Electronics does *not* exist," Shepherd said easily. "Smith-Table is a front you used to fake credentials so you could get aboard *Ponce* last year. Oddly enough, you boarded this ship just about the time the investigation into the attempt to sell the laser to the Chinese got into motion."

Seeley's face morphed quickly into a look of utter shock before he recovered. Rearranging his face, he resumed his mask of neutral indifference.

"I think you've made a mistake, Chief," Seeley said. *This* time his voice carried a note of warning.

"Nope. I had a federal judge on the D.C. Circuit verify the information for me," Shepherd said, watching Seeley gawped openly at that piece of data. "Somehow, your unknown organization managed to use the real Dolus Holdings as a fake parent company to help bolster the Smith-Table fiction. Nicely done, by the way. I'm going to be very happy to find out who you really are and what you want when this is over."

Smith was staring at Seeley with shock, his face white as a ghost. "You're...he's...he's a *fraud?!*"

"Yes, sir," Shepherd said with a sigh. "But, as entertainingly convenient as it would be, he's *not* the man who killed Carl Bacon either."

Seeley glanced behind himself and saw that two MAs had quietly slipped up on either side of him. Looking unsure for a moment, he evidently decided that discretion was the better part of not getting his face smashed into the deck. He sat back and relaxed, Shepherd and Gray both noting he still acted as though he had the greatest 'get out of jail free' card up his sleeve.

The tiniest look from Gray told Shepherd the moment to spring the final blow was at hand.

"It's time to end this tragedy," Shepherd declared. "Wouldn't you agree, Dr. Drummin?"

"What?" Drummin sat frozen, his face a study in disbelief. Sweat ran down his brow, and his shirt was thoroughly soaked with perspiration.

"How does Commander Platter's absence implicate Dr. Drummin?" Smith demanded eagerly, abandoning the anger he held mere moments before.

"You were on emergency leave in August, correct, Commander?" Gray asked Platter.

Almost imperceptibly, Fredriksen and another MA1 began shifting their position. It was very slight, but Shepherd noticed that, right on schedule, they were creeping closer to Drummin.

"I was," Platter said, still horribly confused. "My father passed away."

"I'm very sorry, sir," Shepherd said with genuine sincerity. "And this most recent leave?"

Fredriksen and his partner were now directly behind Drummin.

"My mother is showing signs of dementia," Platter said, his teeth gritted. "We're relocating her to an assisted care facility. What does that have to do with any of this?!"

Shepherd clasped his hands behind his back again. "I just found it very interesting you 'signed' an order shifting the HAZMAT staging area from the flight deck to the starboard side aft line handling room at the same time you were out of state on leave...a shift that, by an amazing coincidence, allowed Dr. Drummin to bring a barrel full of caustic HAZMAT through a space we were searching...and then 'accidentally' spill it, conveniently destroying much of evidence we'd found."

The gathering erupted loudly into a stunned babble for a single heartbeat—

—Drummin leapt to his feet, howling in rage like a feral animal. Seizing his chair, he hurled it with all his might at Shepherd and turned, running full out—

—right into Fredriksen's extended fist.

The impact knocked Drummin backwards. His feet flew out from under him and he arced towards the circle of chairs.

Tate screamed and Hank yelled, both diving out of the way as Drummin crashed into Hank's now vacated seat. The impact reverberated around the mess deck as a dozen side arms flew from their holsters, metallic clicks signaling one and all they were ready to fire.

The weapons were unnecessary. Drummin was out cold.

"Isaac!" Gray hustled to Shepherd as Fredriksen secured Drummin's hands.

"I'm fine," Shepherd, said rubbing his left shoulder where the chair had bounced off him. "He only grazed me. Have to admit I didn't see *that* one coming!"

Drummin was coming around, muttering as he woke up, "She was *dead*. I goddamned *killed* her! There was no pulse!"

His eyes were pure rage as he regained his senses, realizing his hands were bound with heavy plastic zip ties.

"Unfortunately, you're actually correct, Doctor," Shepherd said as Fredriksen hauled Drummin to his feet. "Sniffer *is* dead."

"But, Isaac," Tate said, still breathing hard, a hand on her chest, "You said she was alive."

"I'm very sorry we had to lie to you all," Shepherd said, gesturing towards Drummin. "Unfortunately, we needed this little piece of shit to believe she was alive and cooperating."

Gray took control of the scene, reading Drummin his rights before having Fredriksen and several of the MAs escort him off the ship.

"Chief," Captain Smith walked over to Shepherd, confused. "I...I don't understand. If you had all that evidence...why...?"

"Why do all this?" Shepherd asked, his manner shifting a more military posture. "Captain, if the Navy hadn't embarrassed itself over the false prosecution of Petty Officer Cline, we would have wrapped this up in a much more conventional manner. Unfortunately, the CNO's actions badly complicated the situation. The only way to make sure we nailed Drummin was to goad him into confessing in front of a load of witnesses."

"I see," Smith nodded, clearly unhappy.

Gray walked over, Seeley in tow behind him. Seeley was guarded by two MAs, who were each as big as a small U.S. Army tank.

"Now," Gray said, "Mr. Seeley, you're our next question."

Seeley didn't look at all nervous. In fact, he acted like a man who was being royally inconvenienced. "You guys really *don't* have any idea what you've kicked over, do you?"

"I know you're a fraud who used fake documents and a fake company to get aboard a United States warship while it was testing experimental technology," Shepherd said. "And we know you happened to come aboard *right* when an investigation was begun into an attempt to steal the ANQ45. Not too hard to conclude you're the subject of *that* investigation."

"Chief Shepherd," Seeley said, his voice suddenly light. He was clearly amused. "I *do* have to admit I'm impressed. How the hell *you*, of all people, rumbled me is quite astonishing! I'm sure this fiasco will force The Agency to revise a number of protocols. Unfortunately, however, you and Special Agent Gray really are barking up the *wrong* tree, and I must advise you to cease and desist from this line of inquiry."

Shepherd's lighthearted demeanor dropped when he heard Seeley's terminology.

"The…'Agency?'" Shepherd asked, rolling his eyes and looking at Gray.

Gray suddenly looked like he'd swallowed a rotten egg.

"The Agency," Seeley said, crossing his arms. "You know the term, I suppose?"

"Yes," Shepherd, putting a hand to his forehead in disbelief.

"'The Agency'…?" Smith asked. "Wait a minute...not...?"

"The Central Intelligence Agency." Gray said, shaking his head and looking at Seeley. "You're CIA."

"The investigation that you so loudly proclaimed started up when I came on board started because *I* was conducting it!" Seeley struggled to contain his laughter.

Shepherd and Gray exchanged another look of utter disbelief.

"Still, you both should get some real credit for the level of skill you've shown conducting your investigation," Seeley said with complete sincerity. "I honestly don't think there's ever been an instance where NCIS and some Accidental Detective ever blew an agent's cover, but you two pulled it off nicely."

Staring at Seeley, Smith looked as though he were trying to assimilate yet another impossible piece of information. Anger began bubbling in his voice when he finally spoke.

"You snuck aboard *my ship* and didn't inform me you were conducting an investigation?!"

"Captain," Seeley said with perfect calm, "This is *way* over your head. I was here because we'd picked up chatter indicating someone on *Ponce* was in covert talks with Chinese agents to steal the ANQ45. My own work had not led me as far as Drummin yet, but I had suspicions about Sniffer. I was starting to follow them up when Bacon's murder changed everything."

"I'm afraid you'll have to come with me until we verify this, Mr. Seeley," Gray said. "I know you don't have a secret squirrel identification badge on you."

"I understand," Seeley said sympathetically. "Just be prepared to brief my colleagues when they contact you two."

Gray and Shepherd locked eyes with each other yet again, a silent expression of *"What the hell did we just get ourselves into?!"* passing between them.

"Abe, give me a moment, please," Shepherd said. He was looking at Cline.

"No problem," Gray said. "We'll wait."

Shepherd walked over to Cline and Holder. Cline looked at Shepherd with something resembling awe.

"Chief..."

Shepherd put a hand on the young man's shoulder, a gentle smile appearing on his face. "Jarvis, it's over. *Now* you can start rebuilding your life."

Cline smiled, his eyes holding a glimmer of hope. He still had many tears yet to shed, but they would not be empty anymore.

Holder was at a loss for words. Shepherd smiled and nodded politely before turning so he could rejoin Gray's party.

The captain caught Shepherd's attention, beckoning him over.

"Yes, sir?" Shepherd stepped up to him.

"Chief, I've seen many things during my career, but nothing I've seen comes close to *you!*"

"Thank you, sir." Shepherd said.

Smith rubbed his hands together, "Now, if you'll excuse me, I have make a report to the admiral."

Smith turned and started to leave before being struck by a thought and swinging back around.

"Oh, yes! Chief Shepherd?"

"Sir?" Shepherd too swung back around to face the captain.

"Get the hell off my ship!" Smith ordered coldly before turning on his heel and marching away.

"Aye, sir," Shepherd said coldly, rolling his eyes and then muttering under his breath, "Officers!"

Shepherd was the last to step back onto the pier. Zipping his jacket all the way up, he walked slowly, allowing Gray and the others to pull ahead of him. Unable to simply leave, he stopped and looked back.

"Well, old girl," He said softly, gazing fondly at the aged warrior, "I guess I'll see you later."

He stayed a moment more, listening as the Proud Lion said goodbye in a way only sailors can hear.

Smiling, Shepherd pivoted and strode down the pier, catching up with Gray and the others.

Ponce floated quietly at her moorings, serenely content with the outcome of her final adventure.

Denouement
Friday, October 28; 19:30 hours
Chesapeake, Virginia

"...despite attempts at damage control, Admiral Thomas Donovan resigned as Chief of Naval Operations today. Releasing a statement, the admiral said he had become a distraction after the Bacon controversy, and he would not let the Navy be harmed by continued attacks upon him..."

"The president has already nominated the Vice CNO, Sean," Said Sen. Diego Alejandro. "I know there's been a lot of public pressure clamoring for Admiral Jones to be named Chief of Naval Operations in the wake of his support for Petty Officer Cline, but the president believes the Navy is better served by having Admiral Thurraya Kincaid take over because she can offer a greater sense of continuity..."

"...in other news, former Petty Officer Jarvis Cline, now a student at Middle Bridge University in Nebraska, settled his lawsuit with the Navy for an undisclosed sum..."

"...continuing our coverage of the on-going story out of Norfolk, Doctor Tyler Drummin has been charged with two counts of first-degree murder, one count of conspiracy to commit murder, and one count of conspiracy to violate the Arms Export Control Act. Despite his attorney filing several motions to dismiss the charges based on allegations of entrapment, his trial is set to begin sometime early next year..."

"...turning to market news, GDI Tech stocks fell significantly following revelations one of their employees has been charged with murder and attempted murder in the course of trying to illegally sell experimental Navy technology to a foreign government. In a statement issued by GDI Tech's home office in Seoul, the company said it regrets the actions of Dr. Tyler Drummin, and is fully cooperating with U.S. and South Korean officials investigating the incident..."

The Gray household rang with laughter as Abraham's fingers played the grand piano, he and Shepherd belting out a comedic number he had composed. Abraham sang in a smooth tenor, and Shepherd actually had a respectable baritone for a man with no formal musical training.

Abraham and Sarah had the grill going when Shepherd and Robertson arrived a couple of hours earlier. Sadly, the steaks never had a chance, but the meat's sorrows were drowned in copious amounts of steak sauce as the four ate, celebrating the official closure of the Bacon investigation before repairing to the piano.

Finally, the shindig began to quiet down. Their energy ebbing even though their spirits were still high, the four comfortably curled up in the Grays' living room once the impromptu concert concluded.

"I heard the prosecution is going for life in prison for Drummin," Robertson said, sipping her Chardonnay. "If you ask me that's too easy. I personally think he should be chained up and dropped off that catwalk to *Ponce's* well deck floor head-first, and *then* sent to prison. What a piece of sh—"

"He wasn't even a very good doctor," Shepherd cut in. "Did you guys see the new *academic* charges being leveled against him? He got his two PhDs from Green Hill University in Massachusetts. I saw on the news earlier that he's now under investigation for plagiarizing *both* of his dissertations."

"I saw that, too," Sarah said, leaning against Abraham. "What a piece of work."

"I've got to know," Robertson said, changing the subject, "What happened to the infamous Mr. Cremer, Abe? Chief here told me your boss ripped him a new one. Was that all he got?"

"Nope!" Abraham said. "Cremer has received the *second* official NCIS reprimand. Despite his powerful political connections, Cremer fouled up so publicly this time that his ass is in *real* trouble. He's under an internal investigation, although I don't think that'll do more than slap him on the wrist. However, he's in it so deep that one more screw up *will* force him out of NCIS."

"Good," Sarah said. "That damn snake doesn't deserve to be part of NCIS!"

"Don't hold back, Sarah," Shepherd said. "What do you really think?"

Robertson spoke up.

"I've been wondering something else," She looked at Shepherd. "Chief, when you were attacked on the ship, you said Drummin killed the lights and then hit you. If the lights were off, how could *he* see where to go after you?"

Abraham fielded the question. "Good question, Dionne! We found night vision goggles in his locker on the ship."

"Of course," Robertson laughed.

"So, what's next for you guys at NEPAC?" Sarah asked Shepherd and Robertson.

"Well," Shepherd said, "I have just about eleven months left in the Navy. I'm already starting the separation process, but I still have some work to do. There's a couple of deployments I have get manned up by April, and then Dionne and I have to get ready for Fleet Week New York next May. Once *that's* over I'll really get hot and heavy turning over all my duties and beginning the slow fade to black in September. After that...I don't know. Maybe I should finally go for my own PhD? Of course, I wouldn't mind going back to teach at the DINFOS again, either."

"I've got another year at NEPAC East on sea duty," Robertson said. "Then I roll to shore duty. I'm looking at potential orders now. I'd like to stay here in Norfolk, but Pearl Harbor would be nice to see."

"Unless you pick up chief next year," Shepherd pointed out. "You'll still probably roll to shore duty, but the map will change significantly for you as far as potential assignments."

"Riiiight!" Robertson shook her head. "I've only been up for chief three times, and you know how hard it is to make it in our rate. You're *way* too optimistic!"

"I am not. I made it fourth time up myself. Besides, you've had *me* for a mentor, and that alone should put you over the top." Shepherd spoke as matter of factly as if he was discussing the gravitational constant of the universe.

The other three groaned with good-natured humor.

"A toast," Sarah said, raising her glass.

The others followed suit, looking curious.

"To the Accidental Detective! To his stirring accomplishments, and to his success in reaching retirement from the Navy—and accidentally detecting—in one piece!"

"Cheers!" The other three said, draining their glasses.

Shepherd set his empty glass on a coaster on the coffee table. "My brothers went to Annapolis, but I enlisted because I wanted to experience the Navy as a common, normal sailor. That's obviously *not* how my career turned out. Hopefully, once I retire, I can finally settle into a more normal life."

"Isaac, I don't think you could ever do 'normal,' even it if it walked up and bit you on the ass," Abraham said, the wine giving him a glowing, warm feeling.

Shepherd opened his mouth to playfully retort, but stopped short when he saw the look in Abraham's eyes. Those blue-gray eyes said it all. Respect, affection, even admiration were shining in them.

Shepherd smiled, suddenly feeling embarrassed...and also quite complimented. "Thanks."

"I'm sorry Cline got out," Robertson said. "I was hoping he'd find a way to stay in and rebuild."

"Me too," Shepherd said sadly. "The Navy broke trust with him. Trust me; I know. Admiral Donovan was grade-A stupid. Instead of doing the right thing by protecting his sailors and the Navy, he decided to protect himself. The damage he's done will take a long time to repair."

"I admit I'm somewhat surprised the Navy offered Cline the early discharge. But, then, considering everything that happened, I guess it makes sense," Robertson said.

"I'm not surprised at all," Abraham said, shifting a bit to rest one foot on the coffee table's edge. "The Navy was hoping he'd just kind of quietly go away by letting him be honorably discharged early. Trouble is, that lawyer of his is not the kind to let a matter like this drop, and Cline was too bitter to let it go, either. So, the Navy ended up in court with more bad publicity and had to pay up."

"That's also what put the final nail in the now-former CNO's coffin," Shepherd said.

"At least Donovan had the good grace to retire and set an example that service really *does* come before self," Robertson said.

"Ah...about that..." Shepherd said a bit hesitantly, "He didn't decide to retire. He got fired by the president."

"Say what?" Sarah asked, stunned.

"Yeah, the president literally called him on the carpet in the Oval Office with the rest of the Joint Chiefs of Staff, SECDEF and SECNAV, all present. The president told Donovan to go into the next office and type his resignation up immediately."

"Isaac, how the *hell* do you find out about these things?!" Sarah asked. "I mean, if that's what happened, why wasn't it on the news?"

Shepherd shrugged, "I...have my sources. And...that's all I'm going to say about that."

He and Abraham shared a glance, both thinking of a second text from a mysterious source earlier.

Isaac, nicely done. You and Mr. Gray did Admiral Jones and the Navy proud.

You might want to know the REAL story of what happened to the CNO. The president fired him in the Oval Office with SECDEF, SECNAV, and the Joints Chiefs present. To smooth things over, the president let it be played as the CNO resigning for the good of the Navy.

Be safe. One day we will meet again, and I'll explain everything.

-L

...by mutual agreement, Shepherd and Abraham had decided to keep the mysterious Mr. "L" a secret.

Robertson was talking as Shepherd's mind came back to the present.

"I was hoping Admiral Jones would get the job," She said.

Shepherd shook his head. "I think the president made a good call. Besides, since Kincaid was at a conference in Europe with NATO during most of September, his image hasn't been sullied by the scandal. Don't worry; I'm sure Admiral Jones will be the big boss one day."

"I wonder what Cline's going to study?" Robertson changed subjects.

"Law," Abraham said.

"Can't imagine why," Sarah said sardonically.

"By the way," Sarah asked, "Why Cremer's notes didn't mention the *Mesa Verde* guys seeing the body being dumped?"

Abraham chuckled and shrugged, "That's easy—his work was shoddy and he ignored them."

"Hey," Robertson said suddenly, "You guys never told me what was up with 'Aaron Seeley.' Who was he? What happened with him?"

Shepherd and Abraham exchanged another look and sighed.

Shepherd answered for the both of them.

"He was a federal officer," Shepherd said. "He was on an undercover assignment that inadvertently intersected with our case."

Robertson shook her head in clear disbelief, "Only in the Navy!"

Shepherd nodded, "The Navy: it's not just an adventure, it's a job!"

The joke was corny, but the wine was good, the company warm, and the laughter genuine.

The conversation, and the laughter, continued late into the night.

Fantail
Wednesday, May 9, 2018; 15:30 hours
Philadelphia

Shepherd unfolded his arms and got up off the bollard he'd been leaning on in the shadow of the silent ship. *Ponce* continued to float serenely, a steel psychiatrist who had just spent the last hour allowing her patient a chance to process his memories by reliving the tale.

"It's only been eight months since I retired, and seven months since you retired," Shepherd said to *Ponce*. "But it feels like a few years have already passed. Of course, those six murders *last* year didn't exactly make it the easiest final year of active duty for me."

He stretched his back, his spine creaking under the corduroy sport coat, "But, old girl, *those* are stories for another time."

Shepherd scratched his face, feeling his close-cropped whiskers.

"Oh, yeah, you got lucky, old girl!" Shepherd said, grinning, stroking his whiskers. "I was the master of ceremonies for my friend Ben Foltz's retirement last month on the *Wisconsin*. My retirement gift to him was shaving my beard and getting back into uniform for a day! Took a couple of weeks, but the beard is back!"

Chuckling quietly, Shepherd faded back into silence again and gazed up at the faded number "15" on *Ponce's* bow. Content now, he was ready to move on.

"Hey, you need help?"

Shepherd looked behind him. A worker was climbing out of a white government pickup that had just parked a few yards away next to a warehouse.

"Me?" Shepherd shook his head, pointing at *Ponce*. "Just visiting an old friend. This old girl and I have had quite a unique history together."

"You one of her captains?" The man asked, walking over. He was of medium build and wore jeans, a white work shirt, and a red hardhat set at a jaunty angle on his head. His face bore a look of genuine interest.

Shepherd smiled, "Nothing so grand. I was just one of her sailors. But those were the best of times...and the worst of times."

"We always have vets come out here to see their old ships. They always leave smiling, even if they seem a little sad," The man said warmly. "So, reliving the glory days, huh?"

"Yep, reliving the gory days," Shepherd said.

"Excuse me?"

"Oh, nothing," Shepherd inwardly laughed at the private joke. "Actually, you can do me a favor, if don't mind. Would you get a photo of me next to her?"

"Sure thing, Chief!" The man said, his eyes catching the chief petty officer insignia Shepherd wore as a lapel pin.

Shepherd handed the guy his phone. "One second, though. Let me get the flags out."

"Flags?"

Shepherd pulled open his haversack and extricated an American flag and a Navy flag.

"These were the flags used on *Ponce's* Quarterdeck from at least 2010, when I was first stationed on board her, until she was decommissioned last year," Shepherd said.

"How do you know that?" The man asked.

Shepherd pointed to the small ink marks he had put on the flags' hoists long ago.

"I made those marks in 2010 when I had to use these as backgrounds for some official photos," Shepherd said. "After the ship was decommissioned, I went aboard with a few other *Ponce* vets for a last reunion before she came up here. I found these tossed aside on a table in the chiefs mess. The Military Sealift Command crew told me I could keep them."

The guy laughed, "Nice! And then you brought them here for this visit?"

"More than that," Shepherd said. "I retired myself last year, about a month before *Ponce* did and moved home to Florida. Once there, I decided to get radical and set off on a 'Grand Tour' of the U.S. I saw 22 countries while I was in the Navy, but I'd only seen about 13 of *our* states before I retired. So, I'm on the road for a year, seeing all 50 in one fell swoop."

"I like it!" The man said. "How many you have you seen so far?"

"Let me think," Shepherd did a quick tally in his head, "I started in November...it's May...so...Pennsylvania is state number...state number twenty-two!"

The man laughed as Shepherd draped the two flags over the bollard and stood next to the them.

The man shot several photos for Shepherd.

"Thanks, man, these are great!" Shepherd said, excitedly scanning through the set. "I'm posting photos of the flags in each state I visit on a *Ponce* social media group; these will be *very* well received. I really appreciate it!"

"Don't worry about it; I was in the SeaBees myself," The man said. "Only did one hitch. Kinda wish I'd gone to retirement like you. Hope you have a safe trip!"

"Thank you," Shepherd said, shaking the man's hand. "Oh, hey—what's your name?"

"Jeff."

"Isaac," Shepherd said. "Thanks again, Jeff. Hope the rest of your week is good!"

Smiling, Jeff spun on his heel and headed into the warehouse.

Shepherd glanced up at the warm, blue sky and watched the birds dancing above *Ponce* for a moment. Then he reverently picked up and folded both of the flags, carefully replacing them in his haversack.

"I'd best be on my way," Shepherd said to the ship. "I've got a friend across the river in New Jersey I'm crashing with tonight. Tomorrow I'll take your Quarterdeck flags to Independence Hall and a few other spots in Philadelphia, and then I'll spend a day in New Jersey before heading up into New England. Definitely need to see Lakehurst and all the aviation history up there. And I've wanted to see Maine since I was about six years old and discovered lighthouses!"

Adjusting the haversack and shoving his hands in his pockets. He looked back up at *Ponce.*

"It *was* the best of times and the worst of times, wasn't it, old friend?" Shepherd asked.

Ponce answered silently, in the way that can only be heard by old sailors when they visit their old ships.

Smiling, Isaac Shepherd turned and casually strode back up the pier towards *Sara Jane,* passing the other silent ships that waited for their final fate along with *Ponce.* He was a little sad, yes, but he was smiling.

He never looked back.

***

The Accidental Detective will return in *The Norfolk Murders*

***

***

Appendix 1: Letters from Isaac Shepherd

***

Letter from
Mass Communication Specialist 1st Class Isaac T. Shepherd,
United States Navy,
to
Stephanie Limbani, Chicago Assistant District Attorney

Friday, September 24, 2010
Somewhere at sea aboard USS *Ponce* (LPD 15)

Hey, Steph!

Sorry about the whole "somewhere at sea" thing. I couldn't
resist. It just sounds so dramatic!

We had our change of command today. More on that later.

We're currently in the Mediterranean. You've got enough
military friends to know I can't give you any details or timelines,
but I can say we will eventually head into the Arabian Sea through
the Suez Canal. No big state secret there; the Suez is the *only* way
into the Arabian Sea once you're in the Med...unless you want to
leave the Med and go the long way around Africa. When we do
transit the canal, that'll be my first time through it. I'm excited!

Ponce is indeed named for Ponce, Puerto Rico. Nicely
done! I didn't even know that until I reported on board. *Ponce* is
an *Austin*-class Amphibious Transport Dock, or "LPD" in Navy
shorthand. Basically, we're a small amphibious assault ship with
400 sailors as crew and currently carrying 900 Marines (again, no
state secret; all that was put in our deployment press release last
July). Remind me to tell you about a wrestling match I watched
one night in the Marine berthing over a Charlotte Bronte book (true
story!).

I think it's kind of fitting (if not outright weird) I ended up
on this ship. You know my first *sea-going* command was the F-14
Tomcat squadron VF-213, right? Well, that squadron's emblem is
the Black Lion, made up of the stars from the constellation Leo.
Ponce is my second sea-going command, but this is the first time

I'm actually part of the ship's *crew,* and not just aboard for the mission...and *Ponce's* emblem and nickname is the "Proud Lion."

It gets weirder.

Ponce's keel was laid down in 1966, the year my folks got married, and the ship was commissioned in 1971, the year my brothers and I were born.

Freaky.

After your last case—that DUI with the sailor from Great Lakes there outside Chicago—you said forms of address for enlisted sailors drove you up the wall. Well, get a drink and put your feet up: here's a crash course in Navy and Coast Guard enlisted ranks!

On the DoD pay scale, I'm an E6 (enlisted pay grades run from E1 – E9). I make the same money and hold the same *general* authority and level of responsibility as an E6 in the Air Force, Army, etc. In Navy and Coast Guard terms, I'm a *petty officer* because I sit in the pay grades E4 – E6. By virtue of being an E6, I'm a petty officer first class (or first class petty officer, either works). An E4 is a third class, and an E5 is a second class.

So, if you run into a Navy sailor or a Coast Guardsman with one, two, or three chevrons (or, as we informally call the insignia, "crows"), you are *completely* fine addressing them simply as "Petty Officer."

Now, all military career fields have designations. The Army, Air Force, and Marine Corps use numbers for theirs. The Navy and Coast Guard hew to old tradition and call our enlisted career fields "rates," and your pay grade standing in your rate is your "rating." My *rate* is currently Mass Communication Specialist, or "MC" for short. My *rating* is petty officer first class because I'm an E6, a first class petty officer. So, you can address me formally—and quite properly—by using any of the following terms:

Petty Officer Shepherd

MC1 Shepherd ("MC1" is the short hand for Mass Communication Specialist First Class)

MC1 (no name is necessarily needed)

Hey, Stupid! (at least, that's what my brother Joshua called me during high school)

I know Navy and Coast Guard ratings can be confusing, so if you stick to "Petty Officer" for a sailor or Coast Guardsman who is pay grade E4 – E6, you're doing fine. If nothing else, just ask the person in question.

As I said, the change of command was today. Normally you don't hold a change of command less than 60 days into a deployment, but the Navy had a hard time finding a new CO for *Ponce,* so our previous CO was extended until Cmdr. Donald Ratner took command today. He's been great to the enlisted crew, but you know my job gets me around the ship a lot, and I've already picked up an undercurrent of tension in the wardroom (the officer's community). It's only been one day, and I might be imagining things, but I feel like I've seen Ratner...I don't know. I feel like he's got a slightly snide way of talking to the officers. It might be nothing; our previous CO, Cmdr. Schulz, was extremely popular (I rank him as one of the two best commanding officers I've ever had), so this *might* just be us having to get used to a new guy who committed the "crime" of not being a clone of Cmdr. Schulz.

A weird thing happened today right after the change of command ceremony. We're about 100 miles from land, and a small Indian scops owl landed on the ship. The owl landed right on the starboard ladder leading up from the flight deck to the 02 Level, and would not move. It actually blocked Cmdr. Ratner from going up that way, and forced him to go around to the port side ladder to leave the ceremony. Once he was gone, the owl hung out for a bit, and then flew off. Poof! Gone!

You know I love owls; and this guy was awfully CUTE!

Congratulations on the Jackson conviction! Hopefully you and your team broke the back of that gang. I've been following the news and I know how much damage they've done to the east side. You'll be a chief justice pf the Supreme Court one day yet!

Oh yeah, Bob Wilson emailed me the other day. He lost your new email address, so I passed it on to him. He's got news; he just took over as Winter Garden's fire chief. I admit I had to look it up; Winter Garden is a small burb west of Orlando. But, it's great news for our old high school gang. Another Niceville kid makes good!

Last note: you asked about my brothers. You remember they both got out of the Navy back in 2002? Well, A.J. is finishing his doctorate in volcanology at the University of Washington, so he and his family are in Seattle. Joshua got picked up as the offensive coordinator for the Pittsburgh Steelers starting this coming season, so they just moved to Pittsburgh. Pop is having a hard time with *that* one, seeing as our family have been life-long Dallas Cowboy fans!

Time to close this off and get it in the mail. Hopefully you'll get it in a few weeks.

Stay safe!!

-Isaac

Letter from
Chief Mass Communication Specialist Isaac T. Shepherd, United States Navy,
to
Major Aidan P. Stavenger, United States Air Force

Thursday, 8 November 2012
Naval Exchange, Bahrain

Hello, Old Friend!

I'm sitting in the Bahrain Navy Exchange now, typing away on my laptop. John Stiles, Kelly Tate, and a few other chiefs took me to dinner at the Naseef Restaurant in Manama for my birthday. If you get to Bahrain, Naseef is *definitely* worth it! Can't say I'm happy to turn 41 on deployment, but it's not as bad as turning 26 at boot camp. *That* was depressing!

I'm sorry I took so long to get back to you, but I do want to fill you in on all the "chief season" terminology I've been using in my cryptic and all-to-infrequent emails.

Short backstory: the pay grade of chief petty officer was created Apr. 1, 1893 (yes, Aidan, on April Fool's Day; go on—get it out of your system). Advancement results for the new chiefs this year were announced July 31, which is actually early. Usually results come out the first week of August.

Normally, the commanding officer of a unit personally tells each first class petty officer who got picked up for advancement the good news. As you know, I'm deployed on the USS *Dwight D. Eisenhower* leading the NEPAC East media detachment, and my CO is back in Virginia. We were underway in the Arabian Sea on the 31st, and I hadn't heard anything by 11:00. Not hearing anything that late the morning usually means you didn't make it that year.

The problem was a protocol scuffle. The NEPAC East division officer who's deployed with us wanted to tell me I made it since he's from NEPAC, but the ship's *captain* wanted to tell me since I'm deployed on his ship. They were going back and forth about it in the ward room until the *admiral* commanding the whole strike group settled the thing at 11:50 by calling me to *his* stateroom. I thought I was called up there to get details for a media job since it was so late in the morning.

I about had a heart attack when I realized the admiral kept calling me "Chief Shepherd" while he was shaking my hand. I just stood there like a dope, mouth hanging open while I just shaking his hand. Not my finest moment. Funny, but I reacted the same way when my CO at VF-213 told me I'd made petty officer second class back in 2000.

Anyway, the whole initiation thing lasts about six weeks until everyone selected for advancement to chief is pinned in one big ceremony. All the first class petty officers selected for advancement are called "Chief Selects" or "selectees" as a courtesy. This also begins the sailor's transition from being a "blue shirt" (a reference to the old dungaree uniforms junior sailors used to wear) to joining the senior enlisted ranks.

Some people are immediately *advanced* and get paid straight away, and the others are only "frocked." That means they can wear the uniform, wield the authority, and get the privileges of being a chief, but aren't actually *paid* yet, not until their turn comes up in the line of seniority over the course of the next year. Frocking enlisted people to the next rank until they're actually advanced is a naval tradition that I don't think has a counterpart in the Air Force or Army.

I got lucky; I was ranked so high among the Mass Communication Specialists that I was officially advanced this month. I was the number 3 guy on the list out of 22 new Chief Mass Communication Specialists (my ego is appropriately swollen!).

Back in the day, when the ship's captain decided he needed a new chief, he would consult with the existing chiefs, and then interview the first class petty officers thought to be worthy candidates. Once he picked the new chief, that first class petty officer would start living with the chiefs and spend time with each one taking notes in a notebook (or on whatever he had at hand) of all their leadership wisdom before he was officially promoted to chief. That's how the whole induction tradition started. It's grown in scope over the years to become a nearly six-week long training program.

I had my own personal induction season cut short. We were jogging on the flight deck when a couple of the others guys started goofing around. Well, one of them tripped, fell into me, knocking me clean off the flight deck and down into the catwalk. I landed wrong and wrenched the living hell out of my bad knee (the one I hurt in that motorcycle wreck a few years ago). They very nearly medivaced me off the IKE. After that, there was no physical way I could keep up with my fellow selectees. I had to bow out of everything except for the classroom events and round table discussions.

This is where Master Chief Stiles *really* impressed me.

Several crusty "old school" chiefs started treating me like dog poop on the bottom of their boots. They regarded pulling out of the reindeer games over something as "minor" as a possibly crippling physical injury to be "quitting" and "giving up." You know the type, Aidan—the ones who worship the uniform as a religion and are enslaved to tradition? They tried to keep me out of the classroom activities and even from being pinned during the official pinning ceremony in September.

John Stiles is the IKE's Command Master Chief, so he's *definitely* got some clout. When my own "sponsor" (the chief directly mentoring me through induction) cut me loose for "quitting," John tore that idiot a new one! In fact, John hammered the whole mess (with all of us selectees watching) for over an hour. He said tradition is supposed to *serve* sailors by binding us and guiding us, but we are its master, not its slave (I'll have to remember that when I'm conducting leadership training).

After that, John took over as my sponsor and ensured I was pinned in the ship's main ceremony. John is definitely someone I'm going to stick close to. Frankly, he scares the hell out of me, but I think I can learn a lot from him.

Ok, your last question was about the "charge book." The modern "charge book" started as that notebook I mentioned—the one the first class would carry around writing down notes on leadership from the chiefs before he was pinned.

The selectee's goal with the charge book is to get each chief on the ship (or base, if they're on shore duty) to sign the book with a word or two of wisdom. You can also get any former chief who is now an officer to sign, as well as anyone you look up to as a mentor or example of good leadership. The ship's captain and the strike group admiral are also "targets," but it's hard to get time with them. By virtue of John Stiles taking over as my sponsor, I got time with both...and was the *only* one in my class on IKE to get the admiral to pass on some wisdom!

I better wrap up and go get this printed in the cyber cafe next to the food court. I'll drop it in the mail tonight before we head back to the ship. It should get to you in...what? Two months?

Give Linda a hug for me! I hope the boys are well and still driving you crazy!

Yours,

Isaac

***

Appendix 2: Proud Lion Photo Gallery

***

The Proud Lion heads back to sea following a visit to the Seychelles on Nov. 11, 2010. I got this shot while riding with our security personnel as *Ponce* got underway. (Official U.S. Navy photo by Mass Communication Specialist 1st Class Nathanael Miller / RELEASED)

I got this view of *Ponce* maneuvering with guided missile destroyer USS *Barry* (DDG 52) on Apr. 14, 2011. I was with our visit, board, search and seizure team aboard one of *Ponce's* small boats. (Official U.S. Navy photo by Mass Communication Specialist 1st Class Nathanael Miller / RELEASED)

A view looking aft inside the well deck of *Ponce,* Oct. 25, 2010. I
took this photo as the Proud Lion was flooding the well deck in
order to launch landing craft during exercises off the coast of
Djibouti. (Official U.S. Navy photo by Mass Communication
Specialist 1st Class Nathanael Miller / RELEASED)

Another view inside *Ponce's* well-deck, this time shortly after the ship was decommissioned at Naval Station Norfolk in October of 2017. I took this view standing on aft end of the port side catwalk looking forward. The ramp leading from the well deck floor to the upper level is called "The Beach." An identical catwalk runs the length of the starboard side. The body of Carl Bacon would have been found at the very bottom right corner of this photo. (Personal photo by Nathanael Miller, Oct. 16, 2017)

Ponce was anchored off Kuwait on Christmas Day in 2010. I took this shot during exercises with Kuwaiti forces. This image shows the scale of the well deck, the starboard catwalk 20 feet above the well deck floor, and one of the two hatches to the catwalk from inside the ship (the other hatch is forward just out of sight). (Official U.S. Navy photo by Mass Communication Specialist 1st Class Nathanael Miller / RELEASED)

We held a "Wii" bowling tournament on the mess decks May 8, 2011. I am *not* terribly good at bowling, so I just cheered on my buddies. This is one of the rare personal photos I shot for my own memories during that deployment. The bulk of the *Ponce* images I captured, I shot with the ship's camera while doing my job. (Personal photo of Mass Communication Specialist 1st Class Nathanael Miller)

The now-decommissioned *Ponce* tied up in storage at the Naval Inactive Ship Maintenance Facility, or "boneyard," in Philadelphia on May 9, 2018. The ship was commissioned in 1971 and retired in 2017 at Naval Station Norfolk. (Personal photo by Nathanael Miller)

Myself with the Proud Lion and her Quarterdeck flags at the Philadelphia boneyard May 9, 2018. I was given the flags by the Military Sealift Command personnel when I toured *Ponce* shortly after her decommissioning. After retirement, I spent a year on a road trip seeing all 50 states and parts of Canada. I photographed these flags and two fragments of wood from the old girl's well deck in each state. You can see those photos on my Instagram, @sparks1524. (Personal self-portrait by Nathanael Miller)

THIS PAGE INTENTIONALLY LEFT BLANK

(Navy veterans will get the joke!)

Writer's Notebook

If it needs be said, this is *fiction.* I strive to make these yarns realistic enough to allow even law enforcement professionals enjoy the adventure, but, in the end, this *is* an adventure story. For example, DNA testing is *not* the quick procedure I made it out to be. In the real world, DNA testing takes some time. For the purposes of adventure and pacing, I used artistic license to speed up the process.

A number of fictional commands exist in this universe. For example, the Navy Expeditionary Public Affairs Command (NEPAC) was modeled on the Navy's real-life Navy Public Affairs Support Element (NPASE), but only modeled. The same with Adm. Jones' Atlantic Command, and Master Chief Stiles' Atlantic Forces Surface Command (AFSC). These fictional commands allowed me more flexibility with which to tell the story.

The ships featured here are all real, and you can find all the information I used in everything from Wikipedia to the classic *Jane's Fighting Ships Recognition Handbooks.* All the photos reproduced here are either official U.S. Navy photos I took on active duty that were publicly released, or else my own personal imagery. The Navy regularly makes imagery from its media specialists publicly available at both www.navy.mil and https://www.dvidshub.net/.

USS *Ponce* was launched in 1966, christened in 1970, and commissioned in 1971. *Ponce* was beginning the decommissioning process in early 2012 when the ship was converted for use as an experimental afloat forward staging base. *Ponce* served in this role from late 2012 until her actual decommissioning in October 2017.

Ponce tested the real-life AN/SEQ-3 Laser Weapon System (or XN-1 LaWS) during this period. That weapon was the inspiration for the fictional ANQ45 used in this story. You can watch a great video provided by the Navy of the real AN/SEQ-3 on YouTube at: https://www.youtube.com/watch?v=sbjXXRfwrHg.

None of the characters you met in *Proud Lion* are "stand ins" for real people, but many of these characters' traits were inspired by the remarkable people I've had the privilege of meeting over the years. I have interacted with colorful characters ranging from presidents and emperors to the fascinating owners of small shops in the middle of Montana…including one woman who drove up to Virginia City every summer from her hippie commune in Texas to run the business!

The genesis of Isaac Shepherd strolled into my head one afternoon while I was walking across the campus of Wagner Middle School on Clark Air Force Base in the Philippines back in April of 1985. I was in 7th grade, and the character's original name was Michael McRany (he was very Irish back then). Over the past 30 years, Michael McRany evolved into the Isaac Shepherd you met here. The Irish/Scottish heritage was transferred to Aidan Stavenger, and the Shepherds took on more a Hispanic, French, and Japanese mixed heritage.

The first "Michael McRany" story (and first novel I ever wrote) was a book I wrote in late 1985. The characters were in college and faced a terrorist bombing on an ocean liner. The whole novel was maybe 70 pages long (quite an accomplishment for a 13-year-old). When I yanked the book off the family's old dot-matrix printer, I thought I was ready for the big time! Well, the "big time" took about 35 years to get here….

There's really no rhyme or reason to how characters evolve. All any writer can say is that characters evolve and change in ways that just feel "right." In fact, they can become so real that, even as you write the story, a particular character will "walk up" to you and tell you (in *no* uncertain terms) that they need to perform an action or say a line you had planned for someone else. Dionne Robertson did that in this story. The conversation about Shepherd's failed marriage was originally planned for Abraham Gray to have with Shepherd, but ended up being held by Dionne. As Dionne "pointed out" to me, it strengthened her character and highlighted just *why* Shepherd would rely on her as an ally.

I owe an incalculable debt to my parents. Mom and Pop imparted a very old-fashioned work ethic that eschews illusions of entitlement in favor of hard work and the satisfaction of concrete accomplishments. They also taught me the very valuable lesson of failure: how we face it, accept it, and learn from it (or be crushed by it) are as important to a successful life as any other skill set.

Mom and Pop equipped me to step into adult life far more easily than many of my contemporaries did. I realized this when I was in the dorms at Florida State University. I had several dorm mates ask *me* how to do laundry because I was the only one on the floor who had been taught how to wash his own clothes!

I want to thank Jerry Foltz, a fellow retired Chief Mass Communication Specialist and one of my best friends. I first met Jerry when I was an MC1 and he was my chief at the real-life NPASE East. I had no idea Jerry was a new chief when I first worked for him. He was confident, forthright, and decisive. He didn't quibble or get paralyzed by "what ifs." He quickly became a mentor and, after I made chief petty officer myself, his methods were often the model I followed in approaching different leadership situations. Jerry acted as the ceremonial Boatswain's Mate at my own retirement ceremony, ringing the bell to send me "ashore" according to Navy tradition. The next year, he asked me to be the master of ceremonies at his own retirement ceremony. It was an honor!

I want to thank him not only because he kindly lent me his last name for the Benjamin Foltz character, but also because he acted as editor for this novel. Despite a broken leg, he spent over 120 hours with me during our coast-to-coast video conferences, coaching me and helping me bring this book over the finish life. Most importantly, he worried less about my feelings and more about the quality of my writing. His forthright honesty was critical to helping me polish down some rough edges that I did not see until his keen eye gave me a fresh perspective on this story.

I must also thank Eric Butler, another former U.S. Navy Mass Communication Specialist. Eric took on the commission of producing the final version of the cover art for this book. I designed the cover, but Eric used his considerable skills to scale up my design into a finalized version of sterling quality. Eric is as talented a graphic artist, and he continually produces outstanding work. I am proud to display his talent here!

Isaac Shepherd and Abraham Gray will return.

--Nathanael Miller

About the Author

Nathanael Miller at the Naval Aviation Museum on board NAS Pensacola, Florida, in 2018. The F-14 behind him is one of the actual jets he worked on during his time attached to the VF-213 Black Lions.

Nathanael Miller is a retired Chief Mass Communication Specialist who enjoyed a rich and wildly varied career in the U.S. Navy. Graduating from Niceville High School in Niceville, Florida, Nathanael attended community college before earning his bachelor's degree in history from Florida State University. He worked briefly at the Museum of Florida History until state budget cuts eliminated the position. He enlisted in the Navy in late 1997.

He first assignment was as a yeoman attached to VQ-2 in Rota, Spain, in 1998. While at VQ-2, Nathanael's photography talents placed him in the squadron's public affairs office. Upon graduating the Basic Still Photography course at the Defense Information School in August 2000, his was assigned as a technician maintaining the reconnaissance cameras and associated systems aboard the F-14D Tomcats of VF-213.

Nathanael went on to serve on Guam, teach at the Defense Information School, join the crew of USS *Ponce* (LPD 15), and finally hold several positions at the Navy Public Affairs Support Element (NPASE) East in Norfolk, Virginia. Completing his master's degree in history in 2016, Nathanael retired from active duty in late 2017. He briefly served as a federal civilian for the Navy, accepting an 18-month term position as the staff writer at the Naval Undersea Warfare Center Division, Keyport, in Washington State, before going independent as a novelist and blogger.

Nathanael currently resides in Silverdale, Washington.

Made in the USA
Monee, IL
20 October 2020